PRAISE FOR *THE OTH*

★ "A lovely, moving, and realistic view of the struggles and insecurities—as well as the beauty—that come from being bicultural." —*Booklist*, starred review

★ "Balcárcel's well-rounded characters, complex friendships, and nuanced family dynamics will resonate with many readers. This is a title that will remain relevant long past its publication date. A must-have for all library collections." —*School Library Journal*, starred review

"A touching and oh-so-satisfying story featuring a fierce and tender new Latinx superstar, Quijana Carrillo! Quijana will capture your heart with her defiant spirit and unwavering love for friends and family." —Angela Cervantes, author of *Me, Frida, and the Secret of the Peacock Ring*

"The palpable push-and-pull of Quijana's yearning for her father's homeland, Guatemala, will propel readers through this poetic, deeply affecting debut." —Jenn Bishop, author of *The Distance to Home*

"Bravely told, with notes of vulnerability, brevity, and hope, this is a story that invites quiet courage to speak love, regardless of your native language." —Beth Hautala, author of *The Ostrich and Other Lost Things*

A PURA BELPRÉ HONOR BOOK

A JUNIOR LIBRARY GUILD SELECTION

AN ALSC NOTABLE CHILDREN'S BOOK

WINNER OF THE DEIRDRE SIOBHAN FLYNNBASS AWARD FOR BEST MIDDLE GRADE BOOK

A SPIRIT OF TEXAS (SPOT) READING PROGRAM RECOMMENDED TITLE

AN AMÉRICAS AWARD HONOR BOOK

THE OTHER HALF OF HAPPY

THE OTHER HALF OF HAPPY

BY REBECCA BALCÁRCEL

chronicle books
san francisco

First Chronicle Books LLC paperback edition, published in 2021.
Originally published in hardcover in 2019 by Chronicle Books LLC.

ISBN 978-1-7972-1391-0

The Library of Congress has cataloged the original edition as follows:

Names: Balcárcel, Rebecca, author.

Title: The other half of happy / by Rebecca Balcárcel.

Description: San Francisco : Chronicle Books, [2019] | Summary: Twelve-year-old Quijana is a biracial girl, desperately trying to understand the changes that are going on in her life; her mother rarely gets home before bedtime, her father suddenly seems to be trying to get in touch with his Guatemalan roots (even though he never bothered to teach Quijana Spanish), she is about to start seventh grade in the Texas town where they live and she is worried about fitting in—and Quijana suspects that her parents are keeping secrets, because she is sure there is something wrong with her little brother, Memito, who is becoming increasingly hard to reach.

Identifiers: LCCN 2018037899 | ISBN 9781452169989 (alk. paper)

Subjects: LCSH: Racially mixed children—Texas—Juvenile fiction. | Racially mixed families—Texas—Juvenile fiction. | Ethnicity—Juvenile fiction. | Identity (Psychology)—Juvenile fiction. | Brothers and sisters—Juvenile fiction. | Parent and child—Juvenile fiction. | Texas—Juvenile fiction. | CYAC: Racially mixed people—Fiction. | Ethnicity—Fiction. | Identity—Fiction. | Brothers and sisters—Fiction. | Parent and child—Fiction. | Family life—Texas—Fiction. | Texas—Fiction.

Classification: LCC PZ7.1.B3556 Ot 2019 | DDC 813.6 [Fic]—dc23 LC record available at https://lccn.loc.gov/2018037899

Manufactured in China.

Original book design by Alice Seiler.
Paperback design by Mariam Quraishi.
Typeset in Fazeta and Akzidenz-Grotesk.

10 9 8 7 6 5 4 3 2 1

Chronicle Books LLC
680 Second Street
San Francisco, California 94107

Chronicle Books—we see things differently. Become part of our community at www.chroniclekids.com.

TO MY FRIEND DARYL,

who has lighted my life since seventh grade

(1969–2015)

ONE

I LIVE IN A TILTED HOUSE. A bowling ball on our living room floor would roll past the couch, past the dining table, all the way to the kitchen sink. And if the sink wasn't there and the wall wasn't there and the bathroom behind *that* wasn't there, the ball would roll all the way to my room at the end of the house. That's what it's like being twelve. Everything rolling toward you.

"Quijana?" Mom's voice thuds against my door.

"M'ija," Dad calls.

It's not really our house. We rent. But even if the doors hang crooked and won't close, and even if Mom never comes home till bedtime anymore, and Dad looks tired when he cleans up after supper, I like this tilted house. I get my own room, and there's a backyard swing. There's even a stove with two ovens, the upper one like a dresser drawer. We can bake peach cobbler and cheesy nachos at the same time. Like we might today if we weren't destroying the living room, pulling everything off the walls.

"Quijana, we need another pair of hands, here."

"Is she outside?"

I wish I were. I'd jump on the swing, pump my legs, climb high, and whoosh through the air. Then I'd sing. It's my secret favorite thing, even better than peach cobbler. When I sing out there, something rises up my spine and tingles the top of my head. The notes lift me up until I weigh nothing. I could almost let go and sail over the treetops.

Which is another good thing about this tilted house. We can sing in it. Back at the apartment, way back when my little brother was born, Dad would strum his guitar, and we'd sing ballads in English, boleros in Spanish. Then a neighbor would pound on the wall. Or the ceiling. Apartment walls are nothing but panels of saltine crackers.

"I'll check the backyard."

No one can tell me why this house tilts. The landlady tried. "That ol' Texas sun turns dirt to dust. Can't build nothing on dust." Mom says it's the clay soil that's under the house that slickens in the rain. Dad tells me the builders tried to stairstep a hill, putting each house on a bulldozed shelf. "But no one cheats Mother Earth. She's remaking her hill, filling in the shelves to make a slope again." Mostly I don't notice the tilt. But sometimes, like now, the walk from my room to the kitchen seems steep.

"Quijana." Dad's face appears at my bedroom door.

Of course I should be helping. I hang my head. The thing is, those boleros we sing in Spanish? I've memorized the sounds. But I don't know what they mean. And now Mom and Dad are Spanish-izing the whole house.

Dad looks toward the ceiling as if he'll find a power-up of patience there. Ever since Tío Pancho called and said, "Adiós, Chicago. I got a job in Dallas!" Dad's been different. He's playing more marimba music on his phone. He talked me into taking Spanish instead of Mandarin in school.

Last night, Dad went over to help unload the moving van. We're all going to visit when they get settled. Then I'll meet the whole family: Tío Pancho, Tía Lencha, and three cousins. They've lived in the States for a while now, but we've never been able to visit them in Chicago.

The door flies all the way open, and Memito tumbles in. He thrusts a book in my face and climbs on my lap. He thinks my body is a big chair, just for him.

"He wants to read," I say to Dad. I'd much rather read. A knot kinks in my chest when I think of taking down pictures of me and putting up paintings of Guatemala, the place where Dad was born but I've never been. "Can't we read first?"

"Read afterward," Dad says.

I start seventh grade in forty-eight hours, so I also want to load my backpack. My folders and notebook paper are still slouching in Kroger bags. They'll have to wait. I stand up slowly, tipping Memito onto his feet. "I guess we better."

Dad leaves, but Memito's bottom lip pooches out.

"I know."

He waves the book again and stomps his foot.

"It wasn't my idea."

His face starts to crumple into a cry. "Ride?" I say. He drops the book as I lift him up.

I hear Mom ask, "You didn't tell her, did you?"

Tell me what?

He's almost too heavy, but I hoist Memito over my head onto my shoulders. We march toward weavings and clay pots and volcano pictures—all pretty, but not *home*. We march up, up, up. Up the hill of this tilted house.

TWO

I SET MEMITO DOWN in a room I don't recognize. The walls are in the same places, but everything on them has changed. On both sides of the TV hang curtains of cloth, each zigzagged with sunshiney yellow and fiery orange. On the bookshelf sit two tall pots with red and green painted animals chasing each other around the sides. Dad leans over the computer desk and hangs a photo of people I've never seen before. "My whole family," he says. I guess he means his parents and brothers and sisters, since me and Memito and Mom aren't in it.

"Where'd the baby pictures go?" I ask.

Mom nods toward a cardboard box. "They're online anyway. We'll make a photo book sometime."

"Sometime?" "Sometime" always means "never."

"Hold that side for me, would you, Qui?"

My nickname sounds like "key," but I'm not a key player or a key factor. I'm not keyed up or keyed in. If anything, I'm off-key, especially today.

I hold one end of the large painting Mom is trying to hang. It's a lake surrounded by volcanoes.

"Lake Atitlán." Dad lifts his arms as if he might hug the painting, though it's too big for that. "The most lovely spot in the world. No importa la distancia, siempre habrá un mismo cielo que nos una." Looking at me, he translates. "Distance does not matter. Always the same sky unites us."

"I'm glad we finally framed this," Mom says. "This room needed a revamp."

It looks nice and all, but I miss the baby photos and the picture of the Golden Gate Bridge that came from Target. Only Dad's guitar in its hanger is the same. Memito doesn't mind; he's rolling a toy truck back and forth.

"I liked it before," I say.

"Me too," Mom says, looking around, "but I always felt bad that this stuff was in boxes. It feels like a new house."

That was my point.

"Is it time to get out the package?" Dad asks Mom, his eyes twinkling at me.

"Wait right here," she says. She brings in a white box, the packing tape already cut. "From your Abuela, for your first day at your new school."

Abuela is my dad's mom. She sends birthday cards and letters to my parents, but none of our Guatemalan relatives send gifts. We send them gifts, like Crayola crayons that are hard to get there and American-brand jeans.

"Starting junior high." Dad shakes his head. "I remember my first day of upper school. I wore a new white shirt and polished shoes. At your age, I learned to tie my own tie. Twelve now? You want to stand out and show everyone who you are."

Actually, I'm hoping to *not* stand out. To not embarrass myself. Everybody knows that standing out in seventh grade is bad, as in disastrously, monstrously, don't-be-ridiculous-ly bad, especially the first day. I swallow hard and fold back the cardboard flaps.

A thick, colorful fabric unfolds in my lap. Tropical birds dazzle my eyes. It seems like a tunic or a long poncho. Yellow animals run in a wide stripe across a blue background, and below them, a banner of red diamonds. "Wow," I whisper. It's totally beautiful. And totally out of the question. No one in the history of seventh grade has ever worn something like this to school, at least not in Bur Oak, Texas.

"It is a huipil, m'ija, handmade on a backstrap loom. See the birds? Quetzals. They represent freedom, since they die in captivity. You'll see one on the Guatemalan flag."

"Dad, I . . ." I look to Mom for help, but she just smiles. "I can't wear this."

His face sags.

"I mean, it's great, but . . ."

"You don't want to look especial?" Dad's voice is soft like a velvet balloon and rises at the end.

"Sweetheart, I know it's not what the other kids wear." Finally, Mom takes my side. "But . . ."

Or not.

"It could be a conversation piece."

"A what?"

7

"Something to get kids talking, asking you questions, getting to know you."

"Mom."

"I mean it. Why not?"

I can think of six thousand reasons why not, and thirty of them are going to be sitting with me in each class. Mom is usually more with-it than this. The bright colors must have blendered her brain.

"Try it on," says Dad. "You will see. You will like it."

"I do like it." I run my hand over the cloth, feeling its smooth, close-knit threads. I hate to disappoint them, but I have to. "I just can't wear it to school."

Dad steps back.

"Think about it." Mom puts her hand on my shoulder, then turns to pick up Memito, who is raising his arms.

For a second, a millisecond, I picture walking off the school bus in this outfit. People point and snicker until I'm dizzy just imagining it. I've already planned what to wear on the first day, and it involves denim and machine-made knit.

"Maybe later you'll try on the huipil?" Mom says. "You could wear it next week when we visit your cousins. They'll be moved in by then."

I close my eyes. Right. The Carrillos. All born in Guatemala.

Mom puts her free arm around me. "If you wear the huipil to school, people will see how unique you are." She squeezes me in a half hug.

I'd be unique, all right.

As soon as possible, I tuck the huipil under my arm and slink down the hall to my room, the only unchanged piece of real estate in this house.

I fall onto my bed and look up at my manatee poster on the ceiling. She helps me gather my thoughts. The round body looks comfy and huggable, her eyes patient. I breathe in slowly, hold, and exhale. *Okay. Forget the cousins for now. Forget what Mom and Dad want you to wear. Just get ready for school.* I make a plan: 1) load my backpack, 2) pack my lunch tomorrow night, and 3) bury this huipil in a bottom drawer.

I tackle number three first.

THREE

MEMITO PARKS HIS TRICYCLE by the front door, and a wall of cool air greets us as we step into the house. The four of us walked the entire jogging trail near our house, like we often do on Sundays. September in Texas is still frying-pan hot, so we're all wearing shorts. We pour glasses of water from a pitcher in the fridge. My hair is still sweaty when Dad says, "We cannot let the lawn die in this heat. Let's go buy a sprinkler." I put my shoes back on.

"Take Memito with you, love?" Mom asks. "I need to plan for tomorrow's class." She pulls a pot of rice and beans out of the fridge. "All your teachers are doing the same thing as I am tonight." She winks at me. "It's kinda fun."

"What are they doing?"

"Planning what to say, stuff to do in class, homework assignments. All that."

I think Mom will be a great teacher. I'm almost ready for tomorrow myself. I just need to pack my lunch.

Mom twists a dial on the stove. "I'll warm up these left-overs. Then I'll chain myself to my desk," she jokes. It's close to true. When Mom gets her master's degree, she'll be able to teach college full time. For now, she teaches English in the morning and takes classes in the evening. She comes home late and types on the computer into the night.

Soon Dad, Memito, and I are pulling into the Home Depot parking lot, air conditioner blasting. Inside the giant building, we find an orange-vested man. "Where can we find an esprinkler?" Dad asks.

The man, tall and wide, with thick fingers, squints.

Slowly, my father repeats, "An espr-r-r-rinkeler-r."

The man shakes his head. "I'm sorry?" The man's eyes shift to me.

I myself don't hear my dad's accent, but other people do, and it's only around them that I notice it.

My breath catches in my throat. I wince, not wanting Dad to feel bad about his rolled r's. "Sprinkler," I say quickly, and the orange shoulders relax. I take Memito's hand, and we all follow the man to aisle twenty-two.

Sometimes I wish Dad didn't have an accent. I wish he could be more, I don't know, regular.

I especially wish he'd been to school here. He doesn't know the setup, like how we have lockers and metal detectors. Mom knows. She's a member of the PTA; she knows what student council is. And English is her first language. When she talks to the box at the drive-thru, they get her order right. She knows how things work because, like me, she was born here. Her "sprinkler" and mine is how everything is supposed to be. The English r isn't fancy, but it's like a go-to pair of white socks, matching every word I need. The Spanish *rrr* is orange with pink dots, blinged-out with rhinestones and ribbons.

Dad's good at other stuff. He knows songs. Guitar chords. Philosophers. He knows Spanish authors like Lorca and Cervantes, but nothing useful.

Even our drive home turns into a college lecture. Memito's chewing a fruit bar in his car seat while Dad spins a quote around and around in the air. "Listen to Ortega y Gasset: 'Life is a series of collisions with the future.' What does this mean?" he asks, almost forgetting a stop sign. "It means we run into challenges—bam-bam-bam!—one after another. When I came to this country, I left behind family, friends. I had to embrace new things, bam-bam-bam! Life is a series of yesses. Yes to everything that comes. You will see this at junior high. Challenge will come, but don't be afraid."

"I'll try, Dad," I say, though his words are already pulling apart in my mind, floating away from each other.

Memito falls asleep in his car seat as we turn onto the main road. His neck bends too far, and he looks uncomfortable. But he doesn't stir when Dad's cell phone rings through the radio speakers on Bluetooth. He sleeps right through Dad bellowing, "Hola, Mamita!"

It's Abuela.

Now I'm the one who is uncomfortable. I stuffed her gift into my bottom drawer yesterday, hoping everyone would forget about it. Will I have to thank her? *In Spanish?* My Spanish is somewhere between tourist and two-year-old.

Dad chats with Abuela as he steers the car under the freeway. Maybe he'll keep the conversation between the two of them, so I don't have to say anything. Abuela calls every month, and he always tells her I'm fine. I used to send drawings to Guatemala—stick figures and smiley faces. Now Mom just mails photos. We can't email, since Abuela doesn't have Internet.

The closer we get to home, the more I think I'm off the hook. I sit very still and listen while keeping my eyes on passing cars. I hear a word I know, then another—single raindrops in the word downpour.

Dad taps me on the shoulder. "Thank her," he whispers.

My whole body stiffens. I hear, "¿Quijana? ¿Quijana?"

I clear my throat, my stomach clenching. "Hola, Abuelita." I add the "-ita" to sugar over the fact that I can't say much more than these two words.

"¡Mi amor! Qué tal . . ." I'm lost already. She knows I only understand a little Spanish, but her idea of little is big.

She asks "How is . . ." something or other.

I say, "Bien, Abuelita." Probably true.

"¿Y cómo *something else,* y *I have no idea* de tu Mamá?"

My mind blanks and seconds pass. I need to thank her for the huipil, but now she's asking about Mom. A gap widens between her sentence and the one I am supposed to say next. I wave both hands in the air to get Dad's attention as we come to a stoplight. In a loud whisper, I say, "I can't!"

Seconds pass. Abuela asks, "¿Hola? ¿Hola?" like a ringing doorbell.

"Aquí estoy," says Dad. "Lo siento, tal vez la conexión no está bien." He covers for me, telling her it's a bad connection. "A Quijana le gusta el huipil." He frowns in my direction.

I turn my face to the window, hiding my own frown. Dad's talked to me in English all my life. Why does he act surprised that I don't speak Spanish? I picture Abuela waving at me from the back of a car that's speeding away.

Dad hangs up. He takes a deep breath as if to say something, and I look over. He breathes out, says nothing, and rubs his ear.

The ear. That's bad news. Whatever's coming, it won't be good.

He looks straight ahead as he says, "You know a few Spanish words, m'ija. Maybe you try them out next week when we visit your cousins."

"I can count to ten, Dad. That's about it. Don't they speak English?"

"Some."

"So I'll be the only one who can't understand anything."

I want him to feel bad. *I* feel bad. He's changing the rules on me. If I can't talk to my own family, it's his fault. "You always said English is more important."

He looks back at Memito, which tells me I must have raised my voice. "That was for me, when I was a student," he whispers. "Back then I needed practice."

It's true. After he graduated from college, Dad let up on his English-only rule. But by then I was, like, seven. Even now, he never speaks to me in Spanish, just to Mom. Quietly I say, "Spanish is your secret language with Mom anyway."

Dad twists to look at me, but says nothing.

As we turn into our neighborhood, I notice he's been quiet for three blocks. I know I'm being a pain. Guilt pushes on my chest. Anger pushes back.

FOUR

AS THE SUN SINKS BEHIND THE TREES, Dad takes
Memito to bed, and I start making my lunch for school. If
Mom were here, she'd help. But it looks like she unchained
herself from her desk after all and went to the university to
buy books for her class.

I'm getting out a paper bag when Dad sighs into the
kitchen and slumps into a dining chair. I should say something about Abuela or Spanish, but I can't think what.

I take a sack lunch instead of buying because Mom won't
let me eat "fried whatever and sugary who-knows-what." She
says that becoming a mom changed her eating habits forever.
Not a single Fruit Loop has entered our house since I was
born. I've only seen them in commercials.

I smooth organic grape jelly onto sprouted wheat bread. I
wish I could take white bread instead, but at least PB&J is better than bean and cheese pupusas. Being laughed at in second
grade was the first and last of that. I came home crying, and
Mom promised to pack more common foods—as long as they
were healthy.

Dad watches me rinse the jelly knife and tuck my sandwich into a plastic square box.

"Soon you'll be making your soupcases," he says in a sad-song voice.

"I'm packing lunch, not *suitcases*, Dad. I'm not moving out for years."

He leans on the table, chin in his hand. "I remember the day you started the kindergarten." He's always listening to the fading notes of the past.

I walk over and pat his shoulder. "It's only seventh grade, Dad."

His shoulders drop. "Pues."

This is his word for agreeing. And his word for not agreeing. "Pues" means "well" and "there it is" and "if you say so." What he really means is *seventh grade is the end* and *seventh grade is the beginning* and *why can't we tie down the sun?*

"Don't be sad, okay?" The thing is, I can't stop time. And why would I? My sixth-grade jeans don't fit. Dad's the one who quotes that Spanish knight they named me after, Don Quixote: "In last year's nests there are no birds this year."

And anyway, I can't think about the past right now. My excitement about tomorrow is paper-clipped to worry. I'll be in junior high and practically alone because my sixth-grade friends live across a line that sends them to the other school. Already the school year feels like a carnival ride with iffy seat belts. The only upside is my plan to change my image. I've been the girl who can't tell when people are joking, who takes everything to heart. This year, I'll play it cool.

I walk to the fridge and stow my lunch. I check off a list in my head. Lunch made, backpack zipped. Water bottle, I'll fill in the morning.

Dad takes a deep breath. "You know where to catch the bus?" he asks. "Your phone, it's charged? You have everything you need?"

"The corner. Charged. Yes."

And here I want to whisper, "It's going to be okay, Dad." Either that or shout, "I know what I'm doing!"

I wish he would cheer up. There's no way to tell him I'm stressed already without him being worried, too.

"When you were born, I said to myself, 'I will teach her guitar, the great instrument of Spain.'" His eyes look toward a distant place. "I should have started years ago. By your age, I was serenading the first girl who pierced my heart. I wanted to show you as my father showed me."

"I'll sing in choir, Dad. And I won't be serenading anyone. Guitar can wait."

"Los hijos del zapatero van descalzos," he says to himself.

I know this one—the children of the shoemaker go barefoot. Fine, I'll go barefoot.

He looks up. "As you say, the guitar waits for you."

That isn't what I meant by "wait." The sooner I get to bed, the sooner this conversation can end. I switch off the overhead lights and peer at him in the lamplight. "Going to bed?"

"Not yet, m'ija." He sits up straighter and looks toward the guitar. "How about singing 'El Gallo Ha Muerto'?"

"Now?" Dad taught me to sing that song on a car trip before my brother was born. It's a round, which means Mom began the tune, Dad came in one line later, and I came in last, layering my voice on top of theirs. I had to cover my ears to keep from slipping from my line to theirs. Now I can do "Row, Row, Row Your Boat" and more. I love how rounds chase their own tails.

I'd only known the sounds of what I was singing until I finally looked up the words one time:

El gallo ha muerto, qué dolor.
El gallo ha muerto, qué dolor.
Ya no dirá más cocodi, cocoda
Ya no dirá más cocodi, cocoda
Cocodico-dico-dico-da

I can sing my part, easy-peasy. When I'm not eleven hours from starting seventh grade.

"I guess it's late," Dad says.

The lamp makes an hourglass of light against the dark, one cone spreading out above the shade, one below. Dad, still hunched at the table, sits just inside its glow. "Will you wait up for Mom, then?" I ask, checking the clock that hangs above the sink.

He blinks twice and comes back from wherever he was. "Buena idea. I'll make her some coffee." Mom will read past midnight and get up before I do.

"Good night, Dad," I say, bending in for a chair hug. He squeezes my shoulders, then presses my head against his.

He holds me longer than usual. I know his heart sometimes wishes for impossible things. I guess mine does, too.

I climb into bed and stare at the ceiling fan spinning and churning the air. In a matter of hours, I'll be on the school bus. I should be eager, but I feel pushed off a ledge, falling up instead of down, floating away from everything I used to know.

FIVE

IT'S 7:20 A.M. and wouldn't you know, my first-day hair sticks out on one side. I try to tame it with Mom's straightening iron. By the time I like my face in the mirror, the clock has jumped forward, and I have less than five minutes before I need to leave. Five minutes in which I rinse my cereal bowl, fill my water bottle, hoist on my backpack. Five minutes in which I think, *Will anyone like me? Will I get lost in the new building?* Five minutes in which I kiss Memito, still in his race-car pajamas, while Mom calls out goodbye over the radio's morning music.

"Photo!" yells Dad, running out in his bathrobe.

At the front door, I'm about to protest, but his phone is already poised. I stand up straight in my jeans and scoop-neck shirt. "You look nice," he says, clicking the screen, but I read disappointment in his eyes. *Yes, you're seeing correctly, Dad; I'm not wearing the huipil.* We're standing in front of the Lake Atitlán painting, though, so I can't exactly call this moment a win.

Time to go.

Then I remember my sea turtle. It's a bracelet from Grandma Miller, a tiny sea turtle on a leather cord. I run to my room, where I've tucked it in a tin box made for peppermints. Grandma lives in Florida, and she bought it for me after we went on a sea turtle walk. We trekked with a guide out to the beach at night to watch a mama turtle lay eggs in the sand, then scoot herself back to the ocean with her flippers. Later, the baby sea turtles would hatch and paddle themselves to the ocean.

Looking at my turtle's strong little fins, I think I'll be okay today. *Unless everyone is already friends with everyone else. Unless my clothes look cheap. Unless my hair sticks out again.* I tell myself not to think like that. I fumble, trying to tie the ends one-handed. My fingers slip, and the seconds speed up. "Mom!" I yell. "Can you help me with my bracelet?"

"She's in the shower," comes the answer from Dad.

Dad's thick fingers can't help me.

I hold my breath and try again. Again the ends flop apart. I want to scold myself. *Why didn't I think of this sooner?* I think of hitching it together with a safety pin . . . that I don't have. I think of gluing it, taping it, attaching magnets.

The shower water runs on.

I want to reset my brain to the minute before I cared. Rinse my bowl, kiss Memito, stroll out the door early. Before I thought of the bracelet, I was happy. Now I'm miserable and two minutes late. But I'm the me I'm stuck with.

Each second clangs in my head like a tardy bell. A saying of Dad's pops to mind: "Donde hay gana, hay maña," which means "Where there's a will, there's a way." I look down at the bracelet. My little determined friend. Then I think of Mom and her practical mind. The way she stores items next to where they are used. The breadbox next to the toaster.

"You're coming," I tell my turtle, then shove her into my pocket. "Bye y'all," I yell down the hall, and run for the corner. So much for playing it cool.

The bus bumps us to school, and I walk into a building five times as big as my elementary school. Hundreds of faces stream by. I clutch my backpack straps tighter. Each hall is labeled with a letter, which helps. I bushwhack my way through the first few classes. Rosters, assigned seats, lists of rules that I half-listen to. Texas history, Spanish, algebra. The class I'm looking forward to is choir, but it's last.

The bell rings, and the hall fills with students. How does everyone know where they're going? Changing classes was easier in grade school, where we only switched between three rooms at the end of a dinky hall. I must look silly standing still. *Deep breath.* I look at my schedule. My next class, English, is in Port 3. Where's that? I've heard of airports, ship ports, and USB ports, but none of this helps. I stand at the intersection of four halls looking for a sign or an arrow.

"Can I help?" A man with the school mascot on his shirt guides me out the back door and points toward a blah-colored metal shed with wooden steps. A portable, in a row of portables. One has a big 3 on the side. Port 3.

I wave my thanks and climb the steps.

Inside is a room crowded with desks and walls crowded with posters. A short redheaded woman with a strong voice shouts instructions. "Sit wherever you want. I'll move ya if I have to!"

She starts down the roll, and I'm expecting the usual. Almost every class of my life has started with me giving a tutorial on how to pronounce my name. Not "kwee," but "kee." Not "ja," but "hah." "Kee-HAH-nah." I'm used to it. But Ms. May rattles it off, "Quijana Carrillo," no problem. I almost forget to say "Here."

Ms. May surprises me again when she says, "I never use PowerPoint. Puts a body right to sleep! In this class, no lectures. You'll do the talking. I want to hear you think!"

Looking around the room, I see startled faces. A boy with green eyes sits up straighter. I think I'm going to like this class, too.

My eyes linger on the boy's right fist. He's holding something. All I can see is a string looped around one finger. He catches me looking and opens his hand. A red yo-yo. I smile. When he smiles back, a wave of energy passes through me. Or *something*. Something good.

Ms. May sends us to lunch. "Be back by twelve-fifty, sharp! We'll talk about your favorite songs." *Ohs, oohs,* and *hmms* make up our exit soundtrack.

But when I leave Port 3 and clomp down the wooden stairs last and alone, my confidence wavers. The green-eyed yo-yo boy is nowhere in sight. I sit at the empty end of a lunch table where I'm joined by exactly no one. I tap my sea turtle pocket and try to hear Grandma Miller's voice. She likes to quote a writer who said, "Everything's okay in the end; if it's not okay, it's not the end." All of a sudden I feel like I must be miles from the end. Is everyone laughing with someone except me? I'm a lone grape watching the bunches.

"¿Podemos sentarnos aquí?"

A light-haired girl and her group look at me, all holding their lunch trays.

Before I can process that she's speaking Spanish and that her sentence starts with *Can we,* they're sitting down and saying ten words per second. In Spanish. This never happened at my old school.

"Don't you speak Spanish?" a girl with glasses says.

"Um."

"Aren't you Quijana? From English?" She chews a tater tot.

"Yeah."

The light-haired girl looks over. "Oh, you're one of those. You don't speak Spanish, right? A coconut."

"A what?"

She snorts. "¡No sabe!"

They swerve back into Spanish and speed off, leaving me in their dust.

My sandwich tastes like a stack of notecards. I stuff my lunch sack into my backpack and tramp back to Port 3. It's locked, so I sit on the wooden steps. I'm going to have to make a friend in this class, unless I want to be a lone grape forever.

It's hot. My hair is warm to the touch. Texas summers don't end until almost Halloween.

I pull out my phone and turn it on, which is not allowed. But I'm not technically in the school building or even in the portable, so maybe it's okay. Still, I type quickly. I tilt the screen into the shade to read "coconut: slang term for a Latino who acts white." This isn't me. My mom *is* white. I drop my phone in my backpack, and I look out across the field. What does "act white" mean, anyway? How would I act half Latina?

I twist and untwist the top loop on my backpack. Being a little kid was easier than this. I wasn't half anything. I was a whole continent then, like Pangaea. Unsplit. Now I have tectonic plates. Mom looks at me and sees Grandma Miller's cheekbones; Dad sees the Carrillo nose. I see one land mass, but I'm wrong. My body is Guatemala crashing into the United States. What happens to me, the whole me, when my plates shift, when my continents tear apart? No one told me twelve was earthquake season.

A few kids saunter out from the main building. Then comes a big group. Ms. May opens the door from the inside. "All right, team, find your seats, and start writing the words to your favorite song. You're about to learn rhyme schemes." I'm glad to go in.

26

While Ms. May explains rhyme patterns, I spy the tater tot girl. I see that she has a shiny, stiff backpack, obviously new. My backpack is last year's, and man, it looks like it. Scuffs on the bottom, straps that used to be thick now flattened. I showed it to Mom, but she said, "Plenty of wear left." She's right that I don't *need* a new one. Like Dad says every time we can't afford something, "No perderás lo que no deseas." Mom says it means "You can't lose what you don't desire in the first place." So I shove the wish for a new backpack out of my mind, and try to forget that everyone else seems to have one.

Ms. May struts up the aisle. "Who wants to share their song lyrics and rhyme scheme?"

"Yes, young man," she says to the yo-yo boy. "Remind me of your name."

"Jayden."

I memorize his name and then gasp as he starts reading out loud. He looks over at me, but continues. My face goes hot. We chose the same song. What are the chances? I try not to read too much into it, but I can't help glowing. This day is looking up.

With a bounce in my step, I find the choir room without a hitch. Mr. Green, a man with a bushy beard, a bald head, and round glasses, sorts us into sopranos, altos, tenors, and basses. I'm happy to be an alto; I'll get to sing harmony and not just the easy melody. "We'll learn to read music this semester," Mr. Green says. "And we'll give a concert in about three months."

A fidgety boy in the front row raises his hand. "Only three months?"

"Don't worry. You'll know your parts back and forth and up and down by then. And we won't just sing the notes. We'll make music!"

Inside I'm already singing.

SIX

"QUIJANA! I'M SO GLAD we can finally talk." Grandma Miller's tilting her screen, and I see her white pouf of hair as I sit on my bed with my laptop. Then it's a close-up of her forehead until she relaxes into her chair. "Tell me all about school. And don't tell me *fine*," she says, wagging her finger. "Save that for your parents. How was it really?" Grandma digs for the truth when she talks, her words like shovels.

"Kind of like a roller-coaster—pretty good, but kinda scary," I admit. "The building's, like, huge, and I don't really know anyone. The English teacher seems cool. And I'm in choir. But Mom and Dad made me take Spanish," I grumble. "And . . . I ate lunch alone." When Mom and Dad asked me about school, I left this out, but something makes me tell Grandma everything.

She nods and spares me the advice that grown-ups usually give.

"I took the sea turtle with me."

"Good call," Grandma says. "Remember the night we saw them charge across the beach? I tell you what, we protected those nesting beaches back when I worked for Fish and Wildlife—placed orange cones around the nests, got people to turn off their crazy-bright porch lights. Each turtle should get her chance, right? Tenacious little guys. You keep yours close."

"I will, Grandma."

"Well, sweet pea." Her head tilts and she leans forward. "I have some news, too. I wish it were happier." She looks right at the camera. "I went to the doctor, Quijana. A specialist. She's running a few tests because . . . I'm in some pain."

A falling feeling starts in my head and sinks through my body. "What do you mean?"

"It's not too bad, but I needed to check it out. And I was right, for what it's worth. I'm sick, all right."

"But . . . Grandma. You look fine."

"I know, sweetheart. But inside . . . well, the tests will tell us what's going on."

"But they'll treat it, right? You'll get better." My voice comes out cloggy.

"I think so, sweet pea. They have so many therapies these days. I'm not worried. Remember what I always say."

Tears pool in my eyes. "Everything's okay in the end. If it's not okay, it's not the end."

"Exactly." She smiles at me and I try to smile back. "I wish I could be there in person, little one. I'd hug you until suppertime!"

This makes me laugh, but also makes my tears trickle onto my cheeks.

"Quijana, is there anything you want to know? I will always be honest with you."

Her bravery steadies me, and I wipe my eyes. I shouldn't ask, but recklessness takes over. I want to know the worst. "Could it be, you know, really bad?"

"Well, worst-case scenario, it's cancer. But even that has a treatment."

"Cancer?" I thought she would wrap it in blankets. Now a pang shakes my heart.

"That's only one possibility." She smiles. "Whatever happens will be an adventure, in this world or some other. And you know I like adventures." Her face looks half happy, half mischievous, the same as the day she took off to Nigeria to tag manatees. A marine biologist gets to do that kind of thing. She's even scuba dived in the Philippines.

She doesn't feel sorry for herself, and she won't let me either. Still, my head feels heavy and I let it drop. I'll cry more if I look at her.

"We're at the beginning of this. I'll tell you when I know more. Meanwhile, we'll savor every moment even more than usual! You're coming out to see me for Thanksgiving?"

I raise my head. "Yes, Grandma. Of course."

"Good. We'll have pancakes for breakfast every day."

Pancakes are my favorite. "What about manatees?"

"I'm not sure if we'll see any on this trip. They'll be heading further south, looking for warm springs for the winter."

Since I was little, Grandma has taken me in her canoe to see the manatees. We paddle through shallow water, where

31

their wide backs surface and sink. Sometimes a fat fan tail sticks up or a gray muzzle snarfs a tuft of grass.

"We might spot a few bald eagles," she says. "And the songbirds will be migrating in. Will you help me put out the suet feeders for the woodpeckers?"

"I sure will." It's a relief to hear her talk about the future as if it'll be normal. It has, has, has to be.

When we sign off, I go to my tree-limb swing in the backyard. I sit and dangle my legs, leaning my head against the plastic-coated chain. Darkness falls, and from here, the house windows are rectangles of yellow light. I try to think of good memories with Grandma, but her news smudges everything. My own shoes are barely visible in the gray light, as if I'm being smudged too, rubbed out of existence.

I kick at the grass. I'm here. Here in this world. How could Grandma not be here too?

I see Dad's silhouette move across the kitchen window. With Mom at class, he's making supper by himself. I'm not hungry, but I go in.

"Well, well! Did you enjoy your swinging?"

"Grandma told me," I say.

Dad sets his stack of plates on the table.

"She could die, Dad."

He pulls out a chair for each of us.

"What if I never see . . ." My voice cracks.

"No, no, no," he says, taking both my hands in his. "It may not be serious. That is why they run these tests. And your grandmother, she is strong."

32

I peer into his face. Does he mean it?

He squeezes my hands. "She has much to live for," he tells me. "Much that needs her. The wildlife people want her help with—what do they call it?—coral reefs. Reef restoration. She cannot let them down, yes? And her lights project on the . . ."

"On the beachfront. Where the baby sea turtles hatch," I sniff.

"Yes. She is the one telling people, 'Turn off your lights,' so that the turtles crawl out to sea, not to the houses. She loves that job. It needs her, and she needs it."

"And us, right? She wants to live for us, too."

"Of course she does, m'ija." The outside corners of his eyes look damp, but he tries to smile. "Can you go get Memito for supper?"

I trudge down the hall to Memito's room. He's spinning the wheels on his upside-down Tonka truck.

"Memito, want to eat? Time for supper." He doesn't stop, and I know how he feels, wanting things to stay the same. "Memito, supper." I try to think of something he likes. "Juice?" I could pick him up, but then he'd cry. And I can't take crying right now.

I open his closet and dump over his clothes basket. Dirty clothes can't get much dirtier, right? "Memito," I say, kneeling on the floor and pushing the empty clothes basket right up to him. He climbs in, and I give the basket a push. He's heavier than I remember, and my knees burn on the carpet. In the hall, I stand up and push him fast along the tile. He squeals, and I feel better for the first time since I talked to Grandma.

We eat steaming vegetable soup under the warm dining room light. Maybe Dad's right. It isn't serious. Grandma's strong. And she can't go anywhere while I and her family and all the baby sea turtles in the whole state of Florida need her. Can she?

SEVEN

THE NEXT MORNING, I'm all washed and dressed before I remember Grandma. *Worst-case scenario, it's cancer.* The last word rams into my chest, knocking my breath out. I can't believe I forgot. I woke up thinking about eating lunch alone again. That problem seems small now. I lift my sea turtle bracelet with special care and tie it on.

Everyone's up early. I hear Dad shaving in the bathroom and Mom clinking silverware in the kitchen.

Seeing me plod down the hallway, Memito lets out a happy squeal from his booster chair. He can't tell that I'm sad. He doesn't know he could lose his grandmother. His world is happy.

I let his bright eyes pull me over, and I rub noses with him. "¿Qué tal, hermanito?" This phrase feels cuter than the English, like little balls of sugar in my mouth.

Memito says nothing, as usual. We're still waiting for him to talk. He has some words, but no sentences. My father thinks he's like Einstein, a genius whose brain is building a math machine inside. My mother thinks I help him too much, guessing his words before he needs to say them. Even Grandma says he's quiet for his age. I think he's listening to music in his mind, some delicate melody we can't hear. I just hope he talks before other kids start making fun of him.

He finishes with his breakfast. Mom wipes peach juice off his face and takes the cutting board to the sink. "Sleep well?" she says.

"Sure. Except . . ." I'm not sure how to ask her about Grandma.

Memito kicks his legs and grunts. Mom turns on the faucet. "He might want some water," she calls. "His sippy cup's on the table."

He's pushing at the tray and twisting his body.

He doesn't want water, I know. Me and Memito, our minds are like two strings of Christmas lights, one plugged into the next. Grown-ups don't remember what it's like living at knee level, but I do. "Down?" I say, and his face relaxes.

"Make him say it, Qui," Mom says.

"Down," I say. I stand right in front of him. "Say 'down.'"

He arches his back, straining against the tray. "Aahh!"

I frown. Memito used to do everything I showed him. If I ate my broccoli, he would, too. Wherever I went in the house, he'd crawl behind me. But it's not that easy anymore.

He's twisting his head from side to side. Even angry, he's cute. Cheeks plump as Easter eggs. But I have to catch the bus soon.

Yet I can't leave him stranded there. Dad says Memito is partly my responsibility since I'm the eldest. He actually says that—"eldest." Sometimes his English is more proper than Mom's and mine.

I curlicue my voice like ribbons. "Memito! Lookie, lookie. Up!" I hold my hands high in the air, then whoosh them down to his chin. "Down!"

He gives a half laugh, so I do it again. This time he smiles and bats my hands. The third time, I'm wondering if he will ever let me stop when he says, "Duh." Close enough!

I rip off the tray and he's down and running. Who cares if he was supposed to learn this word a year ago? (True. His teacher told us.)

If he can learn "down," maybe he can learn "water." Maybe "apple." "Brother." Maybe even "big sister."

I check the clock. We still have a few minutes. "Hey, Mom?"

"Mmm?" She dries her hands and starts gathering her schoolbooks and purse.

"Did Grandma talk to you?"

She looks up, pauses, then drops her stuff into a chair. She spreads her arms wide and steps toward me. "She sure did, Qui." She wraps me in a tight hug. "She wanted to be the one to tell you."

I nod. "She told me last night."

Mom pulls away to look me in the face. "First comes testing, then we'll see. We don't know what we're dealing with yet. It could be something simple."

Sounds flimsy.

"I know you're worried." Her voice falters. "I am, too. We'll know more soon." She finger-combs my bangs.

"I'm scared." I surprise myself, saying it out loud.

"I know. We all are. Your grandma's always been so active, so healthy. Traveling the world helping animals. It's hard to believe anything can slow her down. You know what, though?" She lifts her head. "I bet she can beat this."

I let Mom's words stand since I know it's time to go. I guess I feel a little better. She gathers up her books again.

"Hey," she says. "Want me to take you to school? You'll get there way early, but it's on my way."

On any other day, I'd be embarrassed to be dropped off by Mom. But today I say, "That'd be great."

EIGHT

THE FIRST DAYS OF SCHOOL whoosh by. Grandma texts me each morning with a smiley face or "Love ya!" and I'm finally getting the hang of the school building layout.

In English I watch Jayden. Every day I like him more. He does yo-yo tricks before class and even shows other kids how. He and I are always the first to laugh when Ms. May makes a joke. Today when I add a comment to discussion, he says, "Good point!" and I hear nothing for the next two minutes but his voice replaying in my mind: *"Good point!"*

When Ms. May announces lunch, I trudge down the wooden steps of Port 3, picturing the usual kid clumps in the cafeteria. Where will I sit this time? I've stayed away from the Latina girls. Yesterday a girl with cowboy boots and an East Texas twang said, "It's cool with me if you sit here." The day before that I landed in a group of volleyball players. Maybe I should talk to one of the kids in Minecraft T-shirts.

"It's Quijana, right?" Jayden catches up to me and matches my step.

"Right." I feel like a strummed string. "You're Jayden."

"Yup." He opens the door to the main school building and flicks his yo-yo at the same time. "You'd think they could find us a classroom inside the building," he says.

"I like Port 3," I venture.

"You do?"

"It's ugly, but now it's our own little . . ."

"Clubhouse?"

"Yeah, clubhouse. Plus, Ms. May can be as loud as she wants out there."

"Ha! She is loud." His yo-yo zips up the string.

"I like her though. Hey, how did you learn to yo-yo?"

"YouTube. And practice." The yo-yo rolls along the floor for a second before climbing back up to Jayden's hand. "And more practice."

I thought I'd be nervous, but Jayden's easy to talk to.

We unpack our lunches, and the giant cafeteria shrinks to just Jayden and me. The Latina girls are sitting at the next table, but their voices blend with the general noise.

"Hey, look," he says.

We've got matching fruit cups. First the song, and now this!

"Health-nut dad," he says.

"Health-nut mom," I say.

He reaches toward me and we cheers our fruit cups. Our knuckles touch, and I notice his green eyes have a tiny circle of brown around the pupils.

Then a girl with a pink shirt shows up. Bright as July. I recognize her from English, too.

"There you are!" Jayden says as she sets down her tray. He points his chin toward me. "Quijana."

"I'm Zuri. I was looking at your hair clip in class. I sit a couple of rows behind you. Great colors."

"It's my mom's."

"I'm always stealing my mom's hair stuff too! She has wigs and scarves and beads and . . ." She throws her hands up. To Jayden she says, "I had to take a note to the office for Ms. May."

So much for being alone with Jayden. At least Zuri doesn't seem to mind my sitting here. She must not be his girlfriend, or she'd act jealous. Unless she's *that* secure. While I chew on my sandwich, they pick up a conversation that clearly doesn't involve me.

"That picture you sent was amazing," she says.

"Fun, huh?" says Jayden. "Where'd you get an emoji that shows a z-snap?"

I worry that they're a pair, like shoes, chopsticks, windshield wipers. She even calls him Jayday. And she sounds super mature because she talks like she's from England. Her hair makes a smooth, even wedge all the way around.

"So y'all went to the same elementary school?" I ask.

"Since fifth grade," Jayden says. "It's better here."

"Where you can live down the musical?" Zuri says.

Jayden snorts. "Don't remind me."

"Last year's school play." Zuri leans toward me. "We all had to be in it, but Jayden was supposed to be the star."

"Do we have to tell her?"

"Of course!" Zuri turns to me. "So Jayden has memorized his lines, practiced after school, the whole bit. He sounds great in rehearsal."

"I *was* great in rehearsal," Jayden puts in.

"Yes, Jayday, I said that. So all the parents come. The cafetorium is packed."

"Can we skip this part?" Jayden says.

"Shush. The first half goes fine, but then he walks out for the biggest song and FAINTS."

"Faints?"

"I was nervous!" Jayden says.

"Dead away." Zuri slaps the table with her hand with each word.

"I hadn't eaten."

"He fell onto the cardboard tree, which fell on pretty much everybody."

My chuckle turns into a laugh.

"That tree saved me from splitting my head open."

"Well, it didn't do the rest of us much good!" Zuri leans across the table and looks him in the eyes.

"Okay, you're right," Jayden says, his hands up in surrender.

"So, Ms. May?" Zuri asks. "You like her class?"

"I do," says Jayden.

"She's cool," I say. "How about that poem she assigned?"

Zuri bats the air with one hand. "I'd rather do a hundred math problems! I stink at poetry."

Jayden imitates her accent and puts his nose in the air. "Well, ladies, mine will be enchanting!"

Through my laughter, I'm noticing how Zuri sits up straight. Her black skin glistens. I look for a horrible flaw, but all I see are pluses: storytelling talent, princess cheekbones, and math smarts.

"Hey, let's text each other when we finish our poems," Jayden says. "Whoever finishes last has to share dessert! Quijana, what's your number?"

I'm strummed again. As he taps Contacts, I trace the shape of his hand with my eyes. I watch a curl on his forehead as I say the digits.

"Got it! Text you later."

"Great!" His grin makes my stomach flip.

Lunch ends and we trek back to class. Zuri walks next to Jayden, and I make an effort to not care. I wince when they bump shoulders and Jayden grabs her forearm to make a point. *Her shine doesn't take away from yours,* says a voice in my head. It sounds like something Dad might tell me, but I'm not sure where it came from. I walk ahead a little, trying to look more confident than I feel.

We're almost to the door when Zuri asks, "Quijana. Is that a French name? I never heard it before." Her accent makes the r's drop off, and it sounds more elegant than anything I've ever said. *Nevah hud it befoe.*

"It's Spanish," I say without elaborating. The truth isn't cool. I'm not named after a movie star or even a great-grandmother. My namesake is a fictional, delusional knight named Don Quixote who scattershot justice across Spain in the 1600s. No one needs to know that.

"Unique." Jayden flashes a smile, and my head swirls.

"Let's hear it for names that start with rare letters." Zuri toggles her index finger back and forth between us. "We could start a club!"

I like this trio we're making. Does anything come in sets of three? Three musketeers, three primary colors, a trilogy of adventure stories. It could work. At the same time, I picture texting Jayden later. Just the two of us.

After English, I head to choir. Walking toward the far end of the building, I wonder why Zuri's accent sounds fancy while Dad's accent doesn't.

A heavy door opens into the choir room, which is large and echoey, with semicircles of chairs on wide risers. We crowd around the folder slots, reaching for our music. I'm glad we'll really sing today. Voices chatter, feet tromp. Every mind popcorns except mine. Finally, I'm in a place where my mind can settle. I take my seat in the second row.

"Stand up," shouts Mr. Green. "Spines straight!" He sits at the piano and rolls out chords. He lands on a C, and its weight pulls us in. All of us become one pitch. The room stills and we are C. I give myself to the note. C sweeps through my body; worries fall way. A dozen thoughts disappear.

44

Mr. Green cues each section, and sopranos, altos, tenors, and basses take their notes, building a chord. *Ahhh* vibrates my bones.

Mr. Green closes his eyes, and our forty voices hold. I feel popped out of myself and centered in myself at the same time. My eyes scan the room, and I see short hair, long hair, kids with glasses, kids with braces. I see a Minecraft kid, a Latina from lunch, and a boy with cowboy boots next to a boy with high-tops.

The C chord locks, perfectly in tune. For this single wide second, we're all one.

NINE

I FINISH MY HOMEWORK Friday night alongside Mom at the dining table, within sight of two Guatemalan weavings and Lake Atitlán on the wall. I'm starting to like that lake a bit, and the blue volcanoes rising around its edge. A bit.

Normal families do things like watch movies on Friday nights, but we're not all that normal. Dad reads or plays his guitar; Mom studies. When I don't have homework, I do origami or take pictures or do something Mom and Dad think is "productive." Either that, or play. Mom and Dad are big on play. They've always let me play Lego or tea party for hours. Right now, though, I'm playing the big kid and Memito is the one playing games. He spins nearby on his Sit 'n Spin, a toy that whirls him around when he turns a wheel in the middle.

Dad wanders in, wiping his hands on a dish towel. He looks over my shoulder and shouts, "¡Poesía! Why didn't you tell me you were writing a poem?"

"Don't help me, Dad."

He looks a little hurt, but says, "Of course. It must be your own work." He turns to Mom. "'¿Qué es poesía?'" he quotes.

It must be a love poem because Mom looks up from her work and they share a kiss. Sheesh. They're always in Romance Land. Even with Dad holding a dish towel.

My phone vibrates.

Hey Q. Jayden here. How goes it?

My thumbs tingle as I type.

Parents in a lip-lock. Ew.

Haha!

"What's up, Qui?" Mom says. "You look happy as a cow in clover. Who's texting?"

My breath halts. She probably thinks I'll say Kirsten or Olivia, since we hung out last year, but we stopped texting over the summer. I hear the drone of Memito spinning, spinning. "Just Jayden."

"Jayden?" Dad squints. "I want to meet this Jayden."

"*Dad.* He's my friend; he's in my English class."

"I want one of those shirts," Dad says to Mom.

"One of what shirts, mi alma?"

"The ones that say DADD. Dads Against Daughters Dating."

"Not funny, Dad." How hover-y can he be? I just know he'll be impossible when I do date someday.

"Oh, this isn't dating." Mom chuckles, turning back to her work. "I called boys when I was her age. We bought an extra-long phone cord so I could talk in my room."

"See?" I say. *Thank you, Mom.*

Dad frowns. "My father interrogated every boy who came to see my sisters."

47

"You can do that in a few years." Mom gives me a wink. I hope she's kidding.

The next morning, I let the sunshine wake me. Saturday stretches out in all directions, my unexplored island. I sing the choir song as I spin on the swing in the backyard. I imagine writing a movie script, starring Jayden. Memito plays rodeo on his stick horse, and I think about when we took him to the real rodeo. We hauled him to the petting zoo, the milking parlor, and the birthing center where piglets and calves toddle around and nurse, but he spent the whole time covering his ears or his face. Then he pitched a fit and wouldn't ride the ponies. I love him up the hill and down the mountain, but he's definitely different. Sensitive, I guess.

On Sunday, my Saturday shimmer turns to rust.

"Ready to go?" Dad says brightly, poking his head in. It's the worst way to be woken up.

I don't say no, but I think it.

Tía Lencha, Tío Pancho, and my three cousins have settled in across town, and we're invited to a "reunión," which Dad pronounces ray-oon-yone. It sounds like what Mom would call a shindig and I would call a party.

"Will I have to speak Spanish?" I ask.

"You can manage 'por favor' and 'gracias,'" says Mom. "Being polite goes a long way."

"Mom, 'please' and 'thank you' are not going to help much."

"Just do your best. You know more than you think you do."

I don't know what to say to this. The main thing I know is how much I *don't* know.

"You could wear your huipil." She uses the same voice as when Memito won't eat his okra.

"I'm good," I say. I'm sticking with capris and a T-shirt. Even if I'm nervous on the inside, I can be comfortable on the outside.

I hear the apartment even before we get to the building. Man, did Tía Lencha and Tío Pancho invite the whole complex? My breath gets shallow, and Memito whines to be picked up and burrows his head into Mom's shoulder.

When the door opens, the warm smell of corn tortillas greets us. From a cluster of people, a man bounds forward. "Hermano," he says, pulling Dad into a tight hug. Dad hugs his brother for a long time. When they part, tears stand in their eyes. I guess this move is a bigger deal than I thought.

We're barely in the doorway when Mirabel, Raúl, and Crista crowd around me, saying, "Hey! Check this out!" Mirabel clicks a phone app to turn a lamp on and off. They're sixteen, thirteen, and nine. Mom says I met Mirabel when I was little, but I don't remember that. I might have met Raúl if he weren't going to the other junior high. They bundle me off to another part of the apartment. "This is our room," they say, pointing to three mattresses on the floor and a wall full of animal posters.

Tía Lencha calls out something, and they answer in fluent Spanish. Then a few sentences that sound like half English and half Spanish zip between them. I listen hard, but I can't keep up.

"We have our own game system in here," Crista says.

"Have you played *Raft Racer*?" Raúl asks. "What about *Catapult*?"

"Give her some space!" Mirabel says and turns to me. "They're just excited, is all."

Finally, we plop down on a comforter with a unicorn on it; I'm guessing it's Crista's.

"So Quijana, where are the horses?" Raúl asks. His black hair stands thick on his head like a push broom. "I keep asking, but no one will tell me."

"Huh?"

"Is this Texas or what?"

"Oh!" I squelch a laugh. "Most people don't own horses here."

"Yeah, not a single person rode a horse to school." He's shaking his head.

"Not that different from Chicago?"

"I'm really bummed," he says. "*Tssss.*"

Mirabel leans in. She's in high school and wears makeup, and her wavy hair, I notice, is stiff with gel. "Our friends up home were convinced we'd ride to school on horseback."

"I like your hair, Quijana," Crista says.

"Yours is pretty, too," I say. In fact, we have similar hair. Long, dark brown, and thick enough to hang hot on our necks in summer.

"Can I braid it?" Crista asks.

"Hey!" Raúl jumps off the bed. "Rubber-band wars!"

Crista hops up, and even Mirabel runs across the room and reaches behind a dresser.

"What's . . . ," I start.

They pull out giant rubber bands and start stretching them across bars of wood on homemade rubber-band guns. A clothespin on the end of the device holds the rubber band until it's released.

This has possibilities!

"I can share with you, Quijana," offers Crista.

"Wait," says Mirabel. "Here's Dad's," she says, handing me another rubber-band gun.

With the parents buckled into their conversations in the living room, the rest of the apartment is ours. The only rule is no aiming for faces. We run rooms, we climb counters. We hide behind doors and ambush each other. My best move is when I hide behind a recliner and land a rubber band on Raúl's shin, even if I take a double hit from Crista and Mirabel. We fall down on one of their mattress beds laughing. I can't remember the last time I had this much fun.

Finally Mirabel announces, "All right, chicos, I have some people to talk to," and disappears behind her phone.

The rest of us decide to sneak up on the grown-ups. "I'm not shooting Mami," Crista says.

"Of course not," Raúl says. "Just hit the wall near her head. First we'll do some reconnaissance."

"What?" Crista says.

"You know, get the lay of the land. Scope out the enemy."

Crista still looks confused, but I imitate Raúl, who drops to his stomach. A row of folding chairs marks the front lines, and we crawl up to eavesdrop. Crista giggles, which makes me giggle, too.

"Shh!" says Raúl.

"Sorry," says Crista, still laughing. "Shh!" she says to me.

"Shh!" I say back, also laughing. Even Raúl presses his lips together to hold back a chuckle.

It's more giggles and shushing each other until I hear my father mention my name. I listen more carefully. The Spanish is sounding less like a string of noise and more like individual words. I catch a few that I must have learned from children's songs. Then I understand a whole sentence, spoken by my aunt.

"¿Nunca te llama Papi?" *She never calls you Papi?*

My father answers, "No, ella me llama Dad." *She calls me Dad.*

The adults move on, paddling their conversation out of that eddy, but open water stretches between me and my cousins as they turn to stare. "You say 'Dad'?" Raúl asks.

"Sure. Don't you?" I know the answer.

Raúl sits up and looks at Crista, then confirms, "We say 'Papi.'"

"So?" I sit up, too.

"Leave her alone," Crista says, taking my arm.

"But it's weird. Like, he never said 'Call me Dad,' did he?"

"Well, no."

"Then why do you?" Raúl throws his rubber-band gun aside and stands up.

"I was born here," I say, standing up, too.

"But your *papi* wasn't." He shakes his head and wanders to the kitchen.

"Raúl!" Crista shouts, watching him go. "He can be a jerk. Want to keep playing?"

"Nah." I feel a little sick, but I shrug as Crista starts putting away the rubber-band guns.

Why does he care? We've played in English this whole time. Still, *Papi, Papi* repeats in my head. Raúl *is* being a jerk, but what if he's right? Does Dad want to be called Papi? He didn't call his own father "Dad," and he's obsessed with showing me exactly how he did things as a kid. Now the word sounds flat to me: Dad. The "a" seems smashed. Papi sounds rounder, more like a hug. Does more love fit in that open-mouthed *ah*? Why do I suddenly feel like I can't do anything right?

Memito starts crying, bored of Mom's lap and the grown-up talk. "I'll take him," I say. I gather him up, and we step outside by ourselves. Just concrete and parked cars out here, but I don't want to go back in. Memito likes the quiet, too. He squats down to pick up a leaf and looks at it up close.

I send Jayden a text, but he doesn't answer. I reread our texts from Friday night and don't feel any better. A string of silly emojis from Grandma helps a little.

Memito whimpers, and I see that his overall strap is twisted. When I fix it, his face shows relief, but soon he drops his leaf and whimpers until I have to take him in. I think of getting a bottle of bubbles out of his toy bag, but this day is definitely a popped balloon because he immediately wiggles till I put him down, and then he runs straight toward Crista. You're welcome, Memito.

Where's Mirabel? She wasn't part of the Papi-Dad mess, and she has movie stars on the wall above her bed like a typical teen. She and I could breathe blue-jean air and trade Coca-Cola talk. But when I find her in the kitchen, Raúl is already talking to her at the counter, in Spanish of course. Raúl stops mid-sentence when he sees me, but then continues and smirks. Is he talking about me? He leaves the room, still grinning.

Finally, Mom's voice carries in from the living room. "Time to go!" she says. I'm more than ready to leave. I whisk up Memito and walk into the living room just as Mom's saying, "I can't believe we never made it to Chicago!"

"We understand," Tía Lencha says. "All of us, we always working."

Mom agrees, nodding as she hugs Tía. "We'll have to do this again soon!"

Great.

When the cousins line up to hug us, they act like nothing's happened. Nothing really has, for them. I'm the one who can't switch languages like bike speeds. Grandma Miller says to never apologize for who you are, but who even am I? My cousins have something I'm supposed to have, too.

Everyone adioses but me. I stubbornly say bye. I look at Memito. He's lucky. No one expects him to say anything.

In the car, I put my earbuds in. I can't find a just-right song, so I sit in silence. Unfortunately, this means I hear Mom gushing on and on about how amazing my cousins are.

"Those kids are something!" she says. "So polite and speaking English like they're native-born."

"Lencha and Pancho must be proud." Dad shakes his head. "Wow."

I feel a pinch on my heart, and I pick a loud song to drown out whatever they say next.

TEN

I'VE NEVER BEEN SO GLAD to get on the school bus Monday morning. As we jostle along, I check my messages.

Make your day amazing! says Grandma.

You too, I type back.

I snap a selfie, holding my sea turtle bracelet near my face. SEND. The bus turns the last corner, and no new messages. I decide to ask.

Any test results yet? As I exit the bus, my phone vibrates.

Not yet. The spider orchids started blooming down at the bog, the blossoms you called hoodie fairies—a much better name! Remember how you pressed them in the pages of my chemistry book?

I send Grandma a smiley face and a woman-scientist emoji.

Maybe today *can* be amazing, but not until after second-period Spanish. Now that I've heard the Carrillos, learning Spanish seems harder than ever. All three kids can talk the legs off a chair in either language. And faster than Dad. As I walk down the hall, I focus on the black-and-white clock at the end and brace myself for what's becoming my least-favorite subject.

"Bienvenidos, clase!" Señora Francés sweeps out from behind her desk. As soon as the bell rings, she's at the whiteboard and talking. After some chalked charts and a PowerPoint presentation, we're supposedly ready to practice vocabulary and conjugations aloud. I'm not. I read the book's examples again.

"Número uno." Señora Francés looks over the top of her teacher's-edition textbook and sweeps her gaze around the room.

Since we're in the second week of school, there's no more easy stuff like Spanish-izing our names and greeting each other. Last week, it was all about "Suzy" turning into "Susana," Ms. French into Señora Francés, "¡Hola!" and "¿Como estás?"— fun because I knew it all. Now I see that all the Spanish I know fits into one week of class. A thimbleful of ocean.

At least Ms. French is nice. She joked about her name the first day. "My name is Ms. French, but I teach Spanish. I keep hoping I'll meet a Ms. Spanish who teaches French. We'd be mirror twins!" We laughed. Week one was fun.

No one is laughing now.

"Anyone?" Señora asks. I lower my head. "Quijana?"

My skin goes cold because in other classes I am the hand-raiser, the one who likes knowing answers. But now the answer is a dollar lost in the sofa cushions. I'm still searching when she says, "Just say what sounds right to you."

Sounds right? All the answers seem like Monopoly money.

I look up to see a smile that seems to say, "This is easy for you, right?"

An *Oh* unlatches. I see myself as my teacher does. She thinks my dark brown hair knows the answer. She's betting my toasted skin can conjugate verbs. She looks at my name and thinks "Latina."

My mind leaps back to a woman at the park last summer. As I caught Memito on the slide, she said, "You people are so good with children." I like compliments, but that one felt prickly. Was it even a compliment? Now it's happening again, that prickly feeling. *Guess what, Ms. Francés, the* j *in my name doesn't tell me the answers.* At the same time, I shrink in my seat, knowing she's partly right. Look at my name, my dad, my cousins. I can't even get number one? This would give Raúl something to smirk about.

I'm stalled out at the diálogo in our textbook. I don't know what Alberto asks Maria or how to say he was born in Bolivia. What if I can't learn this? I think of Mirabel and Crista talking like bullet trains. Me stuck at the station.

Señora Francés moves on to the girl behind me and makes her way down each row. She runs out of questions before she runs out of kids, but nobody's off the hook because she shouts, "Clear your desks!" A quiz.

I plug in as many conjugations as I can, erasing a few answers before rewriting my original ones. When time is up, I've written at least a guess in each blank, but my head hurts.

"Time to trade and grade," says Señora Francés. She calls out the answers, and the student next to me gleefully marks big x's next to my wrong words.

Suddenly the bell rings, and I'm saved from more embarrassment. Into a recycle bin I drop today's quiz with its huge C on top.

At Port 3, Jayden finds me right away. My day brightens, just seeing him.

"What'd you write about?" he says. We exchange poems, and I read about a hot-fudge sundae. Zuri shows us her pizza poem.

When the bell rings, Ms. May shouts, "Galway Kinnell!"

Is this some new kid?

"He wrote the poem on the screen. 'Blackberry Eating.' Who wants to read it aloud? Notice his vivid descriptions!"

The poem is an ode to deliciousness. It makes me crave lunch.

"Now rewrite your poems, taking Kinnell as inspiration," Ms. May announces. "Imitate his style. Use his structure. Push yourself!"

I'm not sure how to start, so I make my first line almost a copy of Kinnell's. "I love to go to the freezer in late July . . ." Then new pictures come to mind. Vivid words pop in. I follow his poem's path. The plain description I brought to class becomes high-def and surround sound. "Drips of juice trickle / the slushy tip gives way between my teeth."

"Lunch! We'll share these in groups when you return."

I stand up slowly, not wanting to leave the words, not wanting to lift out of the flow. Right now I wish my whole world was this desk.

"You coming?" Jayden nudges me with his shoulder. His touch brings me to the surface, and I walk out with him and Zuri, my mind still drifting.

"Check out my new yo-yo trick!" He throws down the yo-yo, grabs up the string, and makes a triangle. Inside, the yo-yo swings like a pendulum. "Yes ma'am! Rocking that baby."

"Wait, do it again," Zuri says, watching closely.

Jayden goes through each step more slowly for her, then hands her the yo-yo. "Start with Sleeper, then grab. Now spread your fingers. Swing it. Let go. That's it!"

Zuri does it again, then drops the toy into Jayden's hand.

My joy deflates just a little. Her orange shirt splashed with flowers, the British accent, skill with math *and* yo-yos. How can Zuri be so perfect? Even Grandma Miller would like her. *Of course I would!* I imagine Grandma saying. And then, *I love you, too, Quijana. Love isn't a cookie jar that runs out. It's infinite cookies.*

"You want to learn?" Jayden holds out the yo-yo to me.

"Sure!"

"Put your middle finger through the loop. Here, let me tighten it for you." I breathe in Jayden's soapy scent as he bends over my hand. "Now throw it down, then jerk the string up." Instead of snapping back, the yo-yo hangs limply above my shoe. "Try again. It takes a while to get the feel of it."

"Quijana!" Ms. May startles me from the steps of Port 3, and I worry that I'm in trouble. "I bet you're named after Don Quixote!"

Oh no. For once, I wish Ms. May wasn't so loud. Jayden and Zuri look up. "Yes, ma'am," I say.

"Major literary character of Spain. World-famous knight!"

Yeah, famous for screwing up.

Ms. May is off in her own world. "A dreamer, but he always fights for the little guy. He does more than tilt at windmills." Suddenly she's back in my face. "Are you going to live up to your name?"

"I—I'll try to."

"Do! You can." She winks, and I want to say, *You have the wrong girl. I'm not fighting for anyone, and I'm not anything like the insane knight who charges at windmills.*

"So *that's* where your name comes from," says Jayden, taking back the yo-yo as the three of us walk to lunch.

"Yup." I sigh.

"What's wrong?" Zuri says.

"You want the truth?"

"Of course," she says.

"He's not even a knight. His real name is Alonso Quixana. He's an old guy who dresses in ratty armor and rides his farm horse." They slow down and look at me. "The thing is, there hadn't been any knights for a hundred years when he went on his quest. He just read about them. It's all a fantasy. He's crazy."

As we open the cafeteria doors, Jayden says, "Sounds like this dude needs to talk to Batman, get some better gear."

"What's with the windmills?" Zuri asks.

"He thinks they're monsters."

"O-kay . . ." She's getting the picture now.

We sit down at our usual table. "Why would your parents name you after this guy?" asks Jayden.

"Because they hate me?" I laugh, knowing this isn't true, knowing that Mom and Dad love Don Quixote. I'm the hater.

They laugh, and for the rest of lunch I'm trying to listen, but I feel like a smashed can. I'm not doing much better than Don Quixote. My cousins' faces spring up in front of me, then the confusing Spanish book page, and finally the dumb gleam in Ms. French's eye. The knight and I do have something in common; we're both major disappointments. I shake my head to erase the pictures and try to focus on my friends.

As she talks, Zuri's absently folding a paper napkin.

"Hey, can I show you something with that?" I ask. She slides me the napkin, and I fold it in half lengthwise. In a few more folds, I bend the whole thing at the middle and pinch the center between my thumb and index finger.

"A bow tie!" Jayden says, reaching over and holding it up to his neck. "How does it look?"

"Like a professor!" Zuri says.

"Like a hipster," I say. "All you need is black glasses."

"Can you make them out of a napkin for me?" Jayden winks.

I laugh. "I'll have to learn."

"Can you do an animal?" Zuri asks.

Jayden hands me his unused napkin, and I smooth it out. It's nice and square. Can I remember the swan I made for Grandma's birthday party last summer? "It works better with cloth," I say. I make the two folds and stop to think. Then my fingers take over, remembering for me. I fold down the beak and extend the body.

"It's a swan!" Zuri squeals. "Right?"

"Right," I say, swimming it toward her.

Jayden leans over the table to look. "Are these cool or what?"

When we ramble back to class, Jayden walks on one side of me, Zuri the other. It feels good, like we're rock, paper, scissors or an equilateral triangle. Dad once said three is a magic number, and Grandma agreed. "Solid, liquid, gas. Proton, neutron, electron." I wasn't sure there was something special about three, but today, I believe it.

ELEVEN

AT HOME THAT EVENING, Mom gives Memito a bath and reads him to sleep while Dad folds laundry and I make my lunch for tomorrow—PB&J again and a pear from the farmer's market.

I'm flossing my teeth when I hear a question coming from the dining room. "I know this was my idea, but can we afford it?" It's Dad's voice, but he's dialed it down; he thinks I can't hear. I stop and listen.

"It's a great idea. Your mother hasn't seen Quijana since she was a baby," Mom says, "and they've never even met Memito."

My abuela saw me as a baby? I only know her from photos and Dad's monthly phone calls. Plus the letters that used to come in the mail, envelopes with little airplanes on the corners and POR AVIÓN stamped on the front. Inside was delicate paper, thin enough to see through, and blue handwriting wiggling from edge to edge.

Dad drops his voice even lower. "When Pancho talked about our mother yesterday, un anhelo se agitó en mi corazón." I recognize the word "heart." "I miss her. And everyone."

"Por supuesto, mi amor, of course. Will the station give you time off?" Mom asks.

"I haven't taken a day off in . . ." I know Dad is thinking back years. He never misses work. "Since Memito was born." Dad's a sound engineer. At the radio station, he chooses the music that plays between news reports—not whole songs, just clips, to put the story in the right mood. He always picks the right one. A lone violin after sad news and jumpy trumpets after funny stories. "The newscasters speak to the head," he always says. "I speak to the heart."

"Well, I'll check flights to Guatemala City in December." Mom starts clicking keys on the laptop.

Guatemala? The floor drops away from my feet. It's Spanish class all over again, plus those Latina girls, plus Raúl, plus the fact that Guatemala will be crawling with cousins and not one of them speaks English. This cannot happen. I'll be a mute cardboard girl they drag from one gathering to the next.

I march into the dining room. "Mom. Dad." They look at me, their eyebrows arching at the same time. Even surprised, they're like the most in-love couple ever. "If you're talking about going to Guatemala, I can't go. I can't go to Guatemala."

"Honey," my mother starts.

"No," I say.

"Quijanita." My father pours out my nickname, sticky-sweet like pancake syrup.

I picture the daughter they must wish I were. My stomach feels filled with crumpled paper.

"It's not until Christmas, sweetie," my mother coos.

"I don't care when it is. I'm not going. You didn't even ask me first!" Tears form, but I won't let them fall.

"Could she stay with your sister?" Dad says to Mom quietly.

My head lifts. Aunt Jess! She's awesome. She has no kids and talks to me like a grown-up. She has a butterfly tattoo on her ankle. Plus her condo has a pool. I look at Mom.

"No. I mean, of course she *could,* but she should see your side of the family. That's the whole point."

Dad's nodding and rubbing his ear. He knows she's right. Even I know she's right.

The thing is, I wish I did want to go. I wish I wanted to meet these strangers who are actually family. At the same time, I wish there was no Guatemala. No place that would ever make me feel stupid and not-good-enough. I blink fast, trying to stop the tears.

"Quijana," says Mom, "it will . . ."

I'm in my room before they can say anything more. On my bed, I cry into my pillow, wishing the manatee on my pillow-case would come to life and hug me.

When my tears run dry, I text Grandma Miller.

They're planning a trip to Guatemala. Help!

But nothing comes back. She's probably asleep.

"Qui?" It's Mom coming to get my phone to charge it in the living room overnight. This keeps me from using it past bedtime.

"Here." I hold the phone up without looking at her.

She doesn't take it. She sits on my bed and pushes my long hair out of my face, pressing it behind my shoulders. "Why don't you want to go?"

The reasons pile so high that I can't see her. I can't answer.

"The airplane ride will be fun. We'll still have Christmas presents."

None of that matters.

She exhales. "Well, can you take your phone out to the living room?" she says, her voice almost calm enough to soothe me. "Your dad wants to talk to you."

Can this night get worse? I stomp down the hall. Dad's stationed in an easy chair by the charger.

"Quijana," he says, "I know a new country can be . . . frightening. I know it from experience, eh? But we'll be with you. And I want to show you the place I come from," he says, "where I played as a boy, where I went to school. And your family. Your abuela wants to see you."

No one cares what I want.

"Besides, you'll love it. And they'll love you." He smiles as if this solves everything, as if he can change my mind with nothing but good intentions. I promise myself to hate Guatemala.

I plug in my phone and walk back in my room without saying good night. Who cares if I'm sulking? They should have called a family meeting and discussed this. I am not a piece of luggage.

When I try to sleep, I still see Raúl laughing at me—going silent when I come in and then smirking. I'm sure he was talking about me. A drowning feeling makes me gasp for air, and I sit up. I cannot go. I will not.

I slide out of bed and open my laptop. I type *Bus fare from Bur Oak, Texas to Ocala, Florida.* If I tried to run away to Aunt Jess's across town, they would just come and get me. So I have to go all the way to Grandma Miller's. It has to be Florida.

It'll be just like last summer's family trip. We took the bus to Grandma's when airport workers went on strike. I remember the stops and the fast-food places and what the Ocala station looks like—everything I need to know.

A list of fares and dates pops up. Next to BOOK NOW is a dollar sign and a big number, bigger than I expected. $177. I count up my birthday money and allowance in my head. I have about $40. That leaves $137, not including tax.

What if I *could* earn the bus money? Maybe I could sell some stuff or walk neighborhood dogs? I'd buy a ticket and leave on the day of the Guatemala trip. *Wait.* The day before. I have to be gone before they can stop me. Better yet, the night before.

I picture the events in order: I sneak out when everyone is asleep. I get on a night bus and ride to Grandma's and spend Christmas vacation with her.

But is there a bus that leaves at night? The times aren't showing on the screen. I click BOOK NOW to see what happens. A schedule runs down the page. 8:25 a.m., noon, 7:05 p.m., 10:35 p.m.—that's it! 10:35 is after my bedtime. I can pretend to go to bed, climb out my window, and walk to the bus station. I tremble, thinking, *This could actually happen.*

Money is my only problem. And telling Grandma.

I could tell her at Thanksgiving. But then she'll tell my parents. I could say Mom and Dad are letting me stay with her. Tell her it's their idea. But can I lie to Grandma? Somehow lying feels more dangerous than riding a bus a thousand miles by myself. Okay, I could surprise her. Call her from the road. Meanwhile, Mom, Dad, and Memito would be flying to Guatemala without me.

It's not a perfect plan, but it's a start. I can sort out more details later. The main snag is bus fare. Looking around my room in the dark, I don't see anything to sell. But it's only September. I have over three months. *It'll be okay. One thing at a time. Make more plans tomorrow.*

TWELVE

I WAKE UP and make a list of things to sell on eBay. My lava lamp. A snow globe with a music box in the bottom. In my closet, I find old games and puzzles. Nothing's worth much. My bicycle? Too noticeable. In the shower, I remember something else.

The huipil.

A hand-woven top must be worth something. Mom and Dad would never let me do this, but I'm going to anyway. After all, I'll never wear it.

I bring up eBay on my laptop and click Register. I enter my name, my email address. *Oh no.* I have to click "I am at least 18 years of age." My mouse hovers over the box. Well, how would they know? I imagine sirens going off or a voice coming through my computer: "You are twelve! Your computer will now be confiscated!"

I can't figure out how the computer would know that, but I'm still worried. I don't want to know what happens. I "x" that window. I'll have to think of some other way to sell it.

A text comes from Grandma.

You're going to Guatemala? World traveler! Embrace the adventure! Enjoy the day, sweetie. :-)

I should have known she'd think Guatemala would be fun. Sure. As fun as collecting fingernail clippings.

By the time I get to school, I'm a self-doubt sandwich. Normal on the outside, worried on the inside. Where can I sell the huipil? Or how else can I earn money? Will it even work? It has to. I'm so wrapped up in the plan that Mr. Wilson, my Texas history teacher, has to say my name twice before I hear him.

Even English isn't much fun, and I'm glad when lunch comes, though I'm not hungry. I toss my lunch sack on the table, leaving it unopened. Jayden takes the round stool opposite me, and Zuri sits next to him. A soft thud thumps my chest. I was stupid to sit down first. Tomorrow I'll let Jayden sit first, then claim the next-to seat.

They chat about the usual things, but I can't concentrate. Zuri finally notices. "What's up, Q?"

I can't help but grumble. Just thinking about this trip makes my stomach spasm. "My parents want us to fly to Guatemala for Christmas."

"And you don't want to go?" Jayden looks shocked, like he's wanted to tour Central America all his life.

"No way. I won't be able to talk to anyone. It'll be horrific."

"Talking's overrated," Jayden says. "You have a great smile."

The whole cafeteria has magically brightened.

"Your parents can translate for you, right?" Zuri says.

"They could, but . . ." I shake my head. "I don't want to go. I just don't."

"But you have to, right?" Jayden shrugs, and I realize that they don't understand. I want to explain, but no words come. Just a twisting in my gut every time I imagine the trip.

"Hey," Jayden says, "your trip reminds me of an idea I had. A movie!"

"Going to one?" I ask, thinking, *Yes yes yes.*

"Making one!" The light in Jayden's eyes makes me forget Guatemala and buses and money for a second.

But Zuri's face looks like she's swallowed flat soda. "I'm not starring in any more homemade horror movies." She looks so serious, I can't help but laugh.

"Oh, come on," Jayden says. "That was fifth grade. It'll be different this time. No ketchup blood, I promise. Anyway, that old video camera was cool. How could I resist? QuiQui here would have tried it out, right?"

I'm giggling, imaging Jayden behind an old-style camera choosing a location, setting up a shot.

"Admit it; it was fun."

"It was not fun." Zuri drops each word like a brick, but she's grinning.

I count back to fifth grade, when they met. Two years ago. That's four birthday parties, a lot of shared jokes, and at least one homemade horror movie. I can't figure them out. Are they truly just friends? They sit with each other, not a group. Mom says I overanalyze. Can a girl and a boy *be* just friends?

"Okay, fine. No movies. But let's at least do something outside of school for once. What if we took an all-day bike ride?"

A tingle climbs up my spine. "I know a place! There's a bike trail about a half hour from here that goes to Eagle Lake and back. Fifteen miles each way. My Aunt Jess told me about it."

"Perfect!" Zuri says. "Only, do you think our parents will let us do it?"

"We'll be together," says Jayden. "Besides, you and I have biked all over town."

Years of bike rides. How will I ever catch up?

Jayden tilts his head back and looks at the ceiling. "I wish we could go tomorrow. Why is it only Tuesday?"

"How about Sunday?" I want to go soon, too. After this, we *three* will share a memory.

"Sunday's good," Zuri says. "Text when we get the okay from our parents?"

Going to class, Jayden falls into stride next to me, leaning over my phone to see the Eagle Lake trail map. I like the fresh-laundry smell of his shirt. At the classroom door, he says, "I can't wait!"

"Your parents are easier than mine," Zuri reminds him.

I cross my fingers on both hands and make an X with my forearms. I hope we get permission; I hope Jayden will like me as much as he likes Zuri; I hope my life is becoming what I've always dreamed—filled with people and places I am curious about.

In class, Ms. May shouts, "Y'all hush now," and she reads us a poem about two roads diverging in a wood, but I don't see the poem the way she does. A traveler comes upon a fork in the path. He chooses one, and Ms. May says, "Choices create your future." The kind of thing my dad would say.

But the man in the poem sighs. He can't come back to this place and try the other road. He can't take both, only one. I picture my Carrillo cousins walking away on one road, and my friends disappearing around the curve of another. Is there a third road somewhere, wide enough to hold us all?

In choir, we warm up our voices, singing a scale up and down. Sitting up straight and using my voice helps me set aside other thoughts.

"Today we'll put all four parts together," Mr. Green announces. *Yes!* I do a little seat jump. Until now, we've been learning our song's parts separately: soprano, alto, tenor, and bass by themselves, with Mr. Green banging out each one on the piano. "Let's take it slow, all right?" he says. "First chord. Basses, give us the root." The boys in the bass section concentrate and blend their voices into one note. "Now tenors." We stack the chord, then move to the second one. The song unfolds in slow motion. I soak in the sound, listening both to myself and the whole room. As we reach the final phrase, I'm filled with hope. The bike trip, the bus to Grandma's—if I think hard and plan, I know it can all work out.

THIRTEEN

ON THE BUS HOME, I'm picturing how I'll ask Mom and Dad about the bike trip. They *have* to say yes if I show them the map and prove that we're organized. I think about my money plan, too. Maybe I could get a job. If there's a job to get. The people a few houses down have a dog I could walk....

"Quijana, hope your day was good!" says Mom. "Can you make dinner for you and your brother? Dad had to stay late tonight, and I have class."

Ah, a job already. Too bad it's unpaid.

I have to show them how responsible I am if I want to go on the bike trip, so I stand up straight and listen. "There's bread and cheese in the fridge. Rinse the pan when you're done, not only the dishes, and then run the dishwasher. Make sure to wash off Memito's tray by hand." She kisses me on the forehead and cups a hand under my chin. "Thanks, sweetie. You'll be on your own until eight."

That leaves me, the big sister, in charge—watching Memito, flipping cheese sandwiches, and cleaning up. Not to mention homework. No money-planning tonight.

"De tal palo, tal astilla."

I tilt my head.

"From such a stick, such a splinter," Mom says, grabbing her purse. "You're like your dad—the oldest kid and reliable. Of course, it's only the two of you instead of six!" She gives me a wink.

Mom's keys jangle out the door, and Memito raises his arms. "Up!" One of the few words he'll say.

"Okay, little guy." I hoist him up.

"Mama?" he says. That's another.

"No. Just me and you."

Memito is deciding whether to cry, a top starting to wobble.

I give him a new spin with, "Outside?" and he wriggles down. I grab my backpack on our way out.

Memito's favorite toy is a tricycle that he drives between our mailbox and the neighbor's. He circles our driveway and pedals up the sidewalk. Watching him is pretty easy since I know what he likes.

As he makes engine noises, I sit on a plastic yard chair and open my earth science book. Ms. Gupta is serious. Assignments every day. I reread the first section and put a heading on my paper. I answer the first question in a complete sentence. Pretty boring.

I wonder if Jayden or Zuri is doing this same assignment. I think of texting them, but then stop.

It's too quiet.

Scanning the sidewalk, I throw my book into the chair. "Memito?" The yard stands empty. Did he pedal too far to be heard? I follow the sidewalk to the neighbor's, beyond the neighbor's house, and to the next one. Would he go this far? I run past a third house, then turn back, gulping air as I approach our yard again. "Memito!"

If I've lost my brother . . . I can't even think the end of that sentence. "Memiiiiiito!" What if he's hurt, kidnapped, eating a poisonous plant, crossing a busy street, crying, scared? Why did Mom think I could do this?

If he is okay, I think to myself, *I will get 100s for the rest of the year. I will clean his room. I will always help put away groceries.* Worry squeezes my throat.

I catch sight of the tricycle in our side yard. "Memito?" Its seat is empty, but it looks unharmed. I check the backyard. Make a full circle around the house. Where is he?

Then the front door opens and out he toddles, chugging a sippy cup. I whoosh him up, press him close. He smells of apple juice and crayons.

"Qui," he says. Tears spring to my eyes.

"Yes, Memito. I'm Qui. And you are beautiful."

"Full?" he says.

"Yes, '-ful.'" I don't know if boys can be beautiful, but it is the only word with enough syllables, enough length to wrap all the way around us, like the giant towels Grandma Miller wraps us in at the beach.

He goes back to his tricycle, but I can't go back to school-work. I watch him until my stomach nudges me to make dinner.

Inside, we go to the kitchen. I warm a pan and butter slices of brown bread while Memito plays with refrigerator magnets. I cut thick slabs of cheese, like Mom does, add a slice of tomato like Dad. I want to comfort us both. To make the house feel cozy instead of sprawling, lively instead of empty. Windows go gray as sunlight fades. I go from room to room, turning on lights. They help, but I still feel a gnawing emptiness. I think of last night's grand scheme. Can I actually handle riding that bus to Florida alone?

I flip one sandwich too late, the other too early. I'll eat the burned one, I decide, and fasten Memito into his booster seat.

I check the time. The kitchen clock ticks quietly, its hands in no hurry. Dad's still an hour away. Mom, even more. For now, I've landed our rickety airplane. Memito eats fast. I chew slowly, trying to make dinner last as long as possible. I'm ready to give back this pilot's hat.

At the sound of Dad's car, relief floods through me. "Dad!"

He's smiling, but after I hug him, he pulls back and gives me a funny look. "You missed me that much?"

I'm so glad not be in charge anymore that I tell him, "Yes!" even though I feel six years old again for admitting it, even though we're both kind of dippy-dunky happy.

Then just as immediately, I'm clobbered with exhaustion, as if all the stress gave my muscles a workout.

But I still have one more thing to do tonight, so I lie in bed, listening for the garage door.

"Dad, is that Mom?" I say, padding into the kitchen.

"You're still awake?"

"I have to ask you guys something."

Mom bustles in with her book bag and backpack. "Well, you're up late. Everything okay?"

"Sure. But Zuri and Jayden and I, we want to take a bike ride. A bike *trip*."

"A trip, huh?" Mom walks up behind Dad, gives him a kiss on the cheek, and rubs his shoulders. He sips his coffee and grasps one of her hands.

"Yes. A trip. Aunt Jess told me about it—the Eagle Lake trail. Here's the map." I bring out my phone. "We want to go on Sunday. And, oh, we'll need a ride," I add.

Mom nods. "How did it go today?" She looks at Dad instead of me. Are they even listening?

"She did well. Pan washed. Memito fed." Dad gives me a smile. The memory of Memito's empty tricycle comes back to me, and I look away.

"How long is this trail?" Mom asks.

"Fifteen miles out to the lake."

"So thirty miles?" Dad says. "What is that, fifty kilometers?" He's always converting U.S. measurements to metric, like they use in Guatemala. He whistles. "That's a ways."

"Quijana, are you up to that?"

"Google says it takes less than three hours each way." I may not be an expert babysitter, but I can Google all right.

"These young people and their energy," Dad says. "I can drive them out there in the truck. Bikes in the back."

Mom frowns. "So this is Zuri and Jayden? What are their parents saying?"

"I don't know yet."

Mom turns to Dad. "Weren't we going to see Pancho, Lencha, and the kids on Sunday?"

"They won't mind," he says. "And you and I can still drop in for a few hours."

"Mm," she says. "Do you know how to fix a flat?"

"Um . . ." I think quickly. "We'll find a YouTube video and practice."

Mom looks at Dad, who gives a tiny nod. She says, "If the other parents agree, you can go."

"Thanks, y'all!" I give them a joint hug. "We'll be careful. We'll take water bottles. And a lunch."

"I know you'll plan carefully," Mom says.

"Get your friends' addresses," Dad adds, "so we can pick them up."

"By the way, Qui," Mom says, her voice quieter. "I got a text from Grandma today. She's in some pain, so they gave her a new medicine. Just something to keep in mind if she's not on Skype with you so much this week."

I open my mouth and close it again.

She nods and gives me a small smile. "It's okay. I just want you to know, in case she doesn't call very soon."

"We'll all be patient with her, won't we," says Dad.

"We will," I say. I hate to think of Grandma in pain. Not even on purpose, my voice comes out soft, wishing that that alone could help. "Do they know if it's cancer yet?"

"Not yet, sweetie," Mom says. "We'll hear soon."

FOURTEEN

I SEND A ROW OF *X*'S AND *O*'S to Grandma, kisses and hugs. Then I text Zuri and Jayden about the bike trip.

Mom and Dad said YES! As long as yours did.

And they did! At school, we make lists of supplies and watch two YouTube videos on how to fix a flat. Lunch feels five minutes long.

At home, I'm slurping on an apple-juice Popsicle, thinking through our plans, when I hear the car, and Dad brings Memito in from preschool.

"Hey, Dad. Memito!" I swing my little brother around. When I set him down, he turns me into a flagpole and runs circles around me.

"You're in a good mood!" Dad hangs up his jacket.

"I'm excited about our trip! We're all going!"

"I'm excited you're excited finally! We'll see that lake in person." He points over my head to the painting of Lake Atitlán.

No, Dad. "I meant the bike trip."

"Oh." He pulls on his right ear. "Speaking of Guatemala, though, remember we're getting passport photos tomorrow."

"Do I have to?"

He laughs. "Only if you want to be able to leave the country." He starts flipping through the mail.

"But I *don't* want to leave the country."

"Well, you also need a passport to get back in. Unless you want to stay in Guatemala for a few years."

"Dad!"

Finally, he flashes an I-was-kidding smile. I guess I'll have to play along tomorrow—sign a form, I bet, and pose for the camera. But they can't make me smile.

My phone vibrates, and Jayden's number glows on my screen. I could handspring across the house. "Phone," I say, handing Memito off to Dad and bounding toward my room.

"Bike trip!" Jayden yells.

"Bike trip!"

"Okay, but first algebra?"

"Mine's done."

"What'd you get for number sixteen?"

I sit cross-legged on my bedroom floor and pull out my paper. "Eleven."

"Oh no!" Jayden calls algebra a bad marriage between letters and numbers. "But what about the negative?"

"The negatives cancel," I say.

"Where?"

Jayden can do impressions of famous people better than TV comedians and ace Ms. May's poetry tests, but he needs, well, *practice* with math, to put it politely. For me, numbers behave. X hides, but the other numbers point to it until there's only one place to look.

"See that first step," I say. "The 'minus five' becomes 'plus negative.'"

"Oh yeah! Eleven!" he says. "I had the weirdest déjà vu just now. Have we done this math problem before?"

"No."

"I swear I remember this exact conversation."

"First time. Promise."

He hums the opening notes of *The Twilight Zone* theme.

"What do you think it means?" I ask. *I* think it's a sign. We're two factors of a composite number; we're a solution set.

He hits it back to me. "What do *you* think it means?"

My face warms. "Maybe it means we're on the right track. It's like the fruit cups. Like, this is good." By *this* I mean adding our lives together, multiplying the ways we can connect.

"So we should always check our math on the phone?"

"Uh, sure," I say. "And talk and stuff."

"Well, duh. We'll always talk." The word *always* echoes in my head like a repeating decimal. "I just hope it means I'll remember how to do this equation stuff. Hold on," he says.

I lean back against my bed. It's different, this feeling. I've had crushes before—boys I stared at but didn't talk to. Here I am, jokey and comfortable with Jayden. He's a magic number that solves two equations at once, a friend who could (couldn't he?) be a boyfriend. I just hope I'm a magic number for him.

"Back. Had to fill a sippy cup for my brother."

"Been there," I say. "Hey, Jayden?"

"Mm?"

"Have you ever kept a secret from your parents?"

"I guess. Little stuff. Why?"

I close my bedroom door and go into my closet, shutting that door, too. "Have you ever run away?"

"What are you talking about? You're not running away, are you?"

"No, no. I mean . . ."

"Qui. What. Is. Up?"

"Okay. Here it is." I take a deep breath. "I'm not going to Guatemala for Christmas."

"What do you mean?"

"If I go, I'll be miserable. So I'm taking a bus to Grandma's."

"Without your parents? Doesn't she live in Florida? Are you crazy? Does she—do they—know this?"

"I Googled departure times. I'm saving money for the ticket. I can't tell Grandma; she'll tell my parents."

"So you *are* crazy."

"Look, you don't know what it's like not being able to speak Spanish."

"But you're in Spanish class."

"So yeah, I'll be able to count to ten, say what time it is, and talk about the weather."

"How will you get to the bus without them finding out?"

"Sneak out the night before."

"Whoa." He sounds actually serious.

"It's not that big a deal," I snap. "People ride buses all the time."

"I'm just surprised is all," he says. "Hey, how about I walk you to the bus station. It must be two or three miles."

"Okay," I say, letting out a breath I didn't know I'd been holding. "Thanks." I'm glad I told him, even if he does think I'm a little loca.

"Seriously, Qui. Do you think you'll be safe on that bus? And what are your parents going to do? They'll think you ran away."

I sidestep the second part of his question. "I rode that exact bus just a few months ago. There was a kid who rode alone, too. He had a special card around his neck that said Unaccompanied Minor. The driver kept him up front. He was going even farther than we were."

"Too bad you can't ride your bike to Florida!"

"You never know," I say with a laugh.

When I hang up, I feel like I've run a race. I convinced him, but it tired me out. Does he have a point? What if he's right about Mom and Dad thinking I've run away? They might even call the police! I'll have to write a detailed note, explain everything. I can call them from the bus and let them know I'm fine. I open Notes on my phone and type reminders: *Leave a note on my pillow. Call home at their wake-up time.* I should be eight hours down the road by then.

I lie on my bed looking up at my manatee poster. Grandma says manatees were on the verge of extinction when she was my age. It was schoolkids who started a movement to protect them. They voted to make the manatee Florida's state marine mammal, and that brought scientists like Grandma in to make protection plans and safety zones. Because of kids, there are more than triple the number of manatees now.

My bus plan is simple compared to saving a species. No one believes it yet, but I can do this.

FIFTEEN

THE NEXT DAY GOES SMOOTH as jam on a pancake until we go to Walgreens after school for passport photos.

Memito squints and whines at the bright lights. I don't see other kids tearing up and rubbing their eyes, but I do see other customers looking at us, annoyed. "Can you take his picture first?" Mom asks the camera lady. "I'll go next, then take him to the car, I guess." It seems like we're doing things differently for Memito more and more. A few days ago, Dad had to cut all the tags out of Memito's shirts because Memito hunched his shoulders, twisted his head, and pulled at his shirt collar until it ripped.

Mom bundles Memito out to the car, and then it's my turn. Dad says, "Smile, hija. A lovely smile you have." I don't smile. The button clicks. "Wait, do it again," Dad says.

"The U.S. government prefers a neutral expression, sir."

Now I smile.

The lady motions for him to take the stool in front of the white screen. Dad makes his expression "neutral" too.

Outside, Mom takes one car to her night class. The rest of us take the other car home.

After homework, I sit cross-legged on my desk chair and open my laptop. Mom said Grandma's test results were due back in a few days. I hope she's online. She usually checks email after her supper, which is before supper in our time zone. I type,

Hey, Grandma.

Hey, sweet pea. Grandma's message pops up on a chat screen. **How's Jayden?**

I texted her about Jayden a few days ago, pretending he was just a nice kid I met. In two seconds she figured out that I liked him.

He's great.

But . . . ?

Grandma always knows when I'm holding back. The one thing I'm worried about with Jayden is that he's sticking me in the friend zone. Maybe she can help.

How do I get him to like me? I type.

Ah. Little one, right there is your problem.

Where?

You want to know the secret?

Well, duh! I send her just **?**

Don't try.

What?

You can't make him like you. If he likes you, he likes you. If not, fine. Don't "get him" to like you.

I think about this. My cursor blinks.

And if you change yourself to get anyone to like you, *I* won't like you, she types.

You're kidding, right?

Nope. I'll always love you, but I'll only LIKE you if you stay true to yourself.

I reread her sentence. I don't know what it means. Like, love. True to yourself. What if "myself" is boring? Or just lame?

Then figure out what makes you interesting. Do you know what I was doing when your grandpa called me for a first date? I was hiking the Appalachian Trail! My roommate had to take a message.

How long did he wait?

I hiked over 300 miles through four states right after college. I didn't come home for five weeks.

Over a month?

He always said I was worth the wait. But see? Don't wait around. Do something interesting. If you make your life interesting, that boy, and plenty of other people, will want to be part of it. Have you heard of gopher tortoises?

Just separate gophers and tortoises, I joke.

The gopher tortoise is a land turtle we have out here, about the size of your head. It's called a keystone species because when it makes its burrow in the sand, hundreds of other species move in, too, from rabbits to rattlesnakes.

And there's still enough room for the tortoise?

Sure. They dig a long, deep, sandy burrow. Plenty of room. Even owls move in.

I think I see what she's getting at, but I'm not quite sure. **So are you saying I'm a tortoise?**

I'm saying you are a keystone. Just do your thing, and the right friends will come along. If this Jayden doesn't like you, he's not worth it.

I guess.

You guess? What are you afraid of—that he won't like the real Quijana? Don't let fear narrow your life. Be YOU.

WHO IS THAT? I want to type back. But I send her a heart emoji instead.

Grandma seems strong. So strong that I almost forget she's sick. My feelings clear; she's telling me something to remember.

Do something interesting. Don't let fear narrow your life.

We say I love yous, and I'm alone with my laptop—and with a big question mark where my real self is supposed to be. I do love to sing, and I'm even learning to read music in choir.

Do something interesting. I type *learn guitar* into a search engine, surprising myself, since I told Dad no to guitar. But that's because *he* would teach me Spanish boleros, instead of the songs I like. But what if I could play my own music? Sing *and* strum. Compose a song of my own and accompany myself . . . I picture myself on a stage, alone, with a mic and a guitar.

My hand stops in the air above the Enter key. I don't want Dad to find my web history and ask me about it. I can already hear him saying, "¡Estupendo!" and making a big deal. I know he wants to be the one to teach me and pass down the tradition, but I have my own songs to sing. I push Dad aside. I think of Grandma and her adventures. ENTER.

YouTube shows me a long list of how-to videos. I pick "Learn Guitar in Ten Minutes a Day." The lady on-screen demonstrates a chord called G, then C, then D. With these three, she can play a whole song! Then she scrolls a list of songs that can all be played with only these chords. *I can do that,* I think. One set of chords, one song. I'll borrow Dad's guitar while he's picking up Memito from pre-K or when he and Mom come home late. My life is full of secrets all of a sudden, but this is one I'll share someday. Just not until I learn my own tunes.

I pick a song that makes me smile, whose melody is like running up stairs made of sunshine. Not for Dad, not even for Grandma. Just for me.

SIXTEEN

AFTER SUPPER, I TEXT GRANDMA AGAIN. I can't believe I forgot to tell her about the bike trip.

Biking 30 miles on Sunday with J and our friend Zuri.

I attach a map of the Eagle Lake Trail.

Love it! Take water, she writes back.

Dad reads Memito a bedtime story and Mom studies, while I take a walk in the last rays of sun. Green leaves hold to their branches, but I smell a crispness and snap that means fall.

Down the street, I see a man setting up a table in his garage. I stroll closer and find a couch on the lawn, lamps with missing shades, and a ratty recliner perched on the driveway. A woman looks up from a deep box to wave at me.

"Is this a garage sale?" I ask.

"I hope so," she says, wiping her forehead. "It's fixin' to be, anyway."

"You're going to sell all this stuff tomorrow?"

"If we're lucky," says the man.

My thoughts speed up. I choose my words carefully. "I'm Quijana Carrillo. I live up the street?"

"The yellow house," says the woman.

I nod. "I was wondering. Do you need some help? Like, I could help you set up and stuff."

"Well, that's awful nice of you, hon. But we can't pay you anything."

"If I help set up, can I bring some things to sell?"

"How many things?" says the man.

"Four or five."

"Aw, you can bring more than that. I'm Travis Walker. This here's Laurie."

I shake their hands, step into their garage, and start unpacking boxes. I set vases and dishes on the table. I help Mrs. Walker hang a clothesline between two trees, where we'll hang pants that smell like cedar and mothballs in the morning. When the sky darkens to navy blue, I thank the Walkers and head home. I do a little skip as I reach the house. Saturday and selling is going to be as awesome as Sunday and the bike trip.

In the morning, I roll Memito's wagon down the street. I pull it carefully so I don't jostle my lava lamp, the snow globe, a few books, a glass chess set, and a couple of puzzles. I left behind the huipil. I think I can sell it for more money than people pay at garage sales.

Cars are already parking along the curb near the Walker house when I arrive. I add my items to the table and mark the prices with masking tape.

"How much is this?" asks a woman in a wide-brimmed hat.

I pick up the cookie jar and turn it over to find the sticker. "Two dollars, ma'am. Would you like a bag?"

"Nice assistant you've got here," she tells Mrs. Walker.

A teenage boy picks up my lava lamp and pays. Mrs. Walker puts the money in an envelope with my name on it. Later, as the sun turns hot, Mr. Walker brings me a glass of water.

By late afternoon, most of the table is empty and half the clothes are gone. The recliner and couch, too. Everything I brought has sold except for a book.

"Looks like the rest will go to charity," Mr. Walker says. "You were a big help, Quijana."

"Let her take something home, Travis," Mrs. Walker says as she counts coins.

"Why, sure. Take anything you like."

"Thanks," I say, not sure that I actually want anything. I paw through a box of Christmas ornaments, then move to a little tray crowded with knickknacks. Then I see a flash of chrome. It's a dome with a push button, a sales-counter bell. "Can I have this?"

"It's yours. You know, a squirt of vinegar will shine that right up. And here's your take of the cash." Mrs. Walker winks. The envelope feels a little thicker than I was expecting.

"Thank you, Mrs. Walker." It feels impolite to open it yet. "I can put that in the garage for you," I say, pointing to the ornaments.

"Naw. You go on home. The donation truck's due soon," Mr. Walker says. "We sure appreciate your help."

I'm tired, but I run home, too excited to walk. At my desk, I open the envelope and bills spill out. I count $10. Ten! I'm now at $50 for the bus ticket.

To celebrate, I ding my bell. Its clear tone rings through the air. I'm pleased with its round shape, its little push button, its round black base. I take it to the kitchen and shine it up with that spray of vinegar, then tap the button, pretending to arrive at a fancy hotel. *Ding.* In a grand voice I say, "I'd like to check in, please." I pretend my jeans are a drapey dress and diamonds. I curtsy, tap the bell, and say in a British accent like Zuri's, "Here's my credit *cahd.*"

But my T-shirt returns and the diamonds wink away as I notice my brother. When I ring the bell, Memito doesn't look. He's playing cars on the floor and never turns his head toward my London hotel. I tap the bell again. He plays on. I ring three times, like an irate customer. A shrill, repeated pinging. Worry rises like a theater curtain, revealing my little brother downstage, playing in a separate world.

Dad's out mowing the lawn, so I run to Mom. "Hey, Mom?"

She keeps typing. She's probably writing a paper for school. "Mm?"

"It's Memito."

Her hands still hover over the keys, but her fingers stop. "What is it?"

"He's not hearing the bell." She squints at me. "I mean, I got a bell. At the garage sale. But when I ring it, he never notices."

When Mom gets up and sees for herself, I'm relieved, but she's not. She takes on the heavy fact and calls Dad inside. I feel weirdly proud.

They try out the bell again, then call Memito's name. When he doesn't look toward the dinging, they start talking in low voices, using Spanish so I won't understand. They don't want me to worry, but I hear them answer questions with other questions. If he can't hear, it could explain his not talking. Could it also explain why he spins his truck's wheels for hours?

I'm glad to not know every word of Spanish for once. If they find an explanation, they'll tell me in English. Spanish is the inside of the world and English is the outside. Like in earth science. Español is the molten mantle, flowing and shapeable, but Inglés is formed, rigid. I know it can hold my weight. When they switch to English, they'll have a plan to announce, a stable crust for us to walk on.

Memito walks to the coffee table and lines up train cars side by side. I wonder what his teachers see when they look at him. What about other parents?

Finally I hear Dad say, "We can ask Dr. Porter for a referral."

"Tell her we need to see an audiologist."

I look up this word on my phone and find out it's a hearing doctor.

I remember studying the ear in school. With map pencils we labeled the hammer, the anvil, the stirrup, and a spiral whose name I forget. The stirrup looked exactly like a horseback-riding stirrup, but tiny. Fairy-sized. Now it seems obvious that something so small could easily break. Or sounds could get dizzy spiraling their way to the brain, so they arrive garbled and backward.

I cover my ears, trying to imagine what Memito hears. I fold hope like a paper airplane and send it to the audiologist.

SEVENTEEN

I WAKE EARLY, just as daylight washes out the stars. Bike day!

We're so excited on the drive out there that we barely talk at all. And soon enough Jayden, Zuri, and I are unloading our bikes from Dad's pickup at Eagle Lake Trailhead. Morning air meets my face like the cool side of a pillow. The only down part of my up day is bad news that might come about Grandma Miller. She said she'd call today if she got her test results. If the results are good, they won't call her until Monday. If bad, they'll call her today. I know she'd want me to enjoy the bike trip and not worry, but fear tugs at my thoughts.

We attach water bottles, tuck in first-aid and tool kits, then stow food in bike bags, borrowed from Jayden's dad, that now hang on either side of our back wheels. I guess he's a big cyclist. I'm shivering in the dim light, but I know I'll warm up soon.

"You look ready," Dad says as we fasten our helmets.

"Thanks for bringing us, Mr. Carrillo." Jayden gives him a salute.

"I'll pick you up at five." Dad looks at his watch. "Seven hours from now. Your phones have no connection out here, but count on it, I'll be here."

That means I won't know if it's cancer or not until he picks us up. For some reason this is actually comforting.

"You have enough water?"

He's been reminding me that water is more important than food since I was little. "Yes, Dad," I say, trying to sound grateful instead of exasperated.

"Then I give you the big clear."

"The *all* clear, Dad."

"Right. The all clear."

Zuri and Jayden smile but don't laugh.

"Bye, Dad," I say flatly, nudging him to go. I want to start our adventure.

When the crunch of gravel under his tires dies away, none of us says anything. The quiet feels weighted. Thirty miles. On-screen, it looked easy. A bright green line marking a smooth path. Now we see it starts with a steep hill.

"Let's do this!" Zuri says, unfreezing us.

I hold up my phone, stick my head into the camera's frame, and try to get the trailhead sign to show.

"A selfie already?" Jayden says.

"We might not survive," says Zuri, joking.

"Come here." I motion them over.

We clonk our helmeted heads together, and I touch the screen. Three nervous smiles, but all eyes open.

We sweat up the hill, clicking our gears to easier speeds, inching forward. "Okay, I *really* hope the next hill is easier," puffs Jayden.

"I thought I was in shape," I say. My legs are burning.

"Better shape than I am," he says, clicking to first gear. "I've found my Achilles *hill!*"

Zuri groans at his pun as I laugh.

Finally, we coast down a long grade, and Jayden lets out a whoop as the wind rushes past. Tires hum against the pavement. We pedal through dense trees, then open fields. I imagine Grandma cheering me on. I hear the triumphant climax of a choir song in my head. By the time we reach a covered picnic table at the lakeshore, the sun is high. It's supposed to be cool today, but we're hot.

"Get ready for hat hair," Jayden says, taking off his helmet.

"Speak for yourself," Zuri says, her new braids in perfect order, of course.

I hang my helmet on my handlebars, lean my bike next to the others', and pull my ponytail band out. "I think my mane's turned into a mop."

Jayden grins. "Mop-top!"

"Check out this view!" Zuri says.

We've been heading toward the lake for nearly four hours. Now it lies shimmering before us. A deep calm comes over me as I take in the expanse of rippling light. Zuri takes my hand

and squeezes it. "I'm so glad you knew about this beautiful place," she says. A breeze lifts off the water. This is the kind of moment I want to write songs about. "Check it out," Jayden says, skipping a stone across the water.

Zuri and I look for a stone, too. "My dad says flat ones bounce better," she says.

I pick up a flattish, gray one and copy Jayden's technique. The stone plunks into the water. "And a brilliant throw by Quijana," I say in a sportscaster voice. It's such a great day that I can laugh at myself.

"It takes some practice," Zuri says, as her rock jumps three times.

"Like this." Jayden throws again, this time in slow motion. My next rock makes two jumps. "I'm getting it!"

"I'm impressed," Zuri says.

"And I"—Jayden starts, his hand on his heart, his voice ultra-sincere—"am starved!" We all crack up and sit at the picnic table, the shaded metal benches cool under our legs. "Everything tastes better out here than it does at home, I swear."

"It's this fresh air," Zuri says. She waves her empty water bottle in the air and trots toward a spigot sticking out of the ground.

"These live oak trees must be ancient," Jayden says, looking up. The trees rise to the sky. Then he looks into my eyes, and his voice lowers. "Do you ever feel too small to hold a big feeling?"

I nod and hold his gaze. "My body can barely hold my heart sometimes," I say.

"Right? Like the high note of a great song. Or the first morning of summer vacation."

This wasn't what I expected him to say.

"It's like, I don't know, when you overload on sugar and almost keel over!"

I laugh, but my joy dips. I thought he was talking about love, of course. Like I was.

"This place. Totally great!" he stands up.

Just then a shriek pierces the air, and we run toward the sound.

Zuri is on the ground by the water spigot, pushing up off the grass. Then she twists onto her back. She holds one leg straight, keeping her ankle stiff.

"Are you okay?" Jayden asks.

Zuri winces. "My ankle." Her words come out pinched. "I tripped. On that tree root." She points behind her.

"Is anything bleeding?" I ask. "Can you move your foot?" I clasp her hand and kneel by her head.

"I don't think so." She props herself up on her elbows.

Jayden sits in the grass and eases off her sock. The ankle is already swelling. "I better not touch it," he says. "I don't want to make it worse."

"Good idea," I say. A pang of jealousy rises as I see Jayden's hands carefully guide the sock off her foot, and I push the feeling down, ashamed.

Zuri's clearly hurting. Her teeth are clenched and her breathing sounds shallow.

"Do you want to sit up?" I ask. She nods.

We scooch her up so that she leans against me.

A silence falls over us. We look at each other. We look at the bikes. We're fifteen miles from the trailhead.

"You guys should go ahead," Zuri says, her throat tight. "I'll . . . wait here, and you can bring help."

"No way," Jayden says. "It would take us till dark to get back to you."

"We can't leave you alone." I wonder if she can hop on her good foot. "What if we get on either side of you, leave the bikes here, and all walk?"

Zuri looks doubtful.

Jayden stands and walks in a little circle. He stops. "What if we all stay here? Your dad would send help if we didn't show up."

"Or I could go alone," I say, though I don't like this idea much. "I could meet my dad and bring him back here."

We fall silent, still thinking. None of our ideas feel right. Each one has an odd corner that doesn't fit.

"What about this?" I say. "Zuri, you sit on your bike and steer while Jayden and I roll it along, one of us on each side. You can rest your foot on the pedal. We'll leave the other two bikes behind."

"What if I fall?"

"It'll hurt," Jayden says, smiling.

Zuri frowns. "Is that supposed to be funny?"

"Yeah. Sorry."

"Z," I say, "it's the only way we can stay together and keep you off your feet. What do you say?"

We wobble at first; Zuri is heavier than I realized. She needs more speed to stay balanced.

"Let's lower the seat," she says. "Then my good foot can touch the ground." She discovers that she can coast pretty well on her own using her good foot to push herself.

"Are you steady by yourself? Maybe Jayden and I can still ride our own bikes, just slowly."

"What about hills?" Jayden asks.

On hills, Zuri gets off, leans on Jayden, and hops while I push her bike. I wish it was me leaning on Jayden, but it's silly to wish for a broken ankle, isn't it? I focus on doing my part. While Zuri waits at the top, Jayden and I pedal our own bikes up. Soon we are sweating, and we have to stop for water often. Our progress is slow, much slower than walking.

It's obvious we won't make it to the trailhead by five, but we don't talk about it. Dad will be worried sick. With each passing minute, I feel worse for him. We keep moving.

A coyote howls, and I fight an urge to duck. Zuri's eyes go wide. Jayden says, "Oh, don't worry. Coyotes run all over my grandparents' land. They howl to check in with other coyotes nearby."

"Nearby?" I say.

"Wild ones avoid humans. I promise."

"Jayday, you're not very comforting," Zuri says.

We come to a level place and settle into a slow rolling. I'm teetering sometimes from riding so slowly, but we stay together. The farther we go, the more it feels like we're going to make it.

Five o'clock passes, then six. Darkness creeps into the treetops. "Our water is running low," Jayden says. "Z, you drink it."

I can't even tell if her ankle is hurting, she's being so stoic. She takes a sip.

"We're sure going to have a story to tell," I say.

Around the next bend, a light bobs in the distance. "See that?" Zuri says.

"I hope it's my dad." I don't think about what it could be if it isn't.

The light grows. It's moving slowly and seems like a flashlight. "Dad?" I call.

"Quijana! Jayden? Zuri?"

We're all smiles as Dad comes into view, but he practically cries at the sight of us. "¡Gracias a Dios! What happened? Is Zuri okay?" he asks.

"She fell . . . ," I start.

"But we wanted to stay together, and . . . ," Jayden adds.

". . . it hurt too much to pedal," Zuri says.

"But the lake!"

"Definitely the best part."

"I learned to skip rocks! And even the peanut butter in my sandwich tasted amazing. . . ." Our voices layer over each other, telling the story in pieces.

Dad walks us back to the trailhead, and when Zuri hops into Dad's pickup, we feel pride alongside relief. We climb in, different people than when we climbed out this morning. Weirdly, this is one of my favorite days ever.

Fatigue takes over, and we settle into silence as the truck drones over the highway. I'm tired in that good, deep way, and close my eyes.

Grandma!

It's as if I forgot—my mind's been so full until this second. I sit up straight and look at Dad. He avoids my eyes, which is a bad sign.

I blink tears away as the city lights come into view.

At home, Dad and I unload my bike in silence, then walk in slowly. Mom must see my reddened eyes because she pulls me into a hug. "She called this afternoon, sweetheart. It is cancer. But Grandma's going to fight this."

Dad stands close by, looking a little pale.

Mom looks at the clock. "You guys are later than I . . ."

"Well, I had to do a little hiking to find them," Dad says. "When I drove up, nobody. I almost had a heart attack. Thank God you're all okay."

"Except Zuri," I say.

"What do you mean?" Mom's look of concern makes me wish I hadn't phrased it that way.

"She broke her ankle," I say quickly. "Or sprained it."

"But they rolled all the way back together," Dad says. "I started down the trail, and there they came. I about cried when I saw them."

"You did cry, Dad."

He clears his throat, then smiles. "They actually handled it well."

"But Zuri! How did it happen?"

"A root. She tripped on it, and wow, can she scream."

"I'm going to call Mr. and Mrs. Thomas right now." She pulls out her phone.

"They took her to the minor emergency clinic when we dropped her off," Dad says.

"Okay, I'll call them tomorrow. I'm glad you guys figured out how to get back, at least. You make a smart team."

I go to my room and text Grandma, even though I'm sure she's asleep:

So I heard the news. Are you okay?

I even attach the trailhead photo, but my phone stays quiet through showering, brushing my teeth, and putting on pajamas.

"Can I charge my phone in my room tonight?" I ask Mom. Her head swivels between an open book and the computer screen. Another research paper.

"You were with your friends all day," she says, her fingers hovering above the keys.

"Not for them. For Grandma. She might text back."

She turns to look at me and pulls her hands away from the keyboard. She lets out a deep breath, and her whole face softens. "Sure, sweetheart. I hope she does." Her gaze drops to the floor, and suddenly I want to comfort her. We hug, me leaning down, and her squeezing me tight.

"We're not giving up, you know," she says in a strained voice. "She's a strong woman."

"I know," I say. And though it feels odd to be the one saying it, I add, "It'll be okay."

EIGHTEEN

GRANDMA STILL HASN'T REPLIED to my text by the time I go to school, but Zuri has.

Yup, broken ankle. They put on a cast late last night. The parents are letting me sleep in today. Zzzz. Tell me what happens in English, ok?

First period drones on like a TV show rerun. I'm about to sharpen my already-sharp pencil when the fire alarm blares. Yes! We all snap awake. Mr. Wilson rolls his eyes. "Why are these drills always on a Monday? Okay, y'all. Out to the soccer field." I'm relieved to leave behind my map of Texas rivers.

The hallways buzz with quick footsteps and low talking. I check my phone. No text message, only my phone's sea turtle wallpaper, a photo I took on the beach with Grandma.

Pushing through the doors, I look up. It's easy to forget the sky is still out here, arching above our classrooms and all of Bur Oak, stretching even to Florida and past the rim of the world. Just looking up, a piece of me widens into the atmosphere.

We're supposed to stay clumped with our classes, but I see Jayden walking toward me, and today's rating jumps from a two to an eight.

"Hey, Qui!"

My eyes are still smiling into his when I realize that I haven't said anything back.

"Zuri got a cast," he tells me.

"Yeah, she texted me this morning."

"She'll be back tomorrow. But it's just us for lunch. Do you want to eat at the tree?"

"The tree?" A zing corkscrews up my spine. The tree is a towering oak in the courtyard near the cafeteria. Patio chairs and tables cluster underneath. We're allowed to eat out there, but hardly anyone does.

I try to keep the cartwheels out of my voice. *Play it cool.* "Sure," I say. "It's so nice out." Just the idea of being under all this sky with Jayden to myself is making my heart beat fast.

"You won't be cold, will you?"

"I have a jacket," I say.

"Cool," he says. "So in other news, my brother stuck a Cheerio up his nose last night."

"No way! How did it even fit?"

"He's three." Jayden shrugs. "But I found out he can yell louder than all of us put together!"

"Did they get it out?"

"Mom pushed on his other nostril, and the Cheerio came shooting out. Then he wanted to eat it!"

"Gross!" I laugh, covering my mouth with one hand. "Hey, my brother's three, too."

"Well, watch out when he's eating cereal!"

A teacher calls Jayden's name, and he walks backward toward her. "The tree, then?"

"The tree."

He turns and trots toward his class. "See you soon," he throws over his shoulder. "I'm hungry already!"

A surge of happiness expands my chest. Is this what a date feels like? I invent a musical where the boy and the girl sing separate songs about their upcoming meeting. The two melodies unknowingly harmonize, and the singers land on the last note in unison. I know it's just lunch. I know it's just peanut butter and jelly. But it feels as special as white table-cloths and linen napkins.

Fourth period finally comes, and I spend the whole class doodling a treetop, its branches ending in tiny hearts. When the lunch bell rings, I'm beside Jayden in a second. As usual, our conversation is a door that swings open with ease.

"I'm thinking of filming all my yo-yo tricks and posting them online," he says.

"Like on a YouTube channel?"

"Yeah, what do you think?"

"I love it. Will you explain each move or just"—I elbow him in the ribs—"show off?"

"The Jayday way: a little of both!" He grins and elbows me back.

I switch my lunch bag to my left hand so that my right is free. Just in case he wants to brush against it, or hold it. Or grab it and pull me, running, to the tree, then lift me up and swing me around. You never know.

We head to a table for two under the tree. Each iron chair back is a curlicued heart, like the ones in movies with French cafés and striped awnings. All we need is a mustached man to play accordion music.

Of course, when Jayden opens his lunch, no surprise chocolate truffle comes out. No red rose. We're just talking as usual. Eating. And it's great . . . I guess. But it's not him declaring his undying love for me.

Just as I'm feeling like an empty-seat theater and realizing that life is not a show tune, he says, "I've been thinking." He ziplocks his apple core, then pushes back from the table. "Okay, I'm doing it. I gotta take the risk. I want to ask you something."

I hold my breath. Holy cow. Is he about to ask me to prom or something? *Get a grip, Qui!*

"What would you think"—he looks straight into my eyes—"if I tried out for *Sherlock Gets Slimed*."

My accordion music halts. I've never heard anything less romantic. "The school play?"

"Tell me the truth. Would I have a shot?"

Wait—*that's* what this has been about? I struggle to find words for the new track we're on. *Focus, focus. He's waiting for an answer. Would he have a shot.* "Sure you would!

You'd be great," I say, trying to pull myself out of a hole of disappointment.

His eyes lock on mine. "I really, *really* want to be an actor. But just last year, I fainted onstage, remember? I don't know . . ." He looks at the ground. "I'll never be an athlete, that's for sure. Even my dad knows that."

"You're perfect for acting," I tell him truthfully. "You can do voices, accents. You're the ham of English class. And you're about to have a YouTube channel."

"But that's not on a stage. With set pieces to fall into. I know I pretended it was funny, but it, like, really sucked. I wanted to be onstage more than anything, even right before I went on. So why did I faint?"

I can tell he's truly worried. "You know what? You might have locked your knees. Mr. Green always says kids pass out in choir concerts from that. And you said you hadn't eaten. I'm sure it was a one-time thing."

"You think? I really want to do this." As he talks about the audition format and the director, my face is still burning. I'm embarrassed by my selfishness. How could I think this whole lunch was about me? He should definitely try out.

"But what if I don't get a part?" he asks.

What if "myself" is boring? I remember saying to Grandma. "Then you'll work on the set. You'll help people run their lines. Something. But, Jayden," I say, "I think you'll get a part."

He grabs my forearms. "Okay, you've convinced me. I knew talking to you would help. I'm doing it!"

His touch makes my ears fill with applause. As I finish my sandwich, I decide to share a wish of my own. "I have a project, too," I say. "I'm learning guitar."

"Cool! What kind of guitar? What can you play?"

"It's my dad's folk guitar. Just a few chords so far." Watching his eyes light up, feeling his excitement, I can't help but tell him what I've been planning. "I want to write my own song."

"That would be *sweet!*" He looks genuinely impressed, and I feel a charge of confidence. "Just one thing," he says. "Promise to play it for me?"

"Deal."

The bell rings and we start back to class.

"When are the play tryouts?" I ask.

"Auditions," he corrects me, winking. "This week! I have to read the play right away and be ready to read any scene out loud by Friday."

Back at our desks, I imagine Grandma would be proud of me. I feel good about my guitar plan, and I'm not changing myself for Jayden. He likes the real me. I still feel two warm places where his hands touched my arms at lunch. I'm glad I'm not inside a show anymore. Or a made-up musical. Real life is better.

Ms. May breaks into my cozy cocoon. "Okay, people. If you have a smartphone, get it out! Find a fact about Emily Dickinson to write on the board. You have three minutes!"

I take a deep breath and look at the sea turtle on my screen before opening Google. Still no message from Grandma.

Somehow I'm less scared than I was this morning. We'll talk soon. I'll tell her about my plan to write a song. I can already hear her saying, "Wonderful!" I imagine sending her a recording of it, each note making her stronger and healthier.

A dry-erase marker appears in front of my screen. "Okay," says Jayden. "I got one. Emily Dickinson used to load up baskets of gingerbread, then lower them on a rope out her window to neighbor kids. She hardly left her house, but she loved the kids." His eyebrows arch, challenging me to match him. I scroll through the web page I brought up. Nothing but dates and where she lived.

"You win," I tell him, half laughing. But I feel victorious today.

School wraps up, and I text Zuri while I wait in line for the school bus home.

How's your ankle?

Oh, fabulous. This cast is going to look great with . . . nothing!

I'm glad she can laugh about it.

Haha! :-(

Still worth it. Eagle Lake was great.

I'm excited to get home and practice guitar, but as I think forward through the evening, I wonder if Memito will be fussy. He's been harder to keep happy recently.

Hey, I type. **I should know this, but do you have any younger brothers or sisters?**

Just a big sister. Why?

I'm kinda worried about my little brother.

Like how?

He doesn't seem to hear other people. It's like he's in his own world.

I love being in my own world, don't you?

Yeah, I guess. Like, when I sing in choir, everything else disappears.

Maybe he's just concentrating?

Yeah, maybe.

I send her a final yellow heart and slip my phone into my backpack.

I look up to see most of the bus kids clustered nearby. It's odd. We live near each other, but we have nothing else in common. We might have hung out as toddlers on tricycles, but now we've sorted ourselves. We're jocks, popular kids, sci-fi geeks, leftovers. Every day we stand in the bus line like representatives from different planets. I don't even know most of their names. I suspect I'm a leftover.

Today, two brown-skinned boys stride toward us. Brothers? I've never seen them before. They look a little odd with their tucked-in shirts and matching haircuts. They stop short of our group, and I realize, strangely, that we are a group now, just because the button-down boys have stopped two feet away. They're a comet from outside our solar system.

Everyone quiets. One brother says something to the other in Spanish. No one from our group says hey or waves. Well, *I* can't do it. For one, I'm a girl. In the Rules of the Bus

Stop, girls don't approach boys. In grade school, maybe, but not now—now we've got Boy and Girl universes. It is not my fault that seconds tick by with these two new kids looking at their shoes.

A light-skinned boy next to me makes a *tss* sound and hisses "Mexicans" under his breath, as if these neatly dressed kids are space junk.

My ears burn. They have the same stiff, black hair as my cousin Raúl. I don't think they heard. I hope they didn't. Then the mean boy looks right at me and says, "Don't belong here," and I think he means *I* don't belong here—with my amber skin, my dark eyes.

But no. He thinks I'm on his side. I speak with no accent; he hasn't met my Guatemalan dad; he doesn't know my name. He looks at the brothers and spits on the ground.

And what do I do? Nothing. I do nothing, I say nothing.

An us-them gravity pulls the group together. *I'm in.*

For a second, I'm relieved. I'm a local; they're not. I'm American; they're—well, what is American? Maybe they are. Just because they speak Spanish doesn't mean they're not American. I think of my Carrillo cousins and what they would look like standing here.

A crinkly feeling crawls up my arms. I can't meet anyone's eyes. I look at the sidewalk and see one girl's shoe stepping on top of her other one. Maybe she feels it, too. I want to do something, but I can't think what. Should I say something? No words come to mind.

We hear the bus's engine strain up the hill, and this makes it final. The new boys remain a distant moon, our group a home planet. A knot tightens in my stomach. *I'm not the one who said "Mexicans" like an insult,* I tell myself. I didn't do anything wrong. I couldn't have done any better.

We board the bus, and I take the seat with the wheel hump, trying not to notice where the brothers sit.

NINETEEN

GRANDMA TEXTS AT LAST.

School out? One good thing about cancer: it makes small stuff smaller and big stuff bigger. You're some big stuff, Quijana. I love the hiking photo and you, too, sweet one. Any adventures today?

My head clears, and the tingliest part of the day comes back.

I ate lunch with Jayden. I'm going to write a song!

That's my girl!

But I'm worried about you.

The doctors have a long list of plans for me. Everything's okay in the end. If it's not okay, it's not the end.

I ponder that and send three pink daisies.

At home, I shrug off my backpack and find a cheese stick in the fridge. I check the clock. An hour before Dad and Memito come home. I'm in the clear.

I lift Dad's guitar from its hook on the living room wall. My hands are smaller than his, but I manage to press the right strings for a G chord. The strings leave creases on my finger pads, but as I practice the chord, it sounds clearer and bigger, like a full choir in my hands. I strum down, down-up, down, down, the pattern I learned on the video. Notes splash into the air.

I check YouTube for the next two fingerings. C is hard, and my third finger can barely reach its string. Repetition helps, but I move on to D, which turns out to be the easiest. I start a simple song. At each chord change, I stop and position my fingers. Geez, it takes forever to sing one verse. Dad makes it look so effortless.

I practice moving my hands from one chord to the next, cycling through G, C, D. G, C, D. An image of Jayden at the tree today pops into my head, and a melody forms around a sentence. *The more I know you, the more I want to know you more.* My song's first line!

A car door slams.

I silence the strings with the flat of my hand and dash to the hook on the wall. The guitar's neck slides in just as the front door opens. I sprint to the couch and sit, my heart pounding. "Hey, Dad." I wave. He walks in, Memito close behind.

"Hola, m'ija. So glad to be home."

He doesn't notice my fast breathing. Or ask why I'm randomly sitting on the couch with nothing in my hands. Whew.

I stand up, and Memito runs to me for a spin-around, then grabs his dump truck and starts running it in a figure-eight around the couch and the coffee table.

"What's that?" I ask. Dad's unwrapping a rectangular bristly thing. It looks like a brush for scrubbing potatoes.

"A sensory integration brush. Memito's teacher gave it to us. She says brushing his skin might help him be less sensitive."

"Brushing his skin?"

"We'll take it out for a whirl."

"You mean 'give it a whirl'?"

"Yes, m'ija," he says, rolling his eyes and rubbing my head.

I smooth my hair. "Is he going to get his hearing checked, too?"

"Soon."

Memito is still running his dump truck in the figure eight. I get busy lifting down dinner plates.

"Set a plate for your mother, too," Dad says. "Her evening class got canceled. Let's use the dining table."

The dining table! Eating together at the dining table makes this feel like Thanksgiving in October. I'm so excited that I fold paper napkins into special standing fans. Dad lights two candles that flicker at first from the dust on their wicks, but find a steady shine just as we hear the front door open.

"Well, isn't this beautiful!" Mom says. We say a prayer, and a deep peace settles over the room. Even Memito stays quiet.

Nights like this make Dad thoughtful, and sure enough, he starts a story after we eat. "Don Quixote, man of La Mancha."

Again we hear about the crazy knight on his creaky horse on the sun-scorched plains of Spain. This time it's a part of the story where he's rescuing a beaten servant, a boy lashed for bad sheep-herding. I've heard the windmill fight scene over and over, but this part is new.

Don Quixote hears the shepherd boy crying and stops his horse. The boy's master is raising a leather strap in the air. "You, there! Stop!" Quixote says. The man stops, and Quixote lectures him on honor and morals.

"Of course you're right, Don Quixote." The man bows and promises to treat the boy well. But it's a lie. The man picks up his leather strap after Quixote rides away.

"You see how important it is to keep people from abusing their power," Dad finishes.

All my life I've agreed with him, but this story makes me frown. "That's not a good story," I say.

Memito has been chugging his sippy cup, but now he stares at me.

"The boy wasn't rescued!" I'm genuinely mad. "Quixote just thinks he saved the day because he leaves before seeing that he didn't even do anything. Why would that convince anyone not to abuse their power? The bad guy won!"

Every word I think of saying has a spike in it. And the more my father tilts his head to the ceiling and looks into the distance, the more I want to shake him. If Quixote can't rescue anyone, how can he call himself a knight? He's a fake.

"It takes time to understand the stories," Dad says. "In Guatemala, you'll meet an uncle who reads *Don Quixote* every year."

No, I won't. "Quixote never does any good," I counter. Not in any episode I've heard.

My father considers this. He isn't angry, but I wish he were. "It's true," he says. "It doesn't matter, though."

I raise my voice. "It *does* matter." The room goes quiet. I've said enough. I can tell because my mother puts her fork down. But I can't back down. "It matters! Ask the boy. It matters to *him*!" Suddenly I want to scream at them, to fling black bolts of lightning. I try to keep my thoughts from veering to the boys at the bus stop and their open faces. What good is being a knight if you can't change the world, make things actually better? Why is this day falling apart? "You named me after a failure!" The last word comes out cracked. I cover my face with my hands.

I can feel my parents looking at each other and the cheery candlelight mocking me. I've ruined our one family dinner.

Mom turns to Memito. "Go wash your hands, m'ijo," she says as she lifts him down from his booster seat. He scurries down the hallway, and she faces me, takes a deep breath, and then smiles a somehow serious smile. "Quijana, your name comes from Alonso Quixana. He's the man who became Don Quixote."

I already know this and say nothing.

"The man who took up his lance to make things right." My father's voice is too gentle.

I don't look at him. "He screwed up," I say to my plate. "He screws up everything." My cheeks feel hot, and I know I am talking about myself. I picture Jayden realizing that I'm not smart, not interesting, not worth asking to prom, now or ever.

"Out of the fabric of failure, Quixote sews success," Dad says.

"What does that mean?"

"He makes the effort. For its own sake. His heart is true no matter what."

"Think of it this way," Mom says. "The world is always against him, but he tries against all odds."

They must think that I am more loca than the knight, that I am just what schoolkids teased me about back in elementary—too serious. I want to make a real difference, not an imaginary one that only I believe in.

Dad slides his hand toward me across the table. "You don't have to be perfect, Quijana. You are named for an ordinary man. A man who tried his best."

Mom leans in. "Failing is part of life, more common than not. But the try is what matters, Qui."

"That's stupid." I want to kick the table leg. Why can't Quixote win once in a while? I want to do more than fight losing battles. I try to stay mad, but the feeling passes when I look at my father's face, still warm after my coldness. Still soft after my hardness.

"Sometimes the lost causes are the noblest," he says, his voice like warm milk in a mug.

I'm not sure this is so, but a weariness moves through me. I just want to be done with this day.

"Someday, Quijana, you'll read *Don Quixote* and understand. Or, ah! We could read it together. An English translation, of course. One page every night!"

How did we get here? My parents haven't read me bedtime stories for years. Why is he always trying to establish a Spanish colony in my brain? "Dad," I say to the table. "That's the *last* book I want to read."

I feel him looking at me, but I keep my head down. He inhales as if to say something. But then he pushes his chair back and leaves the table in silence. Mom leaves, too, and I hear her long exhale.

And then I do kick the table leg.

TWENTY

I KNOW IT'S CHILDISH, but I stomp to the kitchen and rinse my plate without being careful. I like its clatter in the sink. I'm angry at my father and angry at Don Quixote. Who wants to be famous for losing?

Rubbing my plate hard with a sponge, I play a familiar game: thinking of names I would rather have. Emily. Hailey. Madison. Names that people know how to pronounce. Names with only one dot. Quijana has two, like little eyes that watch for my mistakes.

I lie on my bed and try listening to music. It usually unbuttons a bad mood, but not this time. The manatee poster smiles at me from the ceiling, but I can't even look at her. Instead, I open my sock drawer and pull out the envelope from the garage sale. I count out ones, fives, and tens, putting them in three piles. $52. Bus fare is $177. How can I earn more? Fast.

I hear a knock. *Ugh.* Why can't Dad let me stay mad?

"Can I come in?" he says.

I sweep the money back into the drawer and bounce onto my bed. "Yeah." I pull out my earbuds.

He looks around the room as if he hasn't seen it before. His gaze moves from my stuffed manatee to my origami swan to the bookshelf. From the doorway he says, "School. It's going well?"

I'm about to be annoyed that every conversation seems to start with this question when he sighs and rubs his face. He lowers his head, and I suddenly see my dad as if from far away. He looks like a nice man. A nice man who has something to say.

"School's fine, Dad." As usual, I don't mention the not-fines.

He nods. "Of course it is. Education, so important. You always do well in school, yes?"

"You know I do, Dad." What is he after?

"Yes, because you are lista, Quijana. Since you were little, you always asked questions. Always your eyes stay open." He sits on the edge of the bed and it's hard to stay annoyed, hearing his soft voice. Still, I can't help thinking he doesn't know me. Not the real me.

"I love you very much," he says, looking into my eyes. "No matter what." He means it. I know this, but I'm also thinking it doesn't count. Of course *he* loves me, but can anyone else? Sometimes it feels like I'm nothing but a pile of flaws. A better Quijana would love the Guatemalan stuff on our walls, get *A*'s in Spanish, and stand up for the bus-stop boys. Grandma said to stay true to myself. Is my real self a failed Latina?

"Did I ever tell you about Castel?"

More than once, I say to myself. "One of your grand-mother's horses."

"Yes. My favorite one. He was gray like castle stone, with a soft black nose. Castel was a better friend to me than any village child. He and I spent hours together, exploring the land." My father's face turns even sadder now.

Usually his Castel stories light him up. Maybe I haven't heard this one.

"One day his breathing was coming hard. Something was wrong. He tried to put his nose in my hand, but he could hardly lift his head. A neighbor told me that a certain fruit might save him, and another said an herb might help. I hiked many kilometers to find the tree that made the fruit. Then I traded five eggs from my own chickens for the herb. I mashed these together and brought them to Castel. By now he was very sick. I fed him my medicine, but it didn't help. A hired man took away his suffering with a shotgun."

My father's eyes meet mine, and something softens inside me.

"You see, we do not win every time. But in trying, we show our love. We show the goodness of our hearts."

I see the goodness of *his* heart. I'm not sure about mine. I'm not as good as he thinks. After all, I'm planning to hop a bus in the middle of the night without telling him.

I try to figure out why he's telling me this story right now. Maybe he means that trying really *is* the important thing, even a stuttering trying like mine. Trying to be me, trying to live up to my name—I'm not very good at either one.

He touches the side of my face with two fingers. "Mi Quijanita . . ."

My nickname wakes up a memory: Dad lifting me up to see a blooming branch of redbud. His -ita echoes in my ears. It's a drop of honey in the air, a swirl of cinnamon stirred into my name. I can't help but forgive him for pushing Quixote into my life.

Even so, I wish Quixote could *accomplish* something and not be so weird.

Dad kisses my forehead and hugs my head to his chest, but I still feel alone.

When my computer dings, I immediately perk up. I click open the Skype window, and it's Grandma with her wavy white hair and bright eyes.

"Grandma!"

"Hola, Elizabeth," says Dad. "You and Quijana have fun."

"Bye, Antonio." She waves as Dad leaves the room. "How's my girl?"

"Does anything hurt, Grandma? Do you feel any better?"

"I hope to after surgery, sweetie. It's scheduled for next week," she says. "They'll try to take out all the cancer, and we'll go from there."

My heart lifts. Once the doctors remove all the cancer, everything will be back to how it was. Spring breaks and Thanksgivings and Christmases and summer visits to watch the hatching sea turtles.

"Oh, Grandma, that'll be great."

"It could be. Nothing is certain in this world, except that you are my favorite granddaughter!"

"I'm your only granddaughter," I say with a grin.

"Exactly." She winks. "Tell me, how's the guitar going? Are you writing that song you mentioned?"

"Yeah, I started it. I only have two lines . . ."

"I think the first two lines are probably the hardest ones."

I think about that.

"When I took biology, we started by studying unicellular organisms. Those are organisms made up of only one cell, like algae and bacteria. But all life—beetles and trees and blue whales—it all grows from that one idea. From a tiny building block. So the first two lines are very important."

Grandma makes everything seem possible. But I wonder if she's more worried than she seems. "Aren't you scared, Grandma?"

"About the surgery? No, I've had an operation before—gallbladder."

"About the cancer."

She swallows. "I *am* afraid." She takes a deep breath and looks up, as if searching for words. "But not for myself. Fear comes from resisting what life brings you, from wanting your own way. I've seen a lot of death, Quijana. As a biologist, I know, in a deep way, that my body is mortal. What I worry about are my daughters. And especially, you."

"But we're not sick."

"No, of course. But you'll have to say goodbye to me eventually, maybe very soon. And goodbyes are hard."

I try to process each part of what she's said. "So you're not afraid to die?"

"I'm not. It's natural."

"But you're afraid for me."

"Yes and no. You'll flourish in your life, I'm sure of that. But you'll grieve, too. And not just for me. All your life, you'll be letting go of things. The great secret is to relish the moments as they happen, but let endings happen, too."

"I don't know." I'm not feeling cheered up the way she probably wants me to. "That sounds hard."

"Yes, but listen. I have friends who had cancer years ago and came through it just fine. That could very well be me. Surgery first. Then I'll have some decisions to make. I don't want to be kept alive with, you know, machines and things. I want to live for real, or not at all."

I want her to live, too. Forever. Which is childish, I know. But Grandma sounds strong, like she always does, and surgery will keep the cancer from getting worse. If her friends survived cancer, she can, too. She can get well.

TWENTY-ONE

ALL WEEK, JAYDEN AND I TEXT about the play—which characters he likes, how the set might look, and whether the cast will really wear clothes that look like they're from 1800.

I've decided to audition for three parts, including the lead! he says.

Crossing my fingers for you!

I'm just sure he'll get one of them.

At lunch on Tuesday and Wednesday and Thursday, he explains the play's clever mystery plot, and Zuri and I take turns guessing how it will end. I understand that the play is important to him, but Grandma and her cancer are on my mind a lot. I want to tell them about it, but it never seems to be the right time.

When audition day comes on Friday, Jayden's more preoccupied than ever. Zuri and I sit down at the lunch table to find his nose in the script.

"Um, you guys, I gotta tell you some news," I say.

"It would be cheesy to do an accent, right?" Jayden says, more to himself than to us.

"You could try it," I venture. I'm excited for him, but something about his eating with one hand and holding the script with the other annoys me. "My grandma has cancer," I say.

"Wait, *what*?" Jayden immediately closes the script and Zuri turns to look at me, alarmed.

I feel guilty for using the news to get Jayden's attention, but at the same time I'm relieved to tell them. "She's having surgery next week. Mom says it'll be fine, but . . ." Saying it out loud makes my throat tighten. "I'm not so sure."

"Whoa. That's terrible." Jayden shakes his head. "Is she the woman who hiked the Appalachian Trail?"

"And saves sea animals?" Zuri asks.

I nod. Cancer seems crueler than ever.

"You must be so worried," Zuri says. "My aunt died of cancer."

"Z, don't say that!" Jayden shoots her a frown and leans across the table toward me. "She might be fine. She's too adventurous to die."

I chuckle in spite of my sadness. "She actually said that death would be an adventure."

"Well, it's an adventure that can wait," he says firmly. "Keep us posted, okay? Like, text me when she's out of surgery and all."

"Me too," says Zuri. "I didn't mean . . ."

"It's fine," I say. "It's kind of refreshing to hear someone talk about dying, because it's what we're all thinking, but my parents hardly talk about it. They're being all positive, probably protecting me. Grandma's more honest with me."

"Sounds like her," Zuri says.

Jayden nods, his eyes flowing with concern.

"Thanks, y'all, for just, you know, listening." I feel lighter, like the weight of it is shouldered by all of us instead of me alone.

After school, a text comes through from Jayden.

I got the part of Watson! Totally pumped. I'm turning somersaults!

Congrats!! I knew you could do it!

I add a hand-clapping emoji. I'm happy for him, and even the worry for Grandma at the back of my mind doesn't cancel out the good parts of this day.

Though it's October, summer heat holds on for the next week. It's hot after school when the bell rings. I sure wish the school bus windows could open farther, because Zuri's riding home with me so we can paint our fingernails at my house. She hops onto the bus on her good leg while I carry her knee scooter. She's sweaty before she even sits down.

Still, everything seems exciting with her there, even the green, plastic-y bus seats, the pop songs on the bus radio, and my own front door. When I open it for Zuri, I wince a little at our Guatemalan living room. No TV living room looks like this, and none in the movies either, but Zuri doesn't seem to care. She rides her knee scooter up to the couch and sits on one end.

"You're good at driving that thing," I say.

"Getting used to it," she says. "Except for stairs. And of course my room is upstairs. The first night I slept on the couch! Now I use crutches to get up there."

Out of her bagful of nail polish, we choose the three best colors. Her favorite, my favorite, and a second-favorite we agree on. We line them up like Olympic medalists on the coffee table. She opens the first bottle.

"Pink looks good with your skin," she says, pulling the brush down my thumbnail.

"Yours too."

"Nah. Darker skin needs bolder colors. Like this royal blue," she says.

"Oh." I hadn't thought of this.

"So one green pinkie?"

"Your right one and my left."

When she finishes, I curl my hands and blow on my nails.

"Do you know that Aiden kid? He said I talk funny," Zuri says.

"When was this?"

"Last period." She shrugs. "Probably thinks I'm stuck-up because of my accent. I bet he's never heard of Barbados, much less the fact that it was a British colony. And not everyone's mother went to British boarding schools like mine did."

"Your mom went to boarding school? Wow. But who makes fun of people's accents? That kid has no class." I shake the blue bottle and open it.

"It's happened ever since I came here. I look like I'm from Africa; I sound like I'm from Britain. Black kids, white kids. No one sees me as one of them." Her tone sounds casual, but her shoulders curl forward.

I'm surprised to hear that Zuri has anything wrong with her life. Now I realize that even though she seems perfect, it isn't all peach cobbler and ice cream for her. And our problems aren't that different.

"Same with me. Latino kids know I'm not legit." I press the excess polish off the brush.

"Cause you don't speak Spanish."

"Right."

"You, me, and Jayden—we found each other. We make a group of our own."

"We're like that ice cream with vanilla, strawberry, and chocolate in it," I say.

"Neapolitan!"

"I think I'm more caramel than strawberry," I say, looking at my arm.

She grins. "But your nails are strawberry."

We click a photo of our green pinkies linked together.

We're getting a few likes from classmates when the door opens and Dad's Spanish tumbles through the air. He's streaming clattery words to Memito, trying to stop him from running inside with muddy shoes. "Ay, m'ija. Qué día!" Dad says to me, not noticing Zuri, not seeing the startled look on her face. She knows that my dad speaks Spanish, but I guess he didn't speak this much on our bike trip, and she looks surprised. So am I. He wasn't supposed to be home yet.

I feel like we've transported into a telenovela on the Spanish station. *I was having a nice, normal moment here, Dad. Can't we look like a regular family for once?* I desperately want to change the channel.

"Hey, Dad," I say, my own unaccented English ringing in my ears. He wrangles Memito's shoes off, then turns to Zuri.

"Hello, Zuri! I hope your ankle is healing. You will join us for supper?" My father's friendliness is a sun that burns too warm.

"I wish I could," Zuri says, "but my mom is picking me up."

I'm glad, actually, that she won't stay. She doesn't seem to care whether we're normal or not, but somehow I still do.

Then Memito peeks around Dad's pant leg, showing one brown eye. In a voice like she's talking to a kitten, Zuri says, "Hey."

He ducks away, but then shows both eyes.

"You must be Memito," she says, meeting his gaze.

My annoyance flakes off as my little brother walks to Zuri and touches the top of her hand with one finger. Zuri looks at me and smiles. "He's sweet," she says.

My shoulders relax a little, and I silently thank Memito. He made a bridge between my family and my friend.

"M'ijo, let's brush now," Dad says. Memito runs toward the kitchen, and Dad calls, "Nice to see you Zuri," over his shoulder.

"He doesn't like the brushing," I tell Zuri.

"Teeth?" Zuri asks.

"His skin. They say it might help."

"His skin." Zuri says each word slowly.

"It's supposed to make him less picky about tags in his shirts and rough fabrics. They call it occupational therapy. Since he turned three, Memito hates to wear jeans or anything stiff, even a picture on a T-shirt."

"That's kind of . . . weird?" Zuri says.

"Yeah, definitely. Hey, come see something?"

Zuri rolls after me on her knee scooter. I close my bedroom door behind us and pull the huipil from my bottom drawer.

"Wow. This is beautiful." She runs her hand over the bright colors and fine needlework.

"Yeah, I know, but—how much do you think I could sell it for?"

"Sell it?" She looks confused. "Why would you sell it?"

"Uh . . ." For some reason I don't want to tell her about my trip yet. "I need money. Besides, I'll never wear it. Would you?"

"Yeah, I might." She unfolds it and holds it up to her body. "What do you need money for?"

I decide to trust her.

"You can't tell anyone, okay? Except Jayden."

She makes an X over her heart and sits on the bed.

"My parents want to take a Christmas trip to Guatemala, remember that? But . . . I don't want to go." She nods. "So I'm not going. The night before the flight, I'm sneaking out and riding the bus to my grandma's in Florida."

She pulls back, her face worried. "Can you do that?"

"I checked the bus schedule. Jayden said he'd walk me to the bus depot. But I need more money for the fare."

"But can you DO that? Won't your parents freak out?"

"I have to. I can't go to Guatemala. Maybe if I spoke Spanish, but Zuri, I can't spend two weeks, like, nodding like a puppet and feeling like an idiot. Plus, my grandma in Florida is the one who is sick. We'll see her at Thanksgiving, but I want to see her as much as I can before . . . just, as much as I can. I know it sounds crazy, but I saw a kid traveling alone when we took the bus out there. If he can do it, I can."

Zuri nods. "Okay, then. How much more money?"

"I still need one hundred twenty-five dollars."

"That's a lot, Qui."

"I know." I drop onto the bed.

"Hmm. Let's think about this. My mom makes extra money with a shop online called eArtisans. Have you looked up how much this . . ."

"Huipil. Whee-PEEL."

". . . huipil could sell for?"

I shake my head, and we both pull out our phones.

She clicks and scrolls. "This could work, Qui. Look at these."

The screen shows one huipil for $575, another for $98, and another for $150. She scrolls down and different styles show up, some simpler than mine and costing nearly $100. A wave of excitement rises through me. "That one says hand-made, like mine," I say. "And it's the same style, too. Two hundred dollars." We look at each other with wide eyes. "How do I sell on eArtisans?"

"You need a good photo. Mom always says a good photo is key. Put it on."

"Put it on?" I don't want to put it on.

Zuri rolls her eyes. "For the photo, silly."

I hold the huipil at arm's length, then slip it on over my T-shirt. The thick fabric feels heavy on my shoulders.

"Okay, stick your arms out. Stand in the sunlight." Zuri clicks several photos. "Come see."

The pictures look good. I'm glad to see she's taken the picture without my face in the frame. I doubt Mom shops on eArtisans, but it would be awful, like horrendously awful, if she saw this picture of me somehow. Zuri deletes one that's out of focus. The others show off the fabric nicely, and it looks like something someone would pay a lot for.

"Hey, Zuri?"

She looks up.

"Thanks."

She smiles. "I got your back."

I wake up my phone, click "Sell on eArtisans," and read through the guidelines. "Uh-oh. I don't have a checking-account number and no credit card to pay these setup fees." I have an idea. "What does your mom sell on her site?"

"Bracelets, stuff from antique stores. Cloth purses she makes from African prints."

"Can she buy the huipil from me and then sell it on her site?"

"Maybe." Zuri tilts her head. "I mean, why not?"

"I guess she might want to sell it first and give me the money afterward," I say, biting my lip.

"Oh. I bet she would."

"Well, how long does it take things to sell?"

"Depends. She's at the post office every few days, it seems like. Although there *is* one orange hat she's had up there for a year."

A car horn honks. "Oh, man, what time is it? That's Mom. I have to go," Zuri says.

I grab a bag out of my closet. "We have to try. Here." I slide the huipil into the bag. "Tell her I think it will sell for two hundred dollars, but I only want one hundred forty. She can keep the rest. I'll write this down. You start rolling." I take a piece of paper out of my backpack, write down the numbers, and slip that into the bag, too.

I run out to the living room, where Zuri is scooping up the nail polish and her backpack. I add the bag to her backpack, and she rolls to the door. She twists around and crosses her fingers. I cross mine, too. "Bye, Mr. Carrillo!" she shouts.

It's almost all right that Dad yells, "Adiós!" toward the door at full volume, his sun burning hot as ever. It doesn't bother me like before. I think of the huipil, out of my drawer and zooming farther away every second.

My phone vibrates, bringing me out of my reverie.

Sup Q-zers? It's Jayden!

Great news!

Really? Call me!

Telling Jayden about eArtisans is almost as good as living through it the first time. But when he says, "You're pretty amazing, Qui," I think it might feel even better.

TWENTY-TWO

DAD RUNS ERRANDS on Saturday morning, and Mom takes Memito for new shoes, so I lift the guitar down from the wall. My chords come more easily now, and I can make it through a whole song without stopping if I take it slow enough. I've decided that the song I'm writing is for Jayden. I'll find a way to sing it to him when it's done. Maybe for his birthday.

I daydream and let the first line float around in my head. *The more I know you, the more I want to know you more.* The chords suggest a new line: *And when you fix your eyes on me, I feel my heart expand, fly free.* I sing these two lines back to back and try different variations on the tune. I almost don't hear the garage door opening. I hang the guitar and run to the fridge.

"Our mechanic today was from Puerto Rico" is the first thing Dad says.

Random. "That's nice, Dad," I say, pulling out a nectarine.

Mom and Memito arrive, and after sandwiches, Mom shouts, "Everybody outside!"

I almost forgot. We're supposed to rake leaves today, even though some trees haven't shed any yet. The big Arizona Ash drops its leaves during drought, though, as well as early fall, so we're ankle-deep. Not even Memito is off the hook to help. He swings a child-sized rake that Grandma bought for Mom when she was a kid.

Grandma makes me work hard when I visit Florida. Even when I was really little, I remember her showing me how to wash dishes by hand. She'd always say, "I cooked, so you clean." I'd start by squirting soap in a dishpan, and then she'd come help and we'd end up talking. She'd tell hiking stories while she rinsed dishes, like the time she lost the trail but found a pristine pond.

"Quijana, you start over there." Mom points to the front corner of the yard. "Honey," she says to Dad, "what about you?"

"I'll start under the tree, here," he says. "Quijana and I can handle the whole front yard, right?" He gives me a thumbs-up.

"I bet you can, crackerjackers! We'll start on the side yard. Meet you in the middle."

At first Memito rakes with Mom, but soon he is "helping" by running from one leaf pile to another, adding a single leaf to each one. "Well, thank you, goofy goose," I say to him.

"Qui," he says and hands me a red leaf. As he walks away, it occurs to me that I could test his hearing. "Memito?" He walks on, unfazed.

My phone vibrates, and I take a minute to text Jayden a sad face.

Can't talk. Raking duty.

Dad and I have cleared a small area when Dad's phone rings. "Hola, Mamá!" he says. It's the October call from Guatemala.

I rake vigorously. I hear Dad say the words "work," "audiologist," "Memito," and "Kimberly," Mom's first name. He finally says "Quijana," and I listen harder. *She enjoys singing. She's doing well in school.* This much Spanish I understand.

With these two traits, I imagine Abuela building a Quijana. She makes legs out of singing and good grades. She adds skin and hair from mailed photos, plus light in the eyes from her memory of twelve-year-olds. She builds a heart with Dad's self-discipline and Tía Lencha's warmth. She stuffs all the gaps with good qualities. How disappointed she would be to meet the real me. I'm doing us all a favor by skipping Guatemala.

When Dad passes me the phone "just to say goodbye," Abuela talks to the invented Quijana. The word "abrazos," hugs, is for *that* Quijana. So is "besos," kisses she wants to give me. This is exactly why I don't want to go to Guatemala. I'll be a stranger she's supposed to love. How can she know what to say to a stranger?

But on she goes. Understood or not, Abuela fills the phone with lilts and curls, swishes and swoops. It's pretty great that she's willing to waste all these words on me, knowing I can't understand them. She's obviously in a good mood. It all feels like a hug. I wish I could give her something back. But other than stammering out "te amo"—or should it be "le amo"?—I've got nothing. My heart is a full sink with a stopped-up drain.

Soon she's saying goodbye, and I can only manage, "Adiós, Abuelita." When I hand the phone back to Dad, I'm still feeling swayed by her syllables.

Maybe next time, I can say something. I could plan it out. Use Google translate. Then a pang of guilt passes through me. Abuela sent the huipil as a gift, and I'm about to sell it. But she doesn't understand I can't possibly use it.

My guilt stings harder when I think how I'm using her gift to visit my other grandma.

Dad whistles our doorbell tune. *Ding-dong.* "Are you helping or are you *helping*?" He's already loading leaves into a tall paper bag.

"I'm helping," I say, pulling the rake across the grass.

I let myself imagine Guatemala. In person, I could hug Abuela. I could smile. We could braid each other's hair, look at baby photos of Dad. None of that requires talking, right?

Then I clench, remembering Cousin Raúl's smirk. Guatemala still has cousins in it. I'll still be trapped in my own silent movie once we leave the airport. I hear Abuela's voice again, her syllables like forehead kisses. If only I could get the plane to land in Abuela's living room and take off from her front door.

"Can't we bring Abuela here instead?" I say to Dad.

He stomps the leaves deeper into the bag. "Why?"

I can't think of an answer he'll like.

"We want to see *everyone*," he says. "My brother, three sisters, plus my nieces and nephews. And they want to see you and Memito." He stops and looks up. "I'll show you the house I grew up in! You'll love it, m'ija, I promise."

This is my problem with grown-ups. They're always telling you what's fun, what you'll like, what tastes delicious. It always turns out to be like yogurt—eight ounces of sour for one sweet peach at the bottom.

I pull out my phone and click Zuri's picture. **Any word on the huipil?**

TWENTY-THREE

AFTER THREE WEEKS of waiting for an appointment, Memito's finally seeing the audiologist. We walk into a small office that smells like plastic plants. Mom fills out a stack of forms while Memito plays with the wooden train.

Mom said I could stay home this afternoon. I don't have after-school choir rehearsal, and she said I could pull out our fall decorations. But I want to be here. I want to know if a hearing aid can fix Memito. And if not, what can.

I'm handing him another wooden train track when a lady in jack-o'-lantern scrubs calls, "Manuel?" I almost don't recognize the name as my brother's. We step up to a metal door and Mom goes through, holding Memito's hand. Ms. Jack-o'-Lantern tells me, "You can wait here, little lady."

"No," I say. I stand up straight and speak clearly. "I'm his big sister."

She looks at my mother, who nods, then lets me through. I can tell Ms. Jack-o'-Lantern thinks I'm not important. She might even think Memito is a pain-in-the-butt brother to me, but that's not how it is. I'm the one who watches him when Mom and Dad are cooking or outside, when they're not home or just not paying attention. When he cries, I usually know why.

Inside, we meet a woman at a low table. Her scrubs are a plain, crisp blue. "I'm Dr. Li," she says. She puts headphones on a stuffed bear and then on Memito. She says, "When you hear a beep, raise your hand way up high." Instead of raising his hand, he twists his head back and forth. "Let's try this instead," she says, bringing out a toy boat and a plastic elephant. She trains Memito to touch them when he hears the beeps. This works better. He touches one, then the other. I like her.

Next, she brings out a white handheld instrument that looks like an ear thermometer. "You hold it," she says, giving it to Memito. He puts it to her ear, then to my ear, then to Mom's. He's not afraid. "Now my turn," Dr. Li says. She holds the instrument to Memito's ear and prints the results.

The paper shows a square grid with a barely arched line toward the bottom, like an eyebrow. It looks like something from my algebra book.

"Good job, Manuel." Dr. Li gives him a dolphin sticker and sets a box of blocks on the floor.

"His hearing is normal," she says to Mom, "but this line should look like a hill. A flatter line indicates fluid in the middle ear."

"What causes that?" Mom asks.

"Since he's not sick, I'd say he's allergic to something. Maybe dairy or wheat. Try cutting those from his diet and see what happens."

The woman lists other "-ist" doctors we can see, and Mom takes notes, but I'm stacking blocks with Memito and thinking hard. A hearing problem would be easier to fix, wouldn't it? Like, we could all learn sign language. But with this ear-fluid thing, Dr. Li said changing his food *might* help—like that might not even be the answer. Something more feels off with Memito. He used to let me hug him; now he stiffens. Is that really something you fix with food? He's been curving away from us, and I want him back. My thoughts don't get through to anywhere, smacking flat against my brain like the sound waves smacking flat against his eardrum.

The ride home is quiet. Memito falls asleep. At our drive-way, Mom says, "This is good news. He can hear. So, great. We'll try changing his diet." Her voice sounds peppier than usual. She sounds like she's convincing herself, or rehearsing what she'll tell Dad. I don't say anything.

My phone vibrates. A text from Zuri.

Hey, breaking news. Jayden mentioned getting a girl-friend.

Everything drops through my head's trapdoor except Jayden.

Girlfriend?

Told me yesterday.

I close the car door for Mom as she carries Memito inside. Then I run to my room and call Zuri.

"I thought you'd be interested." She pauses. "I know you like him."

I try to think of something rational to say, but there's no use pretending. I'm practically wailing when I say, "I'm never not thinking about him." I take a breath and lie back on my bed. "My Grandma Miller says not to worry whether Jayden likes me back, but . . ." I trail off. *Hope is born at the same moment as love,* Don Quixote says in my head.

"He does like you. He texts you all the time."

"But does he *like* me?"

She pauses, and I can tell she's trying to be honest. "Hard to tell."

I think how flattened I would feel if Jayden liked some other girl. How 3-D I would feel if he liked me. "Z, I—" I've wanted to ask her this for a while. Now that she knows how I feel, it seems safe. I take a deep breath. "Do *you* like him?"

"Me? No, no. He's like my brother. I don't see him that way at all." She sounds like she's telling the truth, and I breathe a sigh of relief. I've been worried about this since day one. "But he says he thinks *someone* likes him."

"He didn't say who?"

"He didn't."

"What do you think that means?"

"It could be you, and he was just embarrassed to say so, right? Or it could be someone in the play."

Why didn't I sign up for the play? Total missed opportunity. This is not working out like any of the Latino love songs my parents sing.

"You'd still be his friend, no matter who he means." Zuri can tell this is not my first choice at all.

"True," I say with false energy. I push myself up and sit cross-legged, my mind trying to plump up the word "friend" like a pillow.

"So did you talk to your mom about posting the huipil?" I ask.

"That's the other reason I wanted to call you. It's up already!"

"Wow!" I'm thrilled to think it might sell quickly and slightly alarmed that I'm actually doing this. The bus still has seats left, according to the website. I hope they last. "Do you ever help your mom make stuff to sell?"

"It used to be fun to glue on rickrack and stuff. But I'm kind of sick of it, you know? I keep asking Mom to let me use the sewing machine. Then I could make something cool—a scarf or a whole dress, even."

"Maybe she'll teach you."

"I've been sketching designs."

"Ooh, send me pictures!"

"Okay, sure. Hey, how was your brother's appointment?" Z knew I was stressing about this all week. I take the phone out to the kitchen to see if supper is started.

"Well, we found out that his hearing is normal."

"That's good, right?"

Good question. It ought to be good news, but I feel weird about it. "Well, he can hear. But that means we still don't know what's wrong." I see a box of spaghetti on the counter and a jar of sauce.

"Are you sure he's not just, you know, different?"

"He's definitely different. But there must be a name for what he has. Hey, I'm getting the signal that I'm supposed to help make some supper here."

"I gotta go too," Zuri says.

I thank her for everything. I can't imagine seventh grade without her. I shove my phone in my back pocket. As I pick up the spaghetti box, Mom comes in. "Oh, sweetie, hit pause on that. Thank you for starting, but we'll have to give that box away or something. Dad's picking up gluten-free noodles on his way home. Might as well start this diet thing right away. Maybe you can make the salad?"

"Yeah, sure." I hope gluten-free is better than it sounds. Spaghetti *was* my favorite meal. "So, Mom?"

"Mm?" She rummages in the cupboard for the spaghetti pot.

"Is Memito okay?"

"I suppose," she says, filling the pot with water.

"You suppose?"

"He is what he is, Qui. What do you want me to say?"

"Aren't you worried?"

She places the pot on the stove and glances over at me. "Of course I am. Today we got more information. We have to keep looking. Keep trying things, experimenting." She dries her hands on a dish towel and flings it up on her shoulder. "He's getting OT, ocupational therapy, at school now, so that's a good development."

"The brushing?"

"And swinging and other stuff." She turns to face me. "He's lucky to have you, Qui. Now, salad?"

I open the fridge. The lettuce looks like a green submarine instead of a ball. "What happened to the lettuce?"

"It's Romaine. I thought we'd try something besides iceberg. Something different."

Maybe Memito is just Romaine in an iceberg-lettuce world. Just then he dashes through the kitchen pushing his dump truck. The *clack-clack* sound recedes down the hall.

"You know, um, Grandma's surgery is Saturday," Mom says to the silverware drawer. Her voice sounds small, like she's a kid, and for once I swallow my own fear and think about how she must be feeling. Grandma Miller is her mom.

She picks out three forks and a plastic spork for Memito, then pauses over the open drawer. I lay the lettuce on the counter and slip my arm around her waist, and she turns and hugs me.

A new thought makes me feel even worse. "What if Memito never gets to know her?" I choke on the words.

"Oh, Qui. Look, we can't think that way. Some days I can't help it either. I'm afraid I'll up and cry at work. But then I remember all the people who've recovered from cancer. It all depends on if it has spread. We'll know more after this operation."

"But she could die, couldn't she?" Something makes me want to force my mom to say it. I'm sick of her being brave and telling me not to worry. I do worry. Doesn't she worry, too?

"I can't imagine her gone." She shakes her head. "I still need her help."

"But she *could*—"

"Yes, Qui, my goodness." Her tears make me feel like I've won something. "She could. She could die." She puts her hand over her mouth and lets out a sob. I run for the Kleenex box, wishing I hadn't pushed her, my own tears starting. We blow our noses, and Mom tries to smooth her hair. Then Memito calls out, and I'm left alone with moist eyes and blurry lettuce.

TWENTY-FOUR

ON SUNDAY, I TEXT JAYDEN after walking church. That's what Dad calls our Sunday-morning walks on the wooded trail near our house. Sometimes he meditates out there, and prays. Dad always says he's not religious, but spiritual. He also tapes Yoda's words on notecards to our light switches: "Luminous beings are we." Classic oddball Dad. I agree that Yoda's cool, though.

Jayden rehearses all the time now, but I send at least one message every day. **Is the set finished yet?** Truthfully, my imagination is killing me with visions of Jayden texting some new girlfriend from the play, who isn't me. Except for Zuri's message that the huipil has had six views, my phone's been quiet all weekend.

The house is quiet, too. Memito is playing in his sandbox—actually a kiddie pool filled with sand—while Mom and Dad fix a section of fence out back. My fingers are itching for the guitar strings, and my song is running in my head as I pace through the empty house. I lift down the guitar, see Dad through the window, and put it back. It's all I want to do right now, but I don't want to get caught.

It's weird to have a free afternoon. A blank rectangle on my daily planner. Usually I'm what Mom calls "organized" and Dad calls "extra scheduled." My planner is filled with choir rehearsals and assignments. Every hour is labeled. It's great when Monday barrels in like a tornado, and I need to grab the schedule or blow away. The downside is that my phone's clock runs my life. It bosses me through each minute.

My phone buzzes. It's Jayden saying, **Yup! And the last props came in yesterday.**

I type **Where have you been?** but delete it. Too whiny. **Just back from a walk. You been busy?**

Painting sets for the play. Roller-skating with Seth. Sleeping in!

Who's Seth?

The lead in the play. The super-talented Sherlock! Sandy hair, nerdy glasses. I want you to meet him. You'll like him!

Cool.

I guess it's cool that he has a new friend. A new, super-talented friend. I just hope he doesn't forget his old, regular ones. That is, me. There'd better not be any super-talented girls in this play.

What are you up to? he asks.

A little thud lands in my stomach. I want to type something impressive. *Nothing* seems lame. I think about my planner—normally scribbled full, but empty today. I could say I'm playing guitar or writing the song. But why am I thinking of lying?

Taking a siesta.

He doesn't text back right away, so I lie back and relax. Dad says the Spanish take a siesta. It's like an intermission in the day's movie.

I should do that! How's your grandma?

Surgery went okay yesterday, but I can't help worrying.

Oh man, that's intense!

I watch the little bouncing bubbles of ". . ." as he's typing, my curiosity rising. But he just adds, **Gotta run lines with Seth now. Hang in there, Q!**

Ugh. I type **Have fun,** but then hesitate. Should I use an exclamation point?

To tell the truth, I'm bummed. We haven't talked very long. I think of when we used to do homework together on the phone. I guess that's not happening anytime soon. But a period at the end would look sarcastic. A period would look rude. Okay, fine. I'll type it and try to mean it.

Have fun!

I open Notes on my phone and bring up the song lyrics I've been writing. Missing Jayden brings another line to mind, and I write and rewrite it to fit. *Without your love, I'm incomplete. ~~Instead of milk, life's semi-sweet.~~ Togetherness makes life more sweet.*

Skype's water-drop ringtone interrupts my thoughts. Grandma!

"Quijana. I'm glad you're online."

I take in the metal bed rails, the white blanket, and a beeping monitor next to her bed. She's at the hospital. I didn't think they'd let her Skype from there. She's sitting up, but a pillow is behind her head. Her face looks pale—and old. Grandma's never looked so old before. Aunt Jess pokes her head into the frame. "Hey, Quijana. We're doing okay here. I'll call your mom in a minute, okay?"

"Are you all right, Grandma?" I'm sure she hears concern in my voice.

"Oh, don't look at me like that. Do I look that bad?" She smiles, looking more like herself. "They've got me stuck in this bed. But I'm going to eat as much of their chocolate pudding as I can hold!"

"So they're letting you eat?"

"Today I'm on soft stuff. How's the song going? Can you text me your lyrics?" Her body looks weak, but her voice sounds steady.

"Sure. What's that on your wrist?" White tape wraps her wrist like a cast.

"Oh, that's a port. See, this plastic tube lets them pour painkillers in. It doesn't hurt." She pauses for a bout of coughing. "Tell me what's going on with Jayden these days. Is he still lucky enough to have your good opinion?"

I laugh. I wonder if everyone used to talk that way. "Um, yeah. He's in a play at school."

"A thespian! Good sign. But he must be very busy, then."

Leave it to Grandma to go right to the core of the problem. I blow air through my cheeks. "Monumentally busy. We still text, though. And there's school."

"Hmph. And the play is done when?"

"About two weeks."

"Maybe you kids could take another bike ride before the weather turns cold."

"Mm." That's actually a good idea. "I bet we could."

"I talked to your mom on the phone. She's real excited about the Guatemala trip."

"Yeah." She sure is.

"Why the sad face?"

I wish I could tell her everything. My mouth goes dry as I think of what to say. "I won't like it."

"You might."

"You know Tía Lencha? The Carrillos here? I don't fit in. Like, not at all."

She frowns. "So, tell me about it."

I try to explain how out of place I felt to be the only person not speaking Spanish and how all the fun stopped when they found out that I use the word "dad."

"You know what I'm going to ask you, don't you, Qui?"

"Um, no?"

"Well, did you know that manatees shove crocodiles out of their way?"

"What?" Typical Grandma—finding something in nature that makes all our human stuff make complete sense.

"If a croc is in the manatee's path, the manatee just nudges him. No fear at all. The deadly crocodile might as well be a log. Do you know why?"

I shake my head.

"For a long time, I wondered, too. I had to watch for months to understand that crocs *gulp* instead of chew. And they can't gulp a manatee. So a manatee can bully a croc."

"Well, that's good." Why is she telling me this?

"My point is, watch first, understand later. Eventually, you'll see where you fit in. Keep your eyes open, Quijana. This world is vast and beautiful. You'll see amazing things." She leans back and takes a few deep breaths. Her chest moves up and down faster than usual.

"You okay?"

She bats the air with a hand.

"I love you, Grandma."

"I love you, too, little one." Finally her breath slows a bit and she closes her eyes.

"Grandma?"

"Yes?" Her eyes flutter open.

"We'll see you soon, at Thanksgiving, right?"

"I'm planning on it." She smiles. Then she looks offscreen. "I see they're bringing my supper here. I'll try to Skype again when I get home. You be brave. Love you, sweetheart."

"Love you, too."

I take my phone out to the charger in the living room and sink into the couch. Grandma looked thinner. Frail. But she'll go home soon. She'll get better. It's nearly November. Like I said, we'll see her soon.

TWENTY-FIVE

THE NEXT MORNING, I dress for school and check my phone. It shows two messages, but I swipe the screen and send a quick heart to Grandma first. Then I click Zuri's bolded name. **We have a buyer!** is the first message from her at 10:35 p.m. The second one is from ten minutes later. **:-(Her credit card didn't go through.**

Aww. Thx for the update. So close! This proves that there are buyers out there, though. And that our price for the huipil is fair. I bet the next buyer will come along soon.

As I eat Organic O's and almond milk, a thought makes me stop. *Credit card. Buyers need credit cards. How will I buy my bus ticket without one?*

I pull up the bus website on my phone. Nothing about payment in the FAQs. I bring up the schedule. Nineteen more seats left on the 10:35 p.m. I click BOOK NOW and finally find a list of payment options. Visa, MasterCard, American Express. Something called Paypal. Finally I see a printed line in a small font at the bottom. *Cash purchases may be made in person at the bus terminal.* Whew. I'll have to walk over there ahead of time, but at least they'll take my money.

I call out a goodbye and walk to the corner. As I wait for the school bus, I watch the two Spanish-speaking boys. They still wear button-down shirts, tucked in. They still stand together and keep quiet. I wish my cousin Crista were here. She's so smiley and eager, she'd walk right up to them and talk their ears off. Without speaking Spanish—which I am *not* going to do, especially at the bus stop—there's no way I can help them. But I still wish they felt more welcome. They stand tall, looking serious and kind of dignified, like my dad in his First Communion picture. If he were here, he'd make them feel great. That's another difference between us; I didn't inherit his sunny, social gene.

At school, history class seems easy compared to my bus situation. Even Spanish goes smoothly. I'm not even worried when Señora Francés calls me up to her desk after class.

"Quijana, I'm pleased that you're passing Spanish now! I have to confess, when I heard your authentic pronunciation, I assumed you spoke Spanish at home." She pauses, and I realize that this is a question.

"No, ma'am, but my parents do."

"So your parents are fluent?" Two lines form between her eyebrows, and I can tell she's trying to puzzle it all out.

"See, my dad is from Guatemala. My mom learned from school and from being an interpreter there."

"But they didn't . . ."

165

"Teach me, I know." I shrug. Sometimes I wish they *had* taught me. As a baby, it would have been easy to learn. But whatever. I may never be as fluent as my cousins, but at least I'm passing the class.

"Even hearing Spanish actually helps a lot. Your *r*'s are just right." She smiles with too many teeth, and I wonder if she feels sorry for me. "When I learned, I started from scratch. Not even good *r*s. You'll do fine if you keep up with your daily work." So much for feeling sorry for me!

"I will, ma'am."

In English, Ms. May greets us with a discussion question on the board: Describe the personality of the main character in Edgar Allen Poe's "The Tell-Tale Heart" in 200 words. I read the story last night, but the main guy is pretty strange. He murders someone and then can't help confessing to it—it's so not my reality. My shaky letters gain confidence as I write. The guy's so bizarre that he starts to be a little more fun to write about. I hear pencils scratching paper until the lunch bell rings.

"My hand still hurts," says Zuri as we walk to the cafeteria, shaking out our wrists, she with a blue medical boot for her ankle now.

"I thought I had nothing to say about 'Tell-Tale Heart' until I started writing," says Jayden.

"You never have nothing to say," I tell him. "You're, like, a genius with characters and their motives and stuff. And then there's your writing. Ms. May gives you bonus style points on almost every assignment. How can you be all that and a nice person, too?" Suddenly I realize that we've stopped walking, and my friends are staring at me.

Jayden gives a little laugh. "Well, wow. What's with all the compliments?"

Oh no! I've said way too much. "Uh . . ." I wonder if I look as stupid as I feel.

Zuri jumps in. "I'd say all that too, if I didn't know it would give you a big head." She starts us walking again, and I silently thank her. "You're already impossible, Jayday."

Jayden makes some funny comeback, but I can't hear it over my own embarrassment. Heat rises into my cheeks. *Did I embarrass him? What does he think of me now?* I didn't mean to sound like a gum-chewing groupie sticking praise all over him. Yuck.

Zuri makes for the lunch line as soon as we reach the cafeteria. Now I'm afraid to say anything.

Jayden reaches the table first and lifts applesauce out of his lunch bag. I sit down stiffly. It's like my muscles aren't responding. *Can he tell that I like him? Can everyone tell?*

"Whatcha got today?" he says, nodding toward my lunch.

I understand from this that I should skip mentioning the whole episode.

"Nothing new," I say, getting out my pear. As we drive on with the conversation, I pretend to feel completely great. But a sinkhole opens under every word. I'm not relaxed like usual. I'm fidgeting with my food. I feel like we're driving down a road made of lies.

I watch Jayden as he dips a carrot stick in dressing. I love the way his hair falls. I love the shape of his hands. No wonder all this loving leaks out. Maybe it should.

"Jayden," I say, bold as Quixote in front of a windmill.

He looks up.

"The compliments. The reason is . . ."

"You have good taste!" He grins.

"It's more than that. I . . ."

"Man oh man, that line was so long today!" Zuri finally joins us.

Jayden immediately turns to her. "You'll hardly have time to eat," he says.

"I'll get 'tell-tale' heartburn," she jokes.

They laugh, but I can't turn away from my windmill that fast. I was all set to tell Jayden how I feel, but my chance has passed. Even when Zuri disappears to get ketchup, Jayden talks quickly about the play and their first run-through with costumes. He looks up, but never stops talking. It's like he's performing. But why? And why is something in his voice strained, like a guitar string over-tightened?

I think he knows what I was going to say. I bet he's talking right now to keep me from saying it. Maybe he can't relax because he's afraid? This *would* be the day we read "The

Tell-Tale Heart"—a guy who loses his nerve trying to hide the truth. But is Jayden afraid of his own heart or of mine?

I'm off-kilter for the rest of lunch, and I walk a step behind them as we go to class. Pep-rally posters shout action verbs: Charge! Pounce! Win! I want to do exactly that—text him a drastic message, grab his shoulders and look into his eyes. He must know, right? Zuri does.

Jayden texts me every day, hugs me hello, sits across from me at lunch, yet he's like a dresser drawer that won't open all the way. Not for me, at least. Or not yet.

Choir gives me a welcome break. In my usual chair, I feel more like myself. We mark dynamics in our music, noting where we'll sing louder and softer.

Maybe that's the problem with Jayden. I turned up the volume too loud too fast. I'll try a little decrescendo, and see what happens.

TWENTY-SIX

WALKING HOME FROM THE BUS, I turn "Quijana + Jayden" over in my mind like a Rubik's Cube. I line up colors on one side, then mess it up trying to line up another side. His actions never form a pattern I recognize.

At home, in my hour of freedom, I pull down the guitar from its hook and pour my heart into "Tears in Heaven." My fingers have learned what to do now. Sometimes I move them to the next chord without even looking at the frets. Then the chords are like friends singing right along with me.

When I get tired of how sad the song is making me, I sing one version of my Jayden song, using the words I have so far. Then I sing another variation, but no new lines come to mind. How do people write songs? The first lines came to me so easily. But now what? I send Grandma a selfie of my hand on the guitar strings. She sends a **Love it!** right back.

Like usual, I hang up the guitar when I hear a car in the driveway. Dad and Memito come in with corn on the cob, which is almost as good as spaghetti in my opinion. "Yes!" I cheer and get out the butter so it's nice and soft by suppertime.

"Quijana?" Mom's voice carries from the living room. "Come see what else we bought."

She and Dad stand side by side behind huge plastic shopping bags, smiling broadly.

"¡M'ija! What do you think?" Dad unveils four wheeled suitcases. Two stand as tall as Memito, one is smaller, and one is tiny. All are red with black zippers.

Memito squats down and inspects them from a distance.

"Watch this," Dad says. He pulls a telescoping handle out of the littlest one. Memito understands immediately and starts pulling his suitcase around the room.

I lay mine down and unzip each compartment. The biggest section has a new-car smell. I'm already picturing rolling it to the bus station. I see a handy pocket for socks and another for my phone-charger cord. The stiff canvas feels durable. "These are nice, Dad."

He beams, and a twinge of guilt weakens my smile. He has no idea that my plans for this suitcase are very different from his.

Mom says, "Plan to bring a backpack, too, for books and snacks on the plane. That's your carry-on. These, we'll check through as luggage."

I nod, thinking how I'll use her advice for my own trip.

"Guess what else." She disappears into the kitchen and comes back with a manila envelope. "Our passports came!" She pulls out four booklets bound in blue covers. Each has a bald eagle embossed in gold on the front and PASSPORT above it. She hands me mine.

Behind a rigid cover, the first page shows the non-smiling picture we took over a month ago, then my personal information, and at the bottom, a long string of characters that must be my passport number. Across the top, it says The United States of America in fancy letters. A surge of pride in my country shoots through me. Does Dad feel this way about Guatemala? Or America? Or both?

"I'll keep them all together in the desk drawer until we go," Mom says, taking them up. "Isn't this exciting? In a little over a month, we'll be in Guatemala!"

"That soon?" I ask, panicking a little. "What day exactly?" I hope this question doesn't sound suspicious.

"Well, about six weeks. December twentieth."

I make a mental note of the date. It's not the first day of Christmas vacation, and not the date I planned to buy a ticket for.

"You'll miss a day of school, but the airfare was cheaper, and this is important. Educational, in fact."

In the bathroom, I type in the new date on the bus company's website. With relief I see that they run a night bus on December 19, and it has twenty-two seats left. As soon as the huipil sells, I can buy one of those seats. I hope it's soon.

Jayden's text message comes through while we're eating dinner.

Can you talk?

"No phones at the table, please," Mom says as she slices apple chunks for Memito on his tray. Thursday's a no-class night for her, so we're eating together.

I lay my phone in my lap, but my attention follows it. Look at those words: *Can you talk?* I'm nothing but JaydenJaydenJayden and the urge to type *YesYesYes*. I don't hear my dad's next comment or my mom's reply. It's all I can do to stay in my chair. I eat faster.

Mom makes eye contact. "Don't gulp your food, please."

"It's good to keep boys waiting," Dad says, taking more salad. I guess I'm glancing at my phone a little too obviously. Still, annoyance twists my mouth.

"It's not a boy," I lie. In the silence that follows, I'm sure they can tell I'm lying. The lie seems like a new food at the table, taking up space, but I don't care.

Anyway, Jayden isn't a *boy*. Not like that. Not yet. He's a friend. He's not calling for a date.

"Dime con quién andas y te diré quién eres," quotes Dad.

"Yes, so true. Choose friends carefully—you become like them," Mom paraphrases. I huff and roll my eyes at her like I knew what Dad was saying, but I didn't.

I like that idea, though, that you become like your friends. I'd like to be confident like Zuri and clever like Jayden. I chew on, eating the distance between Jayden and me, swallowing the seconds.

Soon evening has dimmed the room, and Dad gets up to switch on the overhead light. I'm biting through a new potato that needs more salt when Memito screams.

We stop our chewing and look at him. Surprise makes it seem like Mom's in slow motion as she checks his tray, the seat strap's latch—anything that might be pinching him. He starts tearing up and covering his eyes, still yelling. Now Dad lifts him up, and Memito's little head burrows into Dad's shoulder. He's writhing and gripping Dad's shirt.

I'm wondering what is hurting him and what I can do when his head-turning makes it clear. "The light!" I say.

"The light?" Mom reaches the switch in one step.

In the sudden dark, Memito goes quiet. We all release a held breath. Memito lifts his head. Mom and Dad exchange startled looks.

"Quijana, thank goodness you thought of that," Mom says. Her eyebrows pull together, like she's still uncertain of why it worked.

"M'ijo, what's wrong with the light?" Dad carries Memito to the switch and says, "You turn it on. You like switches, yes?"

Not today. Memito's body twists away. Dad puts him back in his booster seat. "I guess we eat in the dark tonight." Walking to his own chair, he says, "Extraño."

"Maybe we should check with the doctor," Mom says.

Dad shakes his head, saying, "She already saw him."

"We know his hearing is okay," I say.

Mom searches the ceiling. "But now lights?"

Memito finishes his food, and Mom takes off his tray without making him say "down." No one else seems to be able to eat, including me. At least this takes my mind off wondering what's up with Jayden—until my phone throws glitter into the air with its magic-wand sound. But I'm not in a hurry anymore. I don't move. I don't want to move.

Mom looks up. "Go ahead," she says. "Supper's done anyway."

"It can wait," I say. "I want to know what we're going to do."

But nobody says anything. Finally, Dad pushes away from the table, lifting his plate. "We'll think about this later, won't we Mamá? Talk to your friends, Quijanita. Don't worry."

From my room, I hear Mom reading to Memito. That's a normal thing, but still, everything feels off-balance, like the house is a boat, pitching to one side.

Here, I text, hoping Jayden is still near his phone. While I wait, I type *late talker* into Google. Parenting sites come up, and lists of words that kids should know by age three. Memito, I know, knows only a fraction of them. Maybe it's just his personality, I tell myself. Maybe he's fine. Several people mention that Albert Einstein didn't talk until age four. The Internet always scares people anyway.

Hey. There he is.

Everything okay? I ask him.

My mom's not coming to the play next Saturday.

What?! I'm surprised that any mom would miss her kid's play.

Something at work.

She has to come. Can't she cancel?

You'd think!

I wait to see if he wants to talk about it more. The screen starts to dim.

Play rehearsals good?

He doesn't even answer that.

I'm not sure she's thrilled about my whole acting thing.

What, she wants you on the debate team or something?

Yeah, or the Mathletes.

Now I see why he's upset. **If she came, she'd see how perfect you are for theater.**

You'll come, won't you?

Of course! I wouldn't miss it!

Obviously! I've already planned what to wear. It'll be fun to cheer him on and see him in costume. Then when he quotes a line, I'll know what he means. I hope his mom changes her mind.

I think back to what Zuri said. A girlfriend. Someone likes him.

Tell me about this girl who likes you. I picture each theater girl. Lauren?

Who said any girl likes me?

Zuri.

The reply doesn't come right away. I wonder if he's had to go do something else.

I didn't say that.

Uh-oh. Am I in trouble?

Okay. Sorry. She said you mentioned a girlfriend or someone who wanted to be or something.

I was kidding!

I should be happy, but what is he saying, exactly? A tumbling-down happens in my chest.

So no girlfriend for you, huh?

I hope my half joke hides the fallen feeling I'm trying to ignore. I'm still confused, but I can't figure out what to ask.

Nope.

I'm not sure what to say next. I type in *See you tomorrow*, but backspace over it. Memito toddles back into my head.

Hey, your little brother's three, right? Does he talk a lot?

Again the answer takes some time. I hope he hasn't run off to get a snack. From down the hall, I hear pouring water and clunking plastic toys—Memito playing in the tub.

Jayden's answer hits my screen.

Never shuts up.

I send a smiley face to Jayden, but my heart thuds for Memito. Somehow, hearing about another kid—a real one, who's three, too—makes me realize it's true. Memito isn't a late-talker like Einstein. He's not just different or quirky. Something is *wrong*.

On my way out to the charger in the living room, I stop near the bathroom. Memito is perched on Mom's hip in dinosaur jammies, wet hair pasted to his head. He's double-sweet when he's clean and sleepy.

"Lella, lella," he says.

Mom carries him down the hall.

"Lella!"

I know what he wants. I duck into the bathroom and grab his plastic elephant. As I hand it over, he hugs it to his chest and smiles.

"Thanks, Qui," Mom says.

I wish I could give him something better, though—words.

TWENTY-SEVEN

FRIDAY AFTER SCHOOL, a marimba ringtone xylophones the afternoon air. Dad picks up, and Abuela's on the phone. "¡Hola, Mamá!" he says.

For the first time, I don't dive into a chore or disappear into my room. I have a plan. I have memorized three sentences to say to her. Since I'm not going to Guatemala, I figure I can at least say something. It will surprise her, and Dad, too, because I didn't ask him for help. (If I had, we'd have spent fifteen minutes translating each sentence, talking about every word option and weighing which ones captured the original meaning best, instead of the fifteen seconds it took on a website.)

Plus, I checked my sentences with my Spanish teacher. Señora Francés lit up like a sparkler when I brought over my paper. "Your abuela will be so pleased," she said. I hope she's right.

While Dad talks and paces the kitchen, I rehearse my sentences silently. I stay close by. After all that, I don't want him to hang up.

A half hour later, my chin rests on my folded arms at the table. Memito tugs at my arm. With one finger he points up. This is his signal for an airplane ride. Since Dad sounds nowhere close to saying goodbye, I let Memito pull me to the carpet.

"Okay," I say and lie on my back with my feet in the air. He sets his tummy on the soles of my feet, and I hold onto his hands, then I rock back, raise my legs, and lift him into the air. He's a bird. He's a plane. He's Superman! He giggles as I fly him back and forth, and I feel my eyes crinkle at the corners, remembering when Dad used to do this with me. When my legs get tired, I bring him in for a landing and listen for Dad.

Memito wants to go up again. "No," I tell him. "Later." I point to his dump truck, and he starts running his figure eight as I duck into the kitchen. Dad's still holding the phone up to his ear. Soon he says, "¿De veras?"

Now a long goodbye starts. Every phrase sounds like an ending, but there's always one more. Finally, he mentions my name. "Ella está aquí cerca." *She's here close by.* "Sí, por supuesto."

He hands me the phone. For a second, Abuela's voice washes away my three sentences. I pull my attention back into my head to remember them. As I start to form a word, I worry that she won't understand my pronunciation. I worry I can't do this right. But I figure she can't normally understand me anyway. "Abuela. Hola," I finally say. She starts to talk, but I cut her off. In a rush, I say, "Estoy en el coro en mi escuela.

Me gustan manatíes. No entiendo mucho español, pero te doy un abrazo."

"¡Ay, chica dulce!" she says, and continues with fountains of words that sound smiley. It's over, but I'm trembling. At her first pause, I insert "Adiós, Abuelita," and hand the phone back to Dad. I'm breathing hard; my heart is thumping. I feel like I've dodged an oncoming car.

Dad says more goodbyes, but he's looking at me. Finally he hangs up. I think I did it right because he's starting to smile. I press my lips together, and then a smile spreads across my face, too.

"Well, well!" he says. "You speak Spanish!"

I shake my head. "It's just a few sentences." I look at the floor. All I said was I'm in choir, I like manatees, and I send her a hug.

"But you did it." He calls toward the back of the house. "Kim, come here! Quijana spoke to her abuela."

Oh boy. I didn't want this to be a big deal. But who was I kidding? Dad makes everything a big deal.

Mom comes in from the bedroom and her homework to gush. "Qui!" Exclamations pour out, pats on the back, hair tousling—the works. I almost wish I hadn't done it. What if they want me to speak Spanish all the time now? It's like I've lifted something heavy and have nowhere to set it down.

When they finally calm down, I plop on the couch and text Zuri.

Over-the-top parents alert!

Wanna trade? My parents just started dancing to the elevator music IN THE MALL.

She wins that round. But this isn't how I expected to feel. I just wanted to make up for not going to Guatemala. I didn't mean for them to think that I'm suddenly interested in learning Spanish. This event was a one-off, not the beginning of a series.

As evening arrives, though, Dad's still in a sunny mood. He pulls on his coat and says, "Let's take a walk."

"It's dark already," I say, looking at the grayed-out sky through the window.

"I know, but your mom needs to write lesson plans, and Memito won't let her work. He keeps climbing in her lap and pressing the computer keys."

I believe it. He does the same thing with me. Still. "Why do I have to go?" I want to stay home. I wish I could use the homework excuse, but I have the whole weekend to finish it.

"Let's take flashlights!" Dad's excitement wins Memito over, and *he's* so into it that I laugh. Soon we're walking down our block following Memito on his tricycle.

The street's different after dark. The edges of houses smudge into their backgrounds. Our flashlights make circles on the sidewalk that bounce along as we walk. I stop to snap a selfie of me with a flashlight under my chin and post it. *Muah-ha-ha-ha!* I run to catch up.

Memito looks like such a normal kid, zooming along. No one can tell that he won't wear anything but soft clothes, that we've had to cut out all his shirt tags, that we have to make sure not to shine the flashlights in his face because he still hates bright lights.

As we pass the garage-sale house, Dad says, "I wanted to tell you, m'ija, your pronunciation's very good."

Oh, no. Not Spanish again.

"You know, your mamá first learned from textbooks and classes, too, but then she picked up high-level Spanish by reading books. I could show you a couple at home. We could even order some."

"Dad, I only meant to . . ."

"I know you have far to go. But your three sentences, that's a start."

As we walk on under the stars, I decide not to argue. What can it hurt to let him hope? I'll disappoint him soon enough—like the next time Abuela calls.

Back home, we hang up our jackets and leave our shoes on the shelf by the door. Except Memito. He stomps his feet when Dad reaches for his shoes. "Come on, m'ijo."

Memito bolts down the hall, his shoes still on. "I'll try," Mom says, emerging from her room with a smile, her gaze following the *clomp* of Memito's shoes. "How was the walk?" I can tell she got a lot done because she's really asking, really looking at me.

"Good," I say. "The flashlight made it fun." I don't tell her Jayden "liked" my photo, which was kind of the only good part of the walk.

Mom tugs on the end of my ponytail. "You're a good sister," she says, and then goes after Memito. Immediately, crying carries down the hall from his room. I go peek in his doorway as Mom grabs him up in a big bear hug, pulls up the Velcro straps, and sets the shoes aside. "Sorry, m'ijo. No shoes in the house." Now he's kicking at tantrum-speed, clunking his bare heels on the carpet until they turn red. He tries smushing his feet into the shoes but can't manage the flapping straps or the twisting tongues.

With a determined look, Mom leaves the room. "He's fine, Qui."

He's whimpering and crying himself out on his little race-car bed until I sneak in and help. Mom always says we shouldn't reward bad behavior, but he seems desperate. I put his feet in the shoes, pull the Velcro tight, and relief breaks over his tear-stained face. "Memito," I say, my voice soft. I hope he will look at me, but his eyes close.

When Dad shows up with a bedtime book, Memito is sleeping on top of his comforter, one shoe on each foot. Dad looks at me, and I hold my breath, but I'm not in trouble. He puts his hand on my shoulder. This was more than little-kid dramatics. I know it.

At the dining table, Dad talks with Mom in Spanish. From my bed, I hear keyboard clicks. By now I know the search engine will drive him to another name for what's happening or maybe to one of the names we've seen before. Developmental delay. Sensory integration. Childhood schizophrenia.

Mom's reading a book about allergies and something called leaky gut, and I found headphones for sale that help "auditory processing"—unless that's a scam.

I try blowing all of this away with a deep breath, but worry keeps tapping my shoulder. What if Memito doesn't get better? What if he's never normal again? How will he handle Guatemala, especially without me? Mom and Dad act like everything's under control. I wish it were.

I climb into bed. Under my blanket, I try to feel my feet. I try to feel each toe and the warm air around them. Heels. Arches. Pockets of emptiness where the blanket isn't. I picture what it feels like to have lonely feet, each needing a shoe's squeeze. I'm guessing. I'm imagining. Am I closer to understanding? No one knows.

TWENTY-EIGHT

THE SINGLE DIGITS OF NOVEMBER slip by, and Zuri hasn't mentioned the huipil for a week. I'm nervous to ask her about it, since it's such a big favor, and I don't want to be pushy. At school, our lunchtime talks have been all about final dress rehearsals for Jayden's play and the fact that his mom will be able to go tomorrow night after all. "She canceled her work thing, after all that!" I hope it means she's okay with Jayden's acting. But the thought of money runs behind all my other thoughts because the bus website shows only twelve seats left for my Florida trip.

On Saturday morning, I can't take the suspense anymore. I won't even enjoy the play tonight if I don't know *something* about the huipil. I pick up my phone to text Zuri, and then a better idea comes to mind. I'll call her mom. Since it's the weekend, she's probably home.

"Ms. Thomas? Um, I'm Quijana Carrillo, Zuri's friend?"

"Hello, love. I bet you're calling about that wonderful top."

She doesn't have good news. People haven't shown much interest since the huipil was first listed. "In my experience, reducing the price creates new excitement," she says. "Could you go down to one hundred fifty dollars?"

"That would be okay, except I won't be able to give you as much."

"Never mind that, love. Like I said before, I'm happy to do it. I was wondering . . . Zuri hasn't told me why you're selling it. It's quite beautiful."

"Yes, ma'am. It's . . . it's an extra. My closet has a bunch of these." I feel my cheeks burn red. What am I talking about? My lie sounds dumb.

"Lucky you!" she says, and I feel even worse. "Don't you worry. We'll find the right buyer. And in the meantime, will we see you at the play tonight?"

I inhale rapidly, my mind cascading through the possibilities of her meeting my parents and mentioning this project.

"Quijana?"

"Yes, ma'am. Yes, we'll be there."

The night falls cool and clear as we drive to school to see Jayden's play. One of Mom's college students is babysitting Memito.

We walk in to find the lobby packed. Zuri and I want to sit together, so I text her where to find us. I just hope her parents let her sit with us by herself.

"The enterprising Quijana Carrillo," shouts Ms. Thomas. She waves, and the family of three speeds over. So much for keeping the parents apart.

I hug Zuri, and the four parents shake hands. The Thomases, tall and regal, bend their heads down to greet my petite parents. "I'm *so* enjoying getting to know Quijana," Ms. Thomas says to my mother.

"I'm glad," Mom answers. "And we're so happy when Zuri comes over."

"And Mr. Carrillo, where are you from? I've been asking Zuri, but she never can tell me."

"I was born in Guatemala."

Uh-oh. Zuri and I look at each other, our breath speeding up. This could go toward huipil territory fast. "We better find seats, don't y'all think?" I say.

We shuffle as a group into the auditorium. Ms. Thomas remarks, "The fabrics from Guatemala are so intricate and colorful. I love the—"

"Mom, emergency, can you re-tie my headscarf?" Zuri breaks in, rumpling it.

"Jayden said the play is a comedy," I say randomly, trying to change the subject. "Have you ever been to a junior high school play?" I ask Mr. Thomas.

"No, I haven't," he says, his eyes twinkling.

Zuri and I maneuver to walk between the parents as we make our way down the aisle.

"Were you born in Barbados?" I ask Mr. Thomas, though I already know the answer.

"We both were," he says, taking his wife's hand.

When we get to an empty row, my parents file in. Then Zuri and I take the next two seats, making it hard for the parents to talk across us. I let out a deep breath.

"That was close," she says quietly.

"Nice headscarf emergency." I give her a thumbs-up.

A thick red curtain hides the stage, and the room bubbles with anticipation. Next month, I'll be on the same stage for my choir concert. Zuri points to Jayden's name in the program, and my excitement feels squared by hers. We grip each other's hands. It's exciting to be at school after dark and on a Saturday, like we're breaking some rule or something. I take a picture of her holding the program, and then she takes one of me. I send mine to Grandma, then post it as well.

The theater darkens, and the curtain opens. When the stage lights come up, Jayden stands in an old-timey living room looking like a British gentleman, top hat to wingtips. When he speaks his lines, we're immediately transported to London. I'm amazed at how good he looks in slicked hair and shiny shoes, gliding across the stage—even better than usual.

"Wow," Zuri whispers, and that's what I'm thinking, too.

As more characters enter, I keep an eye out for any cute girls who might like Jayden.

Soon the audience is absorbed in the story, laughing in all the right places, and even I am forgetting he's my Jayden. He's become his part. For a full scene, I forget he's my friend at all. I miss several lines as I realize my map of Jayden is too small. I need to add a sprawling new territory. A mountain range. A river.

The cast takes a bow as the audience roars. I don't think anyone was expecting this play to be actually good, like real-world good, and now we're two hundred hearts wide open. Jayden steps forward, and I'm clapping louder than I've ever clapped before. He's happy in a way I've never seen, smiling with his whole body, eyes glittering.

"Let's go see him!" Zuri is already on her feet.

"What about our parents?"

"I'll go get the car, honey," Ms. Thomas says. "You wait for Zuri."

"I need to visit the ladies' room," Mom tells Dad.

Whew. Crisis averted. The dads might talk, but that doesn't worry me.

We run to the backstage door, ready to hug Jayden, ready to shout how wonderful it was. We thread our way through costumed people and props, and I hear the drama teacher accepting praise from the principal. Finally, we see Jayden, surrounded by cast folk and crew. He's hugging some and fist-bumping others. Students from the grade above us shake his hand.

We're almost close enough to get his attention when the main character from the play, who must be Seth, grabs Jayden in a bear hug. I hear what he says, but it's almost a code, filled with inside jokes. "Where's the seventh Napoleon? Stage left! Don't be naff!" They're laughing back and forth and jostling each other when Zuri bellows, "Jayden, that was fantastic!"

He startles and his face flushes when he sees us approach. He glances at Seth, and then says, "Hey!"

Seth stands close by as Zuri moves in to hug Jayden. "Absolutely brilliant!" she says, hugging Seth, too, even though I'm pretty sure she doesn't know him. "I couldn't stop laughing!"

I set aside a half thought that's forming in my head, focus on Jayden's face, and a surge of happiness returns. "You were amazing!" I say, squeezing him tight, inhaling the cinnamon smell of his hair gel. "I loved it!"

"Thanks, guys," he says. I can tell he knows he did super well. Seth is still with us, so I say, "You did a great job, too," nodding and smiling, a kind of through-the-air handshake.

"No one has timing like Jayden, though. We had that rapid fire going, man!"

Jayden breaks into a real smile again. "See," he explains to Zuri and me. "Seth has to—oh, Seth, this is Zuri and Quijana." He points to each of us. "Seth has to interrupt me in Scene Three, and then I have to talk over him a line later. It has to feel real without confusing the audience. Sometimes we flub it, but tonight—"

"—it went like clockwork." Seth holds up both hands and Jayden meets them in a high ten. "Did you see Amanda in the couch scene?" Seth starts laughing. "She almost didn't pick up the vase!"

Zuri looks at me and I look back. We know it's time to go. The sparks in the room are for the cast and crew. They're all electrified, like a bank of lights. Jayden clearly just wants to talk with Seth.

"Wait, Qui."

I lift my head to see Jayden's green eyes soften.

"Thanks."

"For what?"

"Remember lunch at the tree? I didn't know if I would even try out for this thing. I was worried about—well, you remember." Jayden smiles, and Seth looks at me more closely. "I have you to thank for all of it."

"I knew you'd be great." A little glow warms my chest, and I really wish I could talk to him alone. Now is the time to tell him what I couldn't last week. Now would be perfect.

But the moment doesn't come. Cast members slap Jayden and Seth on the back, and Seth stays right at Jayden's side. Zuri and I say our *See you Mondays* and walk back toward our dads.

The hall of walking coats seems tame, a world without spotlights and applause. I'm happy for Jayden, and I feel special to him, but my heart slumps. I've seen something I didn't expect. The play is Jayden's life tonight, and I am in the wings.

TWENTY-NINE

THE GOOD THING about Jayden's play is that it majorly inspires me to work on more song lyrics after walking church on Sunday morning. I imagine singing the lines to Jayden, his eyes sparkling as I strum. I click Notes on my phone.

The more I know you, the more I want to know you more.
And when you fix your eyes on me,
I feel my heart expand, fly free.
Without your love, I'm incomplete.
Togetherness makes life more sweet.
The more I know you, the more I want to know you more.

Two more lines. That's what it needs. I open up a rhyming dictionary site and skim the most common rhymes, like "-ight." Then I close my eyes and breathe deeply. I think of Jayden onstage, Jayden at the lunch tree, Jayden biking to the lake, Jayden laughing at the lunch table.

Your life inspires; I want to bloom.
A better me lights up this room.

Yes! I read it over again, singing it under my breath.

Three raps on my window startle me. It's Mom in a sun hat and gardening gloves, carrying a tray of winter pansies. "Don't forget, we're having lunch at Tía Lencha's!" she shouts.

I give her a thumbs-up, but my spirits sink.

When we pile in the car later, I ask, "Will Memito be okay at Tía Lencha's?" He looks fine right now, rolling a train engine on the back of Dad's seat.

"I think so, Qui," Mom says. "It's a familiar place."

But I'm not so sure. Lots of stuff triggers him now. Loud laughing, bright lights, crowds of people. His mind is a little bowl that fills up fast. I worry it will overflow.

"What if he gets upset? Will we leave?"

"No, mi angelita," Dad says. "Our job is to help him handle it."

I was partly asking for Memito and partly asking for myself. I'd like to clear out of there as soon as we can.

I text Jayden in the car on the way.

You were so great last night!

He responds right away.

Thanks! Talk later?

Yes!

I hope this means we'll talk more, now that the play is over.

"Okay, phones away, please," Mom announces as she turns off the engine. Dad clicks off his screen.

"One last text to Grandma?" Everyone sits still as I send an image of a fat cat with hearts above its head and **Are you home from rehab yet? I hope so!**

I hold Memito's hand in the apartment building's parking lot, and my breath goes shallow. I'm thinking of the hours to come. It's not just the Spanish that'll be soaring over my head. It's also Tío Pancho using hand gestures I don't recognize, and Tía Lencha speaking English to me that I can't always understand through her accent. She has to repeat two or three times, no matter how hard I listen. I feel like I'm falling through a tunnel of sound, not a single word to grab on to.

But when Tío Pancho opens the door, my worries are replaced by the aroma of frijoles negros and fresh tortillas. Wow. Dad's food never smells this good.

I watch Memito touch every piece of furniture with the back of his hand—yet another new routine of his. Half my attention is on him until he sits down and starts playing with a stack of wooden coasters.

In the warm kitchen, I breathe more deeply. Mirabel and Crista pat balls of harina into palm-sized circles, then Tía cooks them three at a time in her big skillet. She flips them like pancakes and piles the finished tortillas in a basket, keeping them warm under a thick dish towel.

"Hey Quijana, you can help," says Crista. She's wearing a plastic tiara that sits a little crooked.

"If you wash your hands," Mirabel tells me.

I hesitate for a second, but it looks pretty easy.

"Good idea," Dad says. "Learn here so you can help Abuela when we get to Guatemala."

Right. Nothing matters if it's not about Guatemala.

"Guatemala!" says Mirabel. "That's right! When do you go?"

"Next month," I say, then realize November's half gone. A queasy feeling stirs in my stomach. It's way past time to buy my ticket. I really should have thought of a backup plan to selling the huipil.

"I wish I could go." Crista stops her work and looks at a spot above my head. "I remember going to this market, and Don Paulo giving me a stick of candy every time we bought his vegetables."

I wish I could give her the airplane seat I won't be using.

"¡Sí, sí! Es verdad," Tía says and launches into memories in Spanish. Mom and Dad and Tío Pancho join in. A salad of voices tosses around my head.

Worried, I look around for Memito, thinking that all this noise must be bothering him, but he's okay. He's found a quiet corner and a picture book. If he can handle this visit, I should be able to, right?

I scoop up the cornmeal dough and watch Mirabel's hands. I try to form a ball, but the stuff crumbles.

"Here." She sprinkles water onto my cracked wedges. Now it's less grainy and flattens easily.

"That's it," Crista says, straightening her tiara with her wrist. "Easy, yeah?"

It is. Just like Play-Doh.

"So we heard you spoke Spanish to Abuela," says Mirabel.

"What?" I almost drop my dough.

"Your dad told us."

"He did?" Thanks a lot, Dad. Why does everything have to be a family headline?

"Well, what did you say?"

The room stops. Not only Mirabel and Crista look at me, but Tía and Tío, too. "I only said three sentences."

"So say them." Raúl appears from behind his phone.

"Sí, m'ija. Say them." Dad's voice is a drumroll. He smiles as if he's showing his prize pumpkin at a fair.

I try to remember. The two-week-old phrases start to take form, then crumble apart like the tortilla dough. Heat moves up my neck into my face. "I don't remember."

Dad's smile fades.

"Sure you do, honey," Mom says.

"No, I don't." I press the tortilla between my hands hard. Now one of the sentences does bubble up in my mind, but I hide it under my tongue.

Tía Lencha clears her throat. "Eh, Quijana, what grade you are this year? The seven?"

This is my out, my chance to let it go, but I'm still too angry. "I learned those sentences for Abuela, not for any of you," I say quietly.

My parents look stunned, like I've splattered them with drops of hot oil.

Raúl bursts out laughing. "Dang!" he says. "That's cold." This gives everyone permission to unfreeze.

"It's fair," says Tío Pancho, looking at me and nodding. "She has her own mind, this one."

Tía looks at my tortilla dough and says, "Perfecta." She winks to show she's not offended, but the mood of the table has still shifted—because of me. Mom raises her chin and inhales as if to say something, but just moves to bring Memito to the table. Dad doesn't budge. I can't look at him directly, so I watch Tía cook my tortilla and flip it into the basket. I know Dad would say I should feel sorry, but I don't. Sure, it'd be nice to make my dad proud of me and be a daughter he could show off. But I guess she's not me.

The table is too small to hold all of us, so we eat in shifts. Kids first.

Mirabel leans toward me and says, "Sorry, girl. I didn't mean to start a thing. Do you want guacamole?"

I take a spoonful, still feeling cross with Dad. I can feel his disappointment at my outburst from here. Everything he does sharpens my edge. He forgets I'm not like my cousins. He sees our dark heads around the table, a ring of black beans, and thinks I'm another one of a set. Instead, I'm a decoy. Wake up, Dad. See me as I really am. Would that be so disappointing?

After a while I hear Dad's laugh and I know he's recovered. Even though I'm not sorry for what I said, I'm still relieved to know he's not mad.

I stop eating to check my phone—my other life, my real life. Monday sounds delicious right now. But the screen just tells me the temperature and announces an app update. No missed calls. No messages. No way out of here.

Mom says something about Grandma Miller to Tía. "Espero que se mejore pronto," says Tía Lencha. I understand it as "I hope she gets better soon."

"Guess what!" Crista says, leaning over the dining table. She pulls my mind out of its furrow. "Mirabel's in love."

Mirabel startles. "No, I'm not."

"Yeah, right! Then why's the name 'Brian' all over your homework folder?"

"Okay, whatever," says Mirabel. "I like him. But that doesn't mean I'm in love."

"Are you in *like,* then?" presses Crista.

The girls tussle about this as we clear plates. Their easy banter makes me wish I had a sister. I'm delighted by the two of them, but half-distracted listening to the grown-up conversation. I want to know if they're talking about me. Dad's voice wafts through the air, the slow, deliberate tones he uses when quoting an author.

"Wanna see a picture of him?" Mirabel volunteers, and we scamper down the hall and crash on her bed. Mirabel scrolls through the photos on her phone until she finds the one she wants. "I know he likes me," she says, "because he keeps asking my friends about me. Here."

I look at his face. He's decent-looking, but I'm still hearing Mirabel's last sentence. He's asking her friends about her? I have to say, that sounds inefficient. Jayden just talks right to me. He's never been nervous around me. Not even the first day. Maybe that's a good sign.

"Do you like anyone, Quijana?" asks Crista, reading the direction of my thoughts.

"No." I shake my head, but my face reddens.

"Ooh, you do! Who is it?" She pounces in front of me, her tiara shifting.

I smile and a half laugh escapes my mouth. "Nobody, really."

"Tell us!" Crista's eyes light up.

I show them a picture of Jayden on my phone. "Green eyes!" Mirabel says. "Does he like you?"

"I mean, we're friends."

Mirabel squints. "So, no?"

"Well, I . . ." I don't like this conclusion.

"You don't know?" Mirabel says.

The protest on the tip of my tongue dissolves. I guess I *don't* know. I think of our daily chats, texts, and the day we ate lunch at the tree. Here in front of my cousins, none of it looks like strong evidence. I feel like a lawyer with no case. My heart beats faster, and my head sloshes.

"You should send him a note!" Crista says.

"You *would* say that, Crista." Mirabel frowns. "Notes are for elementary school."

"Actually, I've been thinking of asking him about it," I admit.

"You should." Crista's confident in her verdict. I wish she could wave her plastic wand and help me somehow.

"Tell us when you find out," she says. She positions her-self exactly opposite her sister and holds up her hands. "Do 'Chocolate' with me, Mirabel."

Mirabel sighs, but chants through the hand rhyme with her little sister. Their hands clap and pat in unison. Each syllable gets a clap, high ten, or hammer fists. I remember these from the playground. It's fun to watch, but the question of whether or not Jayden likes me wanders behind my thoughts.

The girls say the rhyme faster and faster until they're making mistakes and laughing. "Now you try," says Crista, pivoting to me. She teaches me in slow motion.

Cho-co-la-te. Cho-co-la-te.

Choco choco la la.

Choco choco te te.

Choco la. Choco te.

Cho-co-la-te.

"You're getting it," she says, as my hands learn what to do when. We get it going pretty smoothly.

"Here's one in English," I say.

Say, say, my playmate,

come out and play with me

and bring your dollies three

climb up my apple tree . . .

Before I can finish, Memito rams himself into the bed. "Coco!"

"What does he want?" Crista asks.

"Coco!"

"I think he wants us to do 'Chocolate' again," I say.

"Okay!" Crista loves this. She's so sweet, a little fairy god-mother who loves granting wishes.

We do the rhyme again while Memito watches. "Ga!" he says, meaning "again." We do it twice more.

"Ga, ga!" he says.

After two more times, even Crista is tired of it.

"Coco!"

"That's all," I tell him. "All done."

His lip quivers. Then his mouth opens into a full cry, which of course brings Dad in. "M'ijo, what's wrong?"

"He won't let us stop," says Crista.

"The clapping rhyme," I explain.

"I see. Come here, m'ijo." Dad tries to lift him up, but Memito goes limp and Dad can't get a grip. The crying goes on, and Crista covers her ears.

"Memito!" Dad uses his serious voice. He tries again to pick him up. Finally, he grabs Memito's waist and carries his flailing body to the living room.

I follow them and see Mom stop her conversation with Tío Pancho.

Memito's sobbing drowns out every other sound. "Coco-o-o-o!" he yells. I wish we could all go back to having fun. Why does he so often get stuck on one thing?

Dad puts him down, and he writhes on the floor.

"Memito, sweetie," Mom tries. She approaches him, but he kicks, keeping her away. "Manuel Carrillo." I'm sure Memito doesn't even hear her.

"We should go," says Dad.

Wait. I thought I would want to hear that, but I'm not ready to go. I want to show Crista my hand rhymes. I like hanging out with her and Mirabel.

Mom gathers up Memito's toys, and Dad tries to lift him again.

"Thanks for everything, Lencha. Sorry about this," says Mom.

"The boy, he's tired," says Tía. "No problem. Raúl was the same."

"Coco!" Memito shouts. I doubt this is just about Memito being tired.

I imagine sitting next to this crying machine for five miles. Then I get an idea. "Can I stay?" I ask. "Maybe Tía could bring me home later?"

"Quijana, let's just go," Mom says.

Dad's already wrestling Memito out the door, and Mom hasn't even looked up from stowing Memito's sippy cup and board books. "We can't set this up right now. Maybe another day."

"But there's nothing to set up! I want to stay!"

"We can bring her," Tía intercedes.

I give her an appreciative look.

"No. Thanks, though, Lencha. It's a school night anyway. Quijana, get your coat. And get Memito's, too. Help me out, here, please." Her look to me is half plea, half command. I guess only one kid gets to be crazy at a time.

I stomp to the coats laid on Mirabel's bed. I said this would happen, and Dad said we wouldn't leave. But then, I didn't think I'd want to stay. Looks like we were both wrong.

Mom and Dad are already in the parking lot when I get to the front door. Everyone hugs me, and Mirabel and Crista give me kisses on the cheek that I'm not expecting. "Later, Qui," they call. "¡Hasta luego!"

I see Dad leaning into the car, trying to fasten Memito into the car seat. Mom's on the other side, probably offering him a cracker. This is *so* not normal.

My thoughts go back to the kisses. They were so sweet, like Mirabel and Crista really liked me. Maybe I'll try kissing their cheeks next time. But would it seem fake coming from me, like I'm pretending to be Latina? It's definitely not something I could do at school. But here, with my family, maybe I could. Maybe I would.

THIRTY

ON THE WAY HOME from Tía Lencha's, Memito gnaws on a fruit bar, finally quiet, and I hear from Grandma. **Yes! Happy to be home at last. Have you talked to your mom? Can't wait till Thanksgiving!**

Mm. What does Mom have to tell me?

"You know," says Mom, turning to look at me from the front seat. "Memito wasn't the only one having a little trouble behaving back there."

Ugh. She's not telling me anything about Grandma. It's those three Spanish sentences. I thought they'd been forgotten—and forgiven. "You mean the Abuela sentences?"

"Qui, it's okay that you forgot the sentences or didn't want to tell us. Nobody minds that. But we do mind you speaking rudely."

"I only said that I learned them for Abuela."

"Only that?" She gives me a look that makes me shrink back in my seat.

"Well, no . . . but I didn't mean to hurt anyone's feelings." My voice gets softer toward the end.

"Ladies, this was partly my fault," says Dad. We both look at him in surprise. "I didn't mean to put you, how do you say it, 'on the spot,' m'ija." We stop at a red light, and he looks at me in the rearview mirror. "You couldn't remember. Everyone was listening. I would feel the same."

"You would?" Our eyes smile at each other in the mirror.

At home, Memito runs to his room while the rest of us hang up our jackets. I turn toward my room, too, but Mom touches my hand.

"Quijana, can we chat a minute?" I wonder if she has more to say about the Spanish sentences, but then I notice Dad standing right next to her like they both have something to tell me.

"Is something wrong?"

Mom rests her hand on my shoulder. "We just wanted you to know that Grandma's doctors are . . . worried about some new test results."

"But she's home," I say. "She just texted me in the car."

Dad takes Mom's hand and squeezes it.

"You guys are freaking me out." I take a step back.

"No, it's not—look, she is stronger. They let her go home because she can manage with a nurse coming by for a few hours a day. At the same time . . ."

Dad steps in. "She's not out of the forest."

Mom lets out a little laugh. "The woods, honey. Not out of the woods."

They lean against each other, and Dad kisses the top of her head. I wonder if he mixed up the phrase on purpose because it's made us all less tense now.

"Do you want to fly out there?" Dad asks Mom in a low voice.

"She told me not to come, especially with Thanksgiving so soon. But maybe I should go anyway. Help her out."

Dad adds, "And hug her."

Mom dabs her eyes. "Hug her."

They pull me into a three-way hug, and I close my eyes, willing away the worst. But at least we're in this together. I feel a little better when we part. I'm glad they're willing to talk to me and not hide it. I also understand, for the first time, that Grandma doesn't tell me everything.

Mom tousles my hair and announces, "I'll take Memito for a walk. I could use a walk myself." And then—yes! Dad goes outside to do some yardwork and cover the spigots to protect them from freezing.

This means that the house is empty, and it's safe to lift down the guitar and practice my song. It will be the first time I put all the words to the music. If I can do it, I'll record myself and send it to Grandma.

I get a rhythm going and hum through the melody, thinking the words in my head. I'm ready to start over at full volume when I hear the back door open, and my fingers go cold. I look up. Dad's eyes meet mine. "¡La guitarra! ¡Magnífico!" I feel like a thief caught in the act, but of course he's thrilled, judging from his huge smile.

My thoughts race as I try to think of a way out of this. "I was just . . ." Before I can stand up, he sits next to me.

"I knew you would want to learn! Our whole family played when I was a boy—my uncles, your grandfather. In fact, your earliest ancestor came from Spain with a guitar. Go ahead and strum."

The guitar feels awkward all of a sudden. Its edges bump my ribs now that he's here, but what can I do? I strum a D chord.

"Mira," he says, which means *Here, let me show you.* "That chord can be played with different fingers. More resonant." He closes his eyes to recall his own hand position and starts moving my fingers.

Why couldn't he just be like a normal dad and give me a thumbs-up on his way to another room? Instead, he invaded. This is exactly what I wanted to avoid, exactly what I knew would happen.

"Here's the chord to learn first." He moves my fingers again, trying to place them in the right spots. It's totally unfamiliar to my hand.

"Could you write it down, maybe?" I ask, trying to speed this up. "On YouTube, the lady has a chart with dots to show where each finger . . ."

"A chart?" He snorts. "No, this is faster."

It isn't, but I don't say this. Arguing will only take longer.

"This is how I learned from my own father."

Aha. The real reason we can't write it down.

"What's this chord called?" I'm trying to connect what he's showing me to anything I know.

"Fa."

"You mean F?"

"I don't know 'F,' but we say 'Fa.'"

This isn't help; it's torture. I don't even know which songs use Fa.

"Look at my fingers," he says. I put my fingers on the strings like he has them in the air. "Now you."

This time my chord rings. "Perfect, m'ija. Now, play it again." Three times, four times. Then, of course, he wants to show me another chord. I'm screaming inside. These chords don't even go with my song. This was supposed to be my thing.

Forty minutes later, my hand is aching. Where are Mom and Memito?

"One more, m'ija."

By now, my finger pads show creases from playing so long. My whole hand is weak. I press hard, but the thick strings barely move. "I can't," I say. "I was already practicing for a while before you came in. . . ."

Dad shakes his head, not allowing my comment to settle in his ears. "You can. It's in your blood."

By now, I almost want to fail.

"You know what you need?" Dad says. *A new hobby?* I think. "Your hands, they're small. You need a smaller guitar, with nylon strings. I know just the store."

Torturous guitar days unspool before my eyes. Hours of bleeding fingertips. Afternoons of memorizing hand positions. And Dad standing over me. "No, that's okay, Dad."

"Sure. We can save a little each month. Maybe for your birthday."

"No, really. I don't need one." I shake my head vigorously and fight an urge to run.

"But a Carrillo should have her own guitar. I'll teach you all the boleros. You can play a song for the family in Guatemala!"

My heartbeat slams into overdrive. "No, Dad." I put down the guitar. "I am never going to play guitar in Guatemala." The guitar is for Jayden, and, I realize, for myself.

"But you were learning already. Let me help you, m'ija. You can play like the line of Carrillos before you."

"Not boleros!"

When I was little, I used to cheer to see the guitar come off the wall. It meant Dad doing hilarious voices in "Pecos Bill." It meant Mom and Dad harmonizing Spanish love songs. It meant singing "Row, Row, Row Your Boat" and "El Gallo Ha Muerto" in the three-part rounds.

But now I wanted to keep the fun going in my own way. I wanted to play my favorite songs and write my own. Dad's ruining everything.

The magic-wand sound on my phone saves me. It's Zuri texting both me and Jayden. "Sorry, Dad," I say. "I better answer this. Later!"

He's still in guitar world, tuning the strings and humming— so pleased that I can hardly look at him. I run to my room, close the door firmly, and shut my eyes. *I hope he forgets this ever happened, I hope he doesn't set up a lesson schedule, I hope he gets over the fact that I'm not the daughter he thinks I am.*

I sit on my bed and read Zuri's message.

Still up for yogurt tomorrow?

Yes! Thx for saving me.

From what? It's Jayden.

I type fast. **Having a situation here.**

What's going on? Zuri says.

Dad's forcing guitar on me.

I thought you wanted to learn?

Not his way.

You don't want his help? Zuri's text bubbles stack up on the screen.

How can I explain that Dad's help isn't helpful?

At least your dad cares.

Jayden joins in: **My dad knows nothing about music.**

My blue feelings turn black.

He's taking over, I say.

Whatever. I know I sound ungrateful, maybe even mean, but why aren't they on my side? Dad doesn't get it—no surprise—but I thought my friends could.

Just lie low for a while. He'll forget about it. Jayden's advice.

I scroll through a screen of icons to find a face sticking out its tongue.

Here's MY dilemma. Zuri's yellow text bubble pops up. **The parents said I can have a gummy-candy maker for Christmas or a trip to Austin. I'm leaning toward the trip.**

I'm not ready to think about trips or gummies. I'm still an angry-sad swirl. They don't understand. Maybe I can explain better in person.

But think of the crazy gummy flavors you could make! Jayden says. **Which would you choose, Q?**

I choose to ban parents.

I put down my phone and get a snack. When I come back, I see a new message from Zuri.

Call me!

I do right away. "What is it?"

"Someone bought it! Your huipil sold!"

"What? Really?" I want to run all the way to her house.

"Mom says their payment went through and everything, and she can bring you the money tomorrow after work." Warning lights flash in my head. I can't let her bring it to the house. "Uh . . . can she bring it to the yogurt place? She could give it to me when she picks you up."

"Oh, sure!"

Whew. I'm walking back and forth in my room, too excited to sit. "Awesome! We did it. That was such a great idea, Z!"

"Qui?" Her tone has shifted. "Are you sure about buying this bus ticket? I mean, aren't you scared?"

I am, especially now that it's getting so close and so real. But I keep picturing that little kid riding by himself. If he can do it, I can.

"I guess I'm nervous," I say, "but it's pretty simple, right? All I do is board the bus and get off at the right city. I'll take nuts and raisins and energy bars. It's just like a long car trip." I'm rambling, but listing these details makes me feel better.

"What about when you get there? Is your grandma picking you up at the bus station?"

I try to ignore the voice in my head reminding me that Grandma doesn't even know I'm coming. "If she's well enough to drive. She's home from rehab now, but she's still weak. It's actually good I'm going because I can help her when I'm there. You know, take out the trash and stuff. So I'll probably take a taxi from the station."

"Have you done that before?"

"How hard can it be? I have her address and some cash for cab fare."

"You sound ready, I guess."

"I'm trying to be." I laugh so she'll stop worrying. Part of me stops worrying, too. But another part doesn't.

TH_IRTY-ONE

ON THE MORNING BUS TO SCHOOL, sunlight pours through the window onto my face. It's cold enough that my breath leaves a little cloud of condensation on the glass. I fog the window with a long exhale, then make a dot in the middle with my fingertip. I curve around the dot, making a spiral out to the edge.

Then another finger, drawing a road or something, touches mine. I look up to meet the eyes of one of the Latino brothers peeking over the seat behind me. He gives me a close-lipped smile. *Smile back!* says a voice in my head. But I freeze. Something like fear must have jumped into my eyes because the boy turns back to his window and curves his road in a new direction.

As we run into the school building, I brush the boy out of my mind and think, *The huipil sold, the huipil sold, the huipil sold!*

I rush up to Zuri as we go into English. Seeing her in person makes my trip feel more exciting, less scary. "Yay!" I say, squeezing her arm. "Let's tell Jayden."

"It sold!" I squeal, doing a small hop.

"So you seem a little happy," Jayden jokes. As we take our seats, he whispers, "That's so much money! Good going!"

I barely manage to sit still until lunch, and we walk to the cafeteria in high spirits.

This day feels like wall-to-wall good luck: Memito had a meltdown-free morning, now I'll get J-Z face time, I put a quesadilla in my lunch, in choir we'll prep for the December concert, we'll all go to Gerty's Yogurt after school, and then I'll get the money for my bus ticket. It's a hands-down, definite good day.

When we sit down, Jayden says, "Great to have you back, Quijana."

"Back?" I laugh. "Where did I go?"

"Last night you were, like, low." He overpronounces the last word, letting his voice drop to a bass note.

"I guess I was."

"Really, though," he says. "I was worried."

"Well, dads. You know." I start in on my quesadilla.

Zuri adds, "He sure wants you to play guitar."

"I mean, yeah. But it's more than that. He only wants me to play Spanish songs. He even wants me to sing to my grandmother in Guatemala." It sounds ludicrous even as I say it. "He's taking over this thing that was, like . . . mine. He always does."

"But you're not going to Guatemala," Jayden says.

"Right," I say. "But he doesn't know that."

"Why can't you sing your own songs?" Jayden shakes his head. "Thank you!"

Zuri's chewing slowly, watching me. "Did you tell him this?"

I think back. I guess I didn't tell him, not exactly. Why didn't I? "It's his guitar. I mean, I guess I could ask to use it and just tell him he can't interfere. That I want to do it alone." This sounds iffy. I can see his eyes going either sharp or liquidy—neither one good.

The conversation tilts back to regular school stuff, but I don't listen. Could I actually talk to Dad? Would he hear me?

When the bell rings, Jayden waves his hand in front of my face. "Hello? Yogurt coordination time. Let's meet by the front office after school."

Yogurt. Right. I remind myself that today I'm celebrating.

By the time the school day ends, I've wrestled my mind back onto the Lucky Express, destination: fun.

"Jayday," I say.

"QuiQui!" he says, meeting my fist with his in the air.

"Z!" I say.

"This is going to be marvelous," she says, leading the way.

Gerty's Yogurt is across the street and down a half block. We have all the way till 4:15 before our moms pick us up. Plus, with round tables for three people, I can sit next to Jayden for sure.

"Mahvelous," echoes Jayden. "I love her r-lessness," he says to me in a stage whisper.

But then, the opposite of luck. Seth waves to us from across the yard. "Oh, yeah. I meant to ask you guys. Can Seth come?" Jayden asks.

My hopes take a nosedive, but Jayden's eyes are revved up to extra shine, and Seth is walking toward us. We obviously can't say no.

"Sure?" Zuri looks at me for confirmation.

"Of course," I say, forcing my politeness gears into motion.

"Wanna come for yogurt?" Jayden asks.

"Sounds great!" says Seth. "I'll text my dad."

We shove our hands in our pockets and brave the cold. "My mom said it was too cold for frozen yogurt," I say.

"Nevah!" Jayden says, jutting his index finger into the air.

"All weather is yogurt weather!" Seth pronounces. They're both laughing out loud as we cross the street.

We spiral yogurt into paper cups and find a rectangular table for four. I sit across from Jayden, since Seth takes the next-to seat.

I don't want to talk about the huipil with Seth there, so I say, "Hey, guys, our choir concert date got announced in class today. It's December ninth at seven-thirty. You in?"

"Of course!" says Zuri.

"Great!" I say. "There's this one piece I love especially. One of my favorites ever."

"Is that a Monday?" Seth is shifting in his seat. "Jayden and I usually watch Monday-night football at my house."

"But Seth," says Jayden. "This'll be a big night. I think I should go. We can miss *one* game."

Should. The word sounds louder in my ears than the rest of the sentence.

Seth nods, then gives a little salute. "Whatever you say, Captain Winters."

After that, I have trouble holding up my corner of our four-way conversation. But soon it's mostly two-way. Jayden and Seth talk theater class while Zuri and I just listen.

"What made you think to improv that cell-phone conversation?"

"I just went with what Danielle started."

"No, but then the beach ball!"

"I know. Mr. H is, like, crazy sometimes!"

I keep hoping the guys will touch on something I can add to, but I'm relieved when Zuri asks about Memito. "Last night he figured out how to twang those coil things behind doors," I tell her. "Doorstops. So that was pretty much our evening." She laughs, but it's half-hearted. We listen to Jayden and Seth for a minute.

"You should've been there," Jayden says to us for the fourth time.

"Sounds like it," I say, letting my annoyance show a bit. I don't think they mean to leave us out, but Seth and Jayden have chemistry. They're in sync, like a pilot and a co-pilot. My plastic spoon is scraping the bottom of the cup before I figure it out. Their banter back and forth, their deep smiles. How did I not notice before? They like each other. As in *like* like.

The sky of my heart cracks. Their conversation sounds like it's underwater. I am intensely focused, suddenly, on not crying. Now Jayden's turning to me, demonstrating a crazy tongue twister they say to warm up their voices in theater. Something about a sixth sick sheep, but I don't hear him well—my memory's black box is lining up facts in my brain. Jayden sitting with two girls at lunch. Jayden talking to me without ever flirting. Jayden and Zuri in the friend zone for years. It all makes sense. This flight was doomed from the beginning. Jayden will never fall for me. He's fallen for Seth.

Jayden checks his phone. "Almost four-fifteen. We better stand outside or your mom will flip out, Z."

When she drives up, I'm not nearly as happy as I thought I would be with my thick envelope of huipil money. Thoughts about Jayden have taken all the excitement out of what was supposed to be my moment of triumph. "Are you sure you're comfortable carrying this much cash? I could write your mom a check instead."

"No thanks, Ms. Thomas. My mom will be here in a minute. I won't be carrying it for long."

Thankfully, she accepts this and drives off. Then Seth's dad comes. Normally, I would feel lucky to have Jayden to myself, but I feel like my brain is misfiring.

"Hey, text me tonight," Jayden says.

I make myself say, "Okay."

"I want to hear about your choir pieces. And remind me what time to come."

He's saying all the right things, but I can't figure out how to act. "Oh . . . you don't have to come, really. It's football night." I try to sound like I'm teasing.

"Are you kidding? Of course I'll be there."

He's being a good friend. *So stop being disappointed,* I tell myself. He's been a friend to me all along. Now I need to be a friend to him. I *can* remember how to do this. How to enjoy Jayden for who he is, not just as boyfriend material. *Try,* says a voice in my head. *Try harder!* "I'd love for you to come," I say, looking right into his eyes. It's the truest thing I can say.

"Well, good, 'cause I'll be there with bells on. Jingle bells!"

"No Christmas jokes until after Thanksgiving!" I say, mustering all my energy to sound normal.

"Okay, I'll try to quit *cold turkey.*" He waggles his eyebrows, then his mom pulls up, and he's gone.

I'm relieved. Now I can go ahead and feel like pieces glued together. Thinking of the envelope in my backpack doesn't help much. I go back inside to warm up. My brain skips to another thought, and my heart lurches again. The song. I can't sing it to him now. I've been writing a song that will never be heard.

When Mom drives up, I run through the biting wind to the car. "What flavor did you get?" she asks. I don't even remember.

"You were right," I say. "It's too cold for frozen yogurt."

THIRTY-TWO

AFTER THE GERTY'S YOGURT DISASTER, I want to pull on my flannel-lined leggings, crawl into bed, and listen to music in my room. The one thing I might have energy for is buying the bus ticket. I would have to get to the station and back without being missed, which I think I could do right now, and I bet the brisk walk would clear my head. But that plan's bulb burns out when Mom sticks her head in and says I have to babysit.

"We should be back in an hour or two," Mom says, scooping up her jacket.

I'm feeling staticky when I think about Jayden. I have trouble tuning in to Dad's frequency as he explains where they're going. Something about Aunt Jess having car trouble. Something about one of them waiting for the tow truck and one of them taking her to teach a six o'clock class.

So it's the two of us. We hear the car start, then drive away.

Memito turns from the door and runs to my legs. A bit of cheer drops into my heart like a penny in a piggy bank. I press his head against my jeans. Jealousy passes through me as I picture his three-year-old's life: a little playhouse filled with everything he needs. He feels no pressure to be someone else; he deals with no romance wrecking balls. And by not talking, he gets even more help. Maybe he's figured out that talking only creates catastrophes.

Now he faces the other way and raises his arms. A sign for me to swing him in a circle. I hook my hands under his arms and twirl. "Whee," I say, but only at half volume. I can't muster a full *whee* when I'm in such a bad mood. I twirl until my hands go weak and my legs veer off course toward the coffee table.

"Ga, ga." Again, again. We go around again, until I'm dizzy enough to forget Jayden for half a second.

But only half a second. His voice whispers in my ear. *Text me tonight,* he said at Gerty's. I put down Memito and pull out my phone. "Ga," he says, tugging my arm as I try to click letters.

"Just a minute," I say. I type **Choir concert, Monday 12/9, 7:30 pm.**

My thumbs hover over the screen. I can't decide what else to say. *You broke my heart.* Not that. *Why didn't you tell me?* Deletedeletedelete. I erase back to *pm* and click SEND.

Memito grabs my finger and pulls me to the dishwasher. He loves to roll the empty dish rack back and forth, but it's full right now with a day's worth of plates and glasses.

"No," I say. "Let's play blocks." I try to lead him away, but he won't budge. I try to carry him, but he writhes and whines like a wet seal until I put him down. He stamps his feet and yells, "Sha!"

"No sha," I tell him. That's his word for dishwasher. "Blocks." My phone vibrates in my pocket. **We'll be there!** We. Great. It can only mean that Seth is coming to my choir concert, too. To think that I actually made one of my passwords QuijanaWinters4ever!

"Sha!" Memito bangs on the dishwasher door, and his face turns red. He pulls on the latch to unlock it.

"No, kiddo." I push it back.

He starts to cry as he tries the latch again. "Stop!" This time I pull his hand away, and he pushes me. We push-pull the latch until finally I slam it back into place—and pinch his fingers. His face is immediately a squinting scream, and I've won and lost at the same time.

I try to see if his hand is bleeding or bruised, but he flings it out, whacking my cheek. "Oww!" Instinctively, I push back, and my conscience stabs. Everything is so loud, I'm going to lose it. I kneel on the linoleum with my head in my hands. He's wailing. Why is this so hard? Why aren't Mom and Dad back yet? Memito's gulping sobs press all my raw places, and now I'm crying, too, for him, for myself, for every hour that I thought Jayden could like me.

I barely hear the doorbell. Then comes a pounding knock that rattles my insides. If I answer the door, will Memito open the dishwasher and break everything? Before I can arrive at my next thought, Memito dashes for the door himself. The bell rings again, and I rush after him, wiping my nose with my sleeve, pushing my hair out of my face, reaching the door right as he's opening it.

Two women holding pamphlets stand shoulder to shoulder. Thankfully, Memito has downshifted into a rhythmic whine when he sees them, or else I'd be worried they'd call the cops. His face is splotchy and tear-stained, and my face must look similar, but the women don't seem to notice. The older one fixes her eyes on me. "¿Sabe lo que es el cielo?" she asks in a single, powerful burst. I flinch, and she pelts us with rapid-fire Spanish. I already felt desperate and paper-thin; now I'm pierced with holes.

I shake my head at her and back away from her extended pamphlet. "My parents . . . I mean . . ." I'm not supposed to tell strangers that we're alone. Before he runs again, I grab Memito. The other woman starts talking, too; tears gather behind my eyes. I shout to the women, "I don't speak Spanish, okay? I just don't!" It's not totally true—I understand some of what they're saying. They're converting people, I think; they're from a church. But suddenly, I can't remember even enough Spanish to tell them I don't know Spanish. I picture Dad shaking his head. I picture Señora Francés frowning. "I can't help you!" I yell, slamming the door.

They're gone. For good, I hope. I bet I seemed so crazy they won't come back.

I slide against the closed door to the floor and let go of Memito. I don't care if he goes back to the dishwasher. If every dish becomes shards on the floor, it will be just how I feel. I wrap my arms around myself. The life I want, the person I want to be, is a fading signal, distant and weak. "I can't," I say to the indifferent walls. "I can't do this," I say to the flimsy air. *Grandma, I just can't be a brave sea turtle or a keystone species or a gopher tortoise or whatever.* The only thing I know for sure is that this must not be the end, because I am *not* okay.

TH_IRTY-THR_EE

I'M LEVELED AFTER YESTERDAY'S TEARS, like a field mowed down to stubble. At least Mom and Dad didn't find out that I fell apart. By the time they came home, Memito and I were reading a story. "How was it?" Mom asked, looking at her phone and sounding frazzled herself.

I didn't say, "A disaster! You're lucky we're both alive." I said, "Good enough," not wanting to worry them. Later I was so spent that I didn't even get to the bus station. I still have all my money in my sock drawer.

Now school is happening around me. Students scoot desks, and I realize that Señora Francés has put us in groups.

"Over here, Quijana!" shouts Elena. She rolls her eyes as if she's calling me for the third time. Spanish is Elena's first language, so she acts like this class is for babies. Sometimes she snickers when I give a wrong answer. She even snubs the teacher. "That's not how we say it in Juarez." So Spanish varies from place to place—big deal. Her princesa crown is over-shined today, as usual.

I stand up and slowly push in my chair. "Hurry up!" she says. *Sheesh.* I walk to her end of the room and sit across from her without meeting her eyes.

Carlos joins us. I nod in greeting, but he passes me to sit next to Elena. He touches the bracelet she's wearing, looks intently at her face, and starts purring in fluent Spanish. He is *such* a lover boy, I picture Mirabel saying.

"¡Cállate!" Elena says, shoving his hand away, but then bends toward him and smiles.

Great. I'm stuck with the two native speakers. Why couldn't they be in a class by themselves, or at least with the eighth or ninth graders? To top it off, all they want to do is flirt. I feel like I'm watching Jayden and Seth all over again. That knife plunges deeper. *Don't cry in school.*

"Guys?" I pick up the handout and hold it up. If I focus on what's in front of me, I might be okay. Right now, it's this handout and my grade, which is teetering between B and C. I need these points.

Carlos picks a piece of lint off Elena's shoulder, and she elbows him playfully.

"Okay, let's do this," I say. I let frustration stiffen each word.

Elena's eyes turn to ice. "You do it. You're the one who needs it."

Carlos levels his gaze at me. His lips pucker like he's going to spit. "Pocha."

I pull back as if shoved. My mind spins into the past. I'm with my dad at a special grocery store where everyone speaks

Spanish. We've driven into the city to get here. Dad finds big bananas called plantains and starts to show me how to pick a ripe one, kneeling down and saying how we'll cook them when a woman steers her cart around us, purses her lips, and says, "Pochos," under her breath. My dad leaps to his feet. He asks her a question in Spanish and she sasses back. We leave without the plantains, and he mutters all the way home. It's not until he tells Mom what happened that I understand. "She called us pochos," he fumes. "In front of our daughter!" Even Mom was confused until he explained. "It's slang—someone who has no heritage, who's forgotten where he comes from, who pretends to be white." It was the only time I remember Dad saying "white" like it was something bad. He huffed around the kitchen repeating, "I'm no imposter."

Elena and Carlos are watching me. I straighten my back. "You don't have to be mean," I say, hating how lame it sounds. "This should be easy for you."

"Should we help her?" Elena asks Carlos coyly.

"No way." Carlos crosses his arms, obviously trying to impress her.

They are two doors slammed in my face. I look at the sheet; a block of text blots out the page. I understand about half the words in the first sentence. Less than half in the next one. I imagine my passing grade sinking, disappearing like a coin thrown into a muddy lake. Tears sting my eyes.

"No sabe nada," Elena sneers. This I understand. *She knows nothing.* "Menos que nada." *Less than nothing.* "Hey, wanna hear a joke?"

I look away, disgusted.

"What's brown, but acts white?"

"Shut up." I surprise myself. She shrugs, and fire surges through my body. "Shut up, Elena!" I stretch the middle *eh* of her name, Spanish-style. *Coconut, coconut* thrums in my head. I'm standing now, ready to throw a book at her or kick her or slap her with my bare hand.

"Quijana?" Señora Francés's voice is a stream of cool water, but it steams away as soon as it reaches me.

"You're nothing but a snotty, stuck-up, spoiled brat! You think you're smart, but you're just mean, just vicious, just a total—"

"Quijana! May I see you in the hall?" It's not a question. Señora Francés steps to the door and holds it open, waiting for me to follow. My fire still smokes, but I notice complete silence in the room. Every pair of eyes follows my walk to the door.

On the other side of it, my heart caves in. Shame crackles in my ears. Worse than any punishment is the disappointment that must be on my teacher's face. But I can't even look at her to see it.

"Quijana, this isn't like you. What's wrong?"

My shoulders curl forward. "I don't know," I squeak. Already the shouting feels like it was done by someone else. A ball of thorns rolls around in my stomach.

"What did she say to you?"

My throat closes. All I can think is that I can't, I won't take Spanish next year, no matter what.

"You know you can't shout in class, Quijana. And I can't allow you to insult another student."

I can tell Señora Francés is trying to be as understanding as possible. But all I can do is nod and try not to cry. My nose is already starting to run.

"Quijana, can you look at me?"

I raise my head and press my lips together, trying to keep the tears in.

"Look," she says, her eyes soft. "I know Elena can be frustrating, but you have to be above that." Señora Francés is trying to make this easy for me. I can tell this even though her voice sounds far away. Louder in my ears are my own thoughts. Elena's right. I'll never be a real Latina. Learning to make a tortilla and speaking a few sentences to Abuela doesn't change anything. How could I think that was remotely enough?

"I'm going to let this go this time," says Señora Francés. "I'll put you in a different group tomorrow. Will you be all right, Quijana?"

I'm not sure what to say. The bell rings and saves me from having to figure it out.

Of course, by lunch, Jayden and Zuri have heard that I yelled at Elena in Spanish class. I'd like to forget it, but they drag me through every detail. "What if Señora Francés hadn't stopped you? What would you have said?"

"Uh, I think I was going to say 'witch,'" I lie. What I really think I was going to say was much worse.

"Nothing spicier? I'd like to skewer her with this fork. I bet Seth could whop her upside the head for you." Jayden adds drama to my drama like always.

"She sounds just *dreadful,*" Zuri says. Her word captures it well.

Kids in other classes ask about it, too. "Did you actually yell at her?" I get the sense that a lot of people think Elena is stuck-up because I hear "I bet she deserved it!" from a bunch of people. It's like telling the story of a car wreck over and over. I'm relieved to hear the final bell, even though, weirdly, I feel a little bit like a hero for the rest of the day. Even one of the bus kids whispers about it and points at me. I've never been noticed by anybody but my friends before. I can feel my face get warm, but the attention's kinda cool.

At home, I see a note on the kitchen table.

Dear Quijana, I'll be back after Memito's dentist appointment and grocery shopping. Go ahead and eat a sandwich supper. Mom's at class. See you after 6:00. Con amor, Dad

Okay. Time to buy a bus ticket.

THIRTY-FOUR

I RUN TO MY ROOM, slip on my sea turtle bracelet for luck, and grab the envelope of money. I check Google Maps. It says I can bike the three miles to the bus station in less than twenty minutes. That should put me home in an hour—which will still be a full hour before Dad's estimate. I can do this. I tuck the money in my backpack and click my helmet's chin strap. When I straddle my bike, I can't help but picture Don Quixote mounting his horse, riding into an adventure. Unlike him, I will *not* be fooled by any windmills this time. I stand up and pump the pedals until they spin without resistance.

I've ridden these streets in a car, but everything looks bigger from a bike. Distances between stoplights seem to stretch. Querer es poder, I remind myself. To want to is to be able to.

I arrive safely at the station and lock my bike to a rack out front. I walk in, helmet and all, and stand behind a woman with a baby. After her turn, I step up to the high counter.

"Yes?" says the cashier, looking up. His piercing eyes make me feel younger than I actually am.

Deep breath. "I want to buy a ticket, please." I hear a little shake in my voice and take another breath.

"Destination?"

"Ocala, Florida."

He looks over his glasses at me, but then goes on. "Date?"

"December nineteenth."

"Round-trip or one-way?"

My heart seizes. I didn't think of that. How will I get back home? A voice inside says, *Worry about that later. The adults will figure it out. You can't afford round-trip, so get one-way.*

"One-way," I say, too loudly.

"How old are you?"

I take a chance and tell the truth. "Twelve, sir."

"May I see some proof?"

"Will a school ID work?"

"Yes, that'll do." He holds my ID at arm's length and squints. "Are your parents here?"

"Um, no." My palms have turned hot, and I rub them on my jeans.

"They'll have to sign, you know." I nod, not knowing what they'll have to sign. "Okay, we got an 8:25 a.m., a noon, a 7:05 p.m., and a 10:35 p.m."

"10:35."

"That'll be $135.58, including tax. Make sure you bring this form with you when you travel."

I give him the bills and take the form. Large letters across the top read Unaccompanied Minor.

"Fill that out, and have a parent or guardian sign. Here's your change. And a receipt. Y'all take care." He finally smiles. "Next!"

I look at the form more carefully. It only asks for addresses, but that line for a parent's signature at the bottom makes me wince. *Figure it out at home,* I tell myself. For now, I look at my ticket. My real bus ticket. I slide it into my backpack like a million-dollar check, careful not to bend it, and slip the form on top of it.

The sky goes from beige to gray as I ride home. The thought of the ticket makes my legs pump faster. I'm not even tired when I wheel into the garage and hang my helmet on the handlebars.

The house is still quiet and empty, and I'm slightly amazed that the living room looks the same, since I feel so different. I lug my backpack straight to my room and take a moment to snap a photo of the ticket, then send it to Jayden and Zuri. **Ticket!** Next, I open my sock drawer, but pause. Is there any chance Mom or Dad will see it in there? I need a better hiding place. I look around my room. I look up. My manatee poster smiles down at me from the ceiling. I drag in the stepstool from the laundry room and reach up. I slide the ticket and the form between the ceiling and the poster. From the ground I look carefully and can't tell that they're there.

I put away the stepstool and think about how to get Dad or Mom to sign the form. Maybe I can fold back the

Unaccompanied Minor part and say it's for school. No. Maybe I can forge Mom's signature. Risky. Maybe Jayden or Zuri could sign it? Or maybe it's time to tell Grandma the truth; then *she* could sign it. I'd mail it to her, and she'd mail it back. Or I could bring it with me to Thanksgiving! She'd be happy to sign it and have me come. That's my best plan for now.

At the sink, I fill a glass and take a long drink of water. My heart is still beating fast, and I'm not sure what to do next. Zuri and Jayden have sent a thumbs-up and a smiley face. Now what? A book might calm me down. I don't even take off my ankle boots before I flop onto the bed and start reading.

I open my book and rejoin Harry and his friends at their school for wizards. My breath slows as I drop into their world. The kids enter a giant hall lit with magical candles. They have just taken turns putting on the Sorting Hat when Dad barges in, brandishing the guitar. I must not have heard the garage door.

"I have something for you!" His eyes flash with enthusiasm. He's so excited that he makes me not want to be excited at all.

"I'm trying to read, Dad."

"This song—it's perfect for your Guatemalan debut!" He strums the guitar and starts crooning in the middle of my room.

His voice is loud, but my ears fill with the sound of my own blood pumping hard. First he bursts in without knocking, and now he's pushing another song on me? In what universe is this okay?

235

The song comes to a cutesy ending, and I realize it's not even a serious song. It's for children. I want to scrape his voice off my walls. "Stop!" I shout, throwing down my book. Standing now, I yell. "I'm not a little kid! I'm not doing some silly little kid's song."

Dad pulls back, looking genuinely shocked. "But it's tan chula. A sweet little song."

"I don't care about sweet little songs!"

"Quijanita." I hate the primary colors in his voice.

"I'm twelve! Haven't you noticed? I don't want to play guitar in Guatemala. I don't even want to go!"

"Of course you do."

"No, I don't! I've told you that a hundred times!" Why does every word I say bounce off?

"But you already play guitar. Why not share it con tu familia?" I wish he would stop pleading.

A red power rises in me. "Why should I? I'm just learning—for *myself*. And I'm learning songs that *I* choose, not you." I throw the last word like a dart. "I don't want to sing your stupid song. I don't even know what the words mean! Wait till you get my report card. News flash: I stink at Spanish."

"Qui." He's faltering. "I can tell you what the words mean."

"Who cares!"

"Here," he says, trying to hand me the guitar. "I can show you."

I cross my arms.

236

He's still holding out the guitar, but now he frowns. "You are a Carrillo," he says. "You'll carry the tradition, just like I hoped. You are half Guatemalan and my daughter." He pushes the guitar toward me. "This is your heritage."

"Well, I don't want it. Have you ever thought of that? Maybe I just want to be American. I'm half Anglo, *Dad*." I spit the word at him, and he flinches as if stung. I'm glad.

He sets the instrument down with deliberate gentleness, propping its neck against the low side rail of my bed. It's a battle line between us.

"Quijana." Dad takes a boss-of-the-house tone. "Listen."

"You listen! I'm not going to be your . . . strumming puppet, Dad, just so you get to pretend that I love the song and I love to play guitar and I love Spanish. Just say it. You're ashamed of me! You want me to be like Mirabel and Crista."

My father's face contorts. "That is not the point at all! It never was! Do I wish you would speak español? Por supuesto, pero . . . but . . . you could if you wanted to. You do not even try! Why should my daughter fail Spanish? Because she is not smart? No. Because she does not care! I know you are American, but you will not insult my country, my people, *your* people! Who is ashamed? You are."

"I try hard in that class! How would you know anyway? You have no idea what it's like to be me. All you see is who you wish I was." Teachers, family, friends—everybody wants me to be someone different. In one avalanche, I hear Jayden's

237

laughter with Seth, Memito's crying from pinched fingers, Elena's ugly insult, and Dad belting out the stupid kiddie song. Behind it all, another word is pounding in my ears: Guatemala, Guatemala, Guatemala. I'm tired of being a disappointment, tired of being wrong no matter what I do.

"Quijana Patricia Carrillo, no child should talk to her father this way. Where is your respect? If I even raised my voice to my father . . ."

My chords, my song, my lyrics turn to ash. My world becomes a black whirlpool sucking me down. I have to pull myself out, make it stop, make *him* stop. He's still yelling, still insisting, still arguing. I stomp.

Crack!

Strings twang as my boot lands squarely on the narrowest part of the fret board. The guitar neck breaks in half.

Dad halts mid-sentence. He's silent, raising his arms and then clasping his head. He's whispering, murmuring something in Spanish. It sounds like a prayer. He bends to pick up the pieces as if they are parts of his own body, detached for the first time, and I finally hear what he's saying. "Oh, Quijana, Quijana. What have you done?"

Tears roll down my cheeks, but I don't move.

THIRTY-FIVE

FOR THE NEXT TWO DAYS, the ceilings at home press down on me. Dad's face is tight, and Mom can't look at me without pursing her lips. I know I've done something unforgivable, but at the same time, my own anger is still smoldering. I don't apologize. I pick my way through the house as if through broken glass. I vent to Jayden and Zuri, but leave out the fight. I'm too raw. Then I go straight to my room and stay there as long as I can. In the evenings, I stay in my room with homework and books. I only let Memito in. The guitar's wall hook hangs empty.

I text with Grandma each day, but I can't bring myself to tell her what's going on. My cheerful updates on classwork start feeling like lies. Even though it's late in her time zone, I send a message at bedtime.

Grandma, I did something I shouldn't have.

Want to talk about it?

You're up!

I can't sleep much these days.

Oh.

What happened, sweet pea?

I didn't mean to, but I messed up pretty bad. Had a fight with Dad.

Can you fix it?

If she only knew how much I cannot fix a guitar!

No.

Can you apologize?

But he started it. And before that a girl insulted me at school and before that I found out that Jayden doesn't like me. So everything pretty much sucks right now. Grandma hates the word "sucks." I've never used it in front of her before. But there's no better word.

Can I be honest?

I hesitate. I don't want to be told how inadequate I am. But how can I say anything but yes to Grandma?

Will it hurt?

Probably. :-) But here it is: No self-pity! Act like the wonderful person you are. Ask yourself, What would my best self do? Then do it. I know you can.

I'll try.

At least someone believes in me.

On Friday afternoon, Mom calls me to the table. "Sit down." She remains standing. I know what's coming, and I'm almost glad. I've lived in suspense, wondering what my punishment will be.

In front of me, she sets a piece of paper. It says $400 at the top. "This is what we think it will cost to repair the guitar." I'm thankful that Dad's out with Memito right now. Dad would either yell or cry, while Mom's approach is businesslike, so it doesn't require me to stop feeling self-righteous. I know I shouldn't have wrecked the guitar, but I'm not the one who brought it to my room and forced it on me. Dad's the one who shouldn't have made demands.

"Here's a calculator," she says. "You earn three dollars a week for chores, right? Figure out how many weeks it will take you to pay this."

Fair enough.

I press the buttons and get 133 weeks. That sounds long. I divide by twelve and it comes to two and a half years. That's *really* long. I recalculate to make sure. This means that in one second, I did two and a half years' worth of damage. My body feels heavier in the chair.

Mom's brisk. "If you want to do additional chores, I'll deduct those from your total." I wish I'd known this way to raise money back when I was saving for my bus ticket. Although it would have taken me a year to get out of Texas. "Why don't you write a list of extra jobs you can do around the house, Quijana." Yikes, my whole name. Now I hear anger behind Mom's matter-of-fact tone.

"Mom, if he hadn't . . ."

"Just write, please."

I put my head down and start listing.

Wipe out refrigerator.

Wash windows.

Sweep driveway.

I can't think of many more, but Mom can.

Vacuum under sofa cushions.

Wipe down baseboards.

On it goes. My hand slows as I near the bottom of the page. "You'll do all your regular chores, plus an extra one from this list on Saturdays." I nod.

"Mom, I—"

Her face stays serious.

"I mean . . . I didn't mean for it to happen. I wish I could go back and break something else instead."

Her voice stays hard. "Well, it did happen. Now you have to make it right."

She never even asked me what happened! Doesn't she want to know my side? I didn't go *looking* for that stupid kiddie song. He dragged it in. I thought Dad would at least be a little happy that I was learning to play guitar at all. Isn't *he* the selfish one for insisting that I play the songs *he* likes? Grandma Miller's words flash to my mind: *No self-pity!* Yes. *But, Grandma, this is so hard.*

"You understand, Quijana?"

"Yes, Mom." I look down at the table and scratch a speck on the edge. "I just didn't want Dad to . . . take over like that."

"Oh, Quijana." She lets out a deep breath and rubs her eyes. "I know it feels like that guitar is all about you right now, but think beyond yourself for a second. That guitar. You know when I first saw it? Your father serenaded me when we met. He sang to me every night for a week with that guitar. Before you were born, we went camping with friends and sang around the fire—with that guitar."

I forget that the book of my parents' life started before I came. I'm a middle chapter. "Will the guitar . . . be like it was?" I ask, speaking to the tabletop.

"What?" Mom looks at me, and I try to meet her gaze.

"Will it, you know, sound the same after it's fixed?" I feel a heat behind my eyes that threatens to become tears. I know it's selfish to think of it, but I'm devastated that I won't be able to play the guitar either.

"I don't know."

I look back down. Thinking of all the years Dad played the guitar, I read the chore list and the $400 across the top. I can never truly pay for it. The weight of what I've done makes my head hang.

"Since you're making reparations—that means paying for the damage—you and I don't need to talk about this again. But you and your dad have to work things out—just the two of you."

She hangs the list on the fridge with a rainbow magnet. I wish we had a black-hole magnet. I'd like to drop inside and never come out.

Supper is quick and quiet like it has been all week. Mom and Memito act like themselves, but Dad either concentrates on his food or makes pronouncements like "Good broccoli, Kim" or "Busy day at the station." He even talks to me, but not in the old way, just asks how my classes went today. He tells no stories with exaggerated gestures and dramatic pauses. He quotes no authors or philosophers.

It's cold out here, in the free space I thought I wanted. Dad's changed. Yet I can't imagine that horrible day ending differently. I still don't want to learn a Spanish song I've never heard before. I'm still that disappointing girl.

Mom sets down her fork and clears her throat. "Quijana." Her voice startles me. "I've been wanting to have a family discussion about something. Your Aunt Jess and I have been talking. Me and Dad thought hard about this, too, and it's been a tough decision. I think it's the right thing, although I know you're not going to be happy." She rests her forearms on the table edge and I look up. Am I in yet more trouble? "We feel that Grandma's not ready to host a crowd of people. She's . . . well, she's pretty weak. We've decided to cancel Thanksgiving."

"What?" *Please, no.*

"We'll still have a gathering, but not in Florida."

"But, Mom." I try not to whine, but I can't help it. Not having Thanksgiving in Florida—without Grandma?—is like not having Thanksgiving at all. Plus, I realize with a pang of guilt, I need Grandma to sign that stupid form. "Can't we go anyway? We can do all the cooking, you and me and Aunt Jess. And Dad," I add, uncertain if I should even say his name.

"We thought about it, but Grandma may have to go back to the hospital." Mom's shoulders are slumped, I realize, and her voice is flat. I'm not used to seeing her like this. Mom is one of the strongest women I know. The woman who can do anything with enough Post-It notes and lists. Now she looks exhausted.

"Really? The hospital?" Grandma's texted me almost as much as usual. I thought she was getting better. I may have to help her more than I thought when I get there in December.

"We'll see. I'm going to fly out on Sunday to see her. It's the soonest I could get a flight." This Sunday? Mom's making it sound like an emergency. That worries me.

"I want to go with you," I say.

"It's too expensive, sweetheart."

"We could take the bus."

"Sweetie, I already bought my plane ticket. Look, I'm just going to spend a few days, and we'll have a late Thanksgiving next weekend. Aunt Jess is going with me. She said she'd host a Turkey Day for us when we get back." She turns to Dad. "Watch out, kids. Your dad may have to cook some."

Dad reaches out and rubs Mom's shoulder.

Who cares about a Turkey Day? I just want Grandma.

Before bed, I write her a letter. I ask Grandma to sign the form, explaining that I want to see her and that I can't face Guatemala. Then I send her a book-length text, telling her about my song, about how I think Jayden likes Seth, my Memito worries, and how I blew it with Dad.

245

Thanksgiving won't be the same without you, but we'll see each other soon.

I don't mention the letter or the form in the text. I can't mail them yet since Mom will be there. I'll send it after Thanksgiving.

My phone makes its magic-wand sound. It seems too late for Grandma to message me. I swipe my sea turtle screen. It *is* Grandma!

I hate to hear of life being so tough for you, sweet pea. I wish I could cheer you up with some pancakes! When you're ready to hear advice, listen to your heart. You'll find answers there. I have heard your father say, "Fortune always leaves some door open to admit a remedy." A quote from Don Quixote, I believe. You'll see an opening for a solution, I'm certain. Meanwhile, my love is with you always. XXOO

The memory of Dad's disappointed face floats in front of me, and I hear his *What have you done?* over and over. Then I remember his yelling, his insisting. The feeling that I would be bent and twisted into something unrecognizable if he won. I look for an open door, but I don't see one.

THIRTY-SIX

WITH MOM IN FLORIDA, Dad and I have no one to talk to. We can't talk to each other until one of us apologizes. It won't be me. Maybe when the guitar is repaired, it'll feel easy again, like it used to. As for now, he's fizzy with Memito, but goes flat when he asks me to take out the recycle bin. The weirdest thing is the silence during times when Dad would normally strum or sing. After supper, I'm used to hearing him pick out a melody. I'm still not sorry.

Jayden and Zuri text me from their relatives' houses, where they're having real Thanksgivings. Jayden's silly selfies make me smile, though a sadness rises up, too.

Mom texts me only once, but she calls Dad every night. Tonight I stop reading my book to listen to the half conversation.

"Good idea," Dad says. "The right medication will make all the difference." He pauses. "A turkey. Can't I thaw it in the sink?" Loud noises erupt from the other end of the phone. "Okay, okay. The fridge, got it."

Thanksgiving Day passes like a normal day, except for a big group video call. Grandma looks more like herself with her living room in the background and her regular clothes. "It's so good to see you, dear Quijana," she says.

"I wish I could hug you through the screen!" I say.

Friday night brings Mom home, and on Saturday we trundle down the road to Aunt Jess's for "Thanksgiving." She's invited us and a few friends. The strangers will make Memito withdraw, which could be good. He'll cling to Mom and not get into trouble. The rest of our Carrillo family won't be coming. They went on vacation to San Antonio, so Mirabel, Crista, and Raúl are probably snapping photos of the Riverwalk and mariachi bands, having fun. I'm surprised to almost wish I was with them. Without Grandma Miller with us, it doesn't seem like we should have fun.

I feel better when I smell pecan pie. "I followed Mom's— your grandma's—recipe exactly," Aunt Jess tells us. As the pie comes out of the oven, I take a picture and send it to Grandma. **Your pie looks yummy. Missing you.**

Dad brings in the cooked turkey, and after a few minutes of reheating, it comes out golden. He's proud of making the main dish, and I have to admit he did well. He's better at following YouTube directions than I thought.

But he still won't look me in the eyes.

We sit around a big table and everyone gets quiet. We all look at Aunt Jess. I think we're waiting for a prayer.

"Let's make this ecumenical," Aunt Jess says. Her friends seem to know this word. "You know, include everyone's spiritual path." So Mom says a Christian prayer. "Heavenly Father, we thank you for your many blessings, especially the love of friends and family near and far. May your love spread around this table and around the world. Amen." Aunt Jess raises her hands, closes her eyes, and chants "Om" loudly, three times, sending good energy into the universe and to every soul.

Dad quotes a Mayan prayer: "From the center, from the source, which is everywhere at once, may everything be known as the light of love."

Grandma would have liked it all. Mom and Aunt Jess said she was stronger by the time they left. Next year, everything will be back to normal.

After we eat, Aunt Jess calls everyone into the living room. "I have a game for us!"

"Scattergories? Apples to Apples?" Mom guesses.

"Nope. Pho-Doh! I invented it. It uses photos and Play-Doh. Get it? Pho and dough." Crazy games are so Aunt Jess.

She brings out a stack of family photos and lays them out in a grid. "Bring me that basket, would you, Qui?" I lug it to the coffee table and find it's full of Play-Doh canisters. "Teams guess which photo the sculptor is creating," she explains. "You get three minutes!"

She's on my team and shapes the Play-Doh into fingers dripping from a flat surface. "Conan's Pizza!" I shout, thinking it looks like melting cheese. She keeps making fingers. "Mama's Pizza?" The timer is close to running out as she adds some stumpy fingers coming up from the bottom. Those aren't cheese, they're stalagmites! "Inner Space Cavern!" We fist-bump, and I put the photo of us at the cave in my team's stack. When a photo of me on Dad's shoulders comes up, he looks away, but I don't. He used to let me be myself. That's the real me in the picture, and it's the real me sitting here, too. He's the one who moved the goalposts.

As we play, Memito takes the Play-Doh and makes balls out of four different colors. When he smooshes them together, I try to stop him, but Aunt Jess says mixing the colors is part of his "creative process" and doesn't mind. Of course, he yells when he realizes his hands are coated with Play-Doh dusties and stickies, but he seems to have come around to the idea by the time Mom carries him to the sink to rinse.

The day feels empty without Grandma, like a living room missing its couch, but it's not as bad as I thought it would be. And she's recovering, I remind myself. She'll be even better by the time I get there. When I check my phone, I see she's sent a string of different-colored hearts.

On Sunday morning, I bundle up and walk to the grocery store to buy an envelope and stamp. I slip the form inside the envelope and drop it in the mailbox in the parking lot. It'll go out tomorrow. Once Grandma signs it, they'll have to let me board the bus. I bet Dad won't even mind that I'm not in Guatemala. He'll be glad because I won't embarrass him.

I unzip my coat and hang it on the hook in the entryway. "I'm back from my walk," I call. Mom meets me with damp cheeks and a hug.

"What is it?"

She pulls back and looks me straight in the eyes. "I'm so sorry, Qui. I wish there were a good way to say this." Fear squeezes my heart, and I swear it stops. "This morning, Grandma didn't respond when the nurse rang the doorbell. A neighbor let the nurse in the house, and . . . Grandma passed away in her sleep last night."

Died? I don't cry. It doesn't seem real. For some reason, the first thing I think is *She won't get my letter.* "You said she was better."

Mom nods, tears standing in her eyes.

"I thought she was better, Mom," I repeat, not sure how this news can be true.

Mom hugs me again and leads me to the living room. Dad's there with his head in his hands. Slowly, bits of loss float down. No more homemade cinnamon rolls. No more canoeing on spring break. My mind bumps against no-mores for what feels like hours. We sit in the living room in silence, except for Memito's little chirps as he rocks in a big plastic rocking fish from Aunt Jess. My thoughts rock back and forth, too, between believing it and not believing it, thinking of happy times and remembering all over again that she's gone. Dad puts his arm around me and actually talks. "She loved you so much."

I want to thank him. I want to say, *It feels so good to have you love me again, even for a minute,* but I don't trust my voice. In my room, I take out my sea turtle bracelet. Tears pool in my eyes. Did she know how much I loved her? Will I ever be as brave as she was? Will I remember all her wisdom? I sit on my bed, clutch the bracelet, and let the tears fall.

Evening darkens the windows before I realize: *Guatemala. I'll have to go to Guatemala.* I wince as I think how selfish I am. Legitimate sadness is what I should be feeling—all the conversations we'll never have and the hugs I'll never give her. But legit sadness mixes with selfish sadness—the form she can't sign, the bus I can't take, the plane I'll have to board. My head spins, and I guess I zombie-walk through changing into jammies and brushing my teeth. I don't remember any of it.

At some point, I text Zuri and Jayden to let them know. Before long, they each call, but I can't bring myself to answer. As night shrouds the house, Mom and Dad appear at my bedside. We say a prayer together and send our love to Grandma, but I don't feel any better. I go back to crying. I don't remember falling asleep.

I wake up to a bright bedroom. Mom has let me sleep late. No school for me today, I guess.

"I made pancakes," she says. Grandma's breakfast.

"Thanks, Mom."

Between flipping pancakes, she adds items to a list on the counter. "So many details," she says, sighing. Instead of tears, she pours out pencil marks. I can't believe she's in planning and tactical mode after only one day. Maybe she's tired of crying.

I take a pancake, but I can't eat more than half. The syrup turns sour in my mouth. Memito eats two. He doesn't understand why today is different from every day before it.

Mom and Dad spend all day on their phones. I hear them tell the story to different people, sniffling each time. Mom talks to Aunt Jess three times, first to plan a memorial service, later to schedule some legal thing, and again to plan how to pack up Grandma's house in Florida. I wander from my room to the kitchen and back. Not even my phone tempts me. I can't bring myself to care what the rest of the world is doing.

Finally I carry the step stool to my room and close the door. I position it under the manatee poster and step up. The bus ticket pulls out easily from between the ceiling and the poster. I hold it, stare at it. This little piece of paper would have taken me to Grandma. To her wise eyes and adventurous soul at 10:35 p.m. on December 19.

I rip the ticket in pieces and drop them in my trash can. There goes that idea. What a waste. Hopefully no one will ever ask to see the huipil.

I tramp to the backyard, where the grass has turned brown for the winter. I kick Memito's red ball against the brick wall of the house.

The ball bounces back to me, and I kick it again. Each time it comes back, I kick harder. I kick over and over. I kick the doorbell that went unanswered in Florida. I kick the phone that brought the news. I kick the tears. I kick the cancer. I kick until I am nothing but a kicker, my ears filled with my own pumping blood and the *bam, bam* of ball on wall. *Bam!*

On flattened leaves, the ball sits at my feet. It's stubbornly unaffected; completely undented; a round, permanent fact. I give it one more kick, then wander to the swing. I'm hoping to be alone and pump hard into the air, but Dad brings Memito to the door and calls, "Can you watch him, Quijana?"

Before I can answer, Dad disappears into the house. I sigh. Is it wrong to want a day off from being a big sister? Memito runs to the swing and pulls on the chains. "My turn," I tell him. "I'm swinging. Go to your sandbox." He pulls at my fingers, trying to uncurl them from the chain. "Look, there's your ball." I point. He pushes on my back and grunts. "Okay, fine." I get up, and he goes stomach-first onto the swing. Is this what life really is, one thing after another being taken away? I sit on the concrete square by the back door until Memito's ready to go in.

Mom talks through supper. Cremation arrangements in Florida. A meeting at the bank. Moving companies, flights, storage. When she's finally out of words, Dad says, "Kimberly," and her poise gives way. They stand and hold each other. I come to join them, hoping Dad can love me right now. We're a triple hug. Mom's and Dad's hands are warm weights on my shoulders. Not heavy enough to still my heart's shuddering, but solid enough to hold me close.

THIRTY-SEVEN

FOR GRANDMA'S MEMORIAL SERVICE, I zip myself into a dress. Under Memito's chubby chin, I re-clip a bow tie every time he rips it off.

Finally, Mom says, "It's okay. Leave it off." She smiles at Memito, but her tears start. "Today's not a good makeup day," she laughs, wiping her eyes. "I'll cry it off before we even get there." Seeing Mom cry in dress-up clothes makes the world melt a little.

It's a weekday, but it feels like an un-day, a day in an alternate time line. I'm not in school; Dad's not at the radio station; Memito didn't get dropped off at preschool. Mom is dabbing her eyes in the front seat of the car instead of teaching a class.

We drive down a street I recognize to a building I don't. "When did this get here?" I ask. A wood-sided chapel has materialized next to the bank we use. I must've passed it in the car and on the school bus a hundred times, even walked by it as Mom pushed Memito in a stroller. I never saw it before.

Aunt Jess greets us in the foyer. "Oh, Kimmy," she says, hugging my mother. The two sisters look into each other's eyes, seeming to send silent messages they both understand. Aunt Jess kisses me on the cheek, then my father. Her lip is quivering, but she keeps her tears in check. I can tell she's trying to be strong.

Tía Lencha is here, too, with Tío Pancho, Raúl, Mirabel, and Crista, all dressed in church clothes. Raúl pulls at his collar, but the girls envelop me in their arms. "Quijana, you must be heartbroken!" Their tears wet my shoulder, and I feel bad that I'm not crying. But for some reason, I can't. Maybe I'm all cried out.

I remember something Dad told me about Guatemala. When someone dies, wailing women follow the casket to the graveyard, sobbing loudly. When the departed spirit hears the wailing, it understands that it's on the other side. I guess that explains why Tía Lencha is wringing Mom's hand, choking out loud words between tears, sobbing and waving her Kleenex. "Pobrecitos!"

Dad keeps blinking tears, too. He told me to expect this, saying, "We express openly."

Only I am wooden. Only I seem to be watching this moment instead of living it. I feel less Carrillo-like than ever. I can't stop touching my sea turtle bracelet to make sure it's there.

Ushers hand each of us a carnation as we step into a plush-carpeted room. Grandma's death blooms into reality when I see a picture of her at the front, and I grip Mom's hand. Grandma's body is being cremated in Florida, but the large photo makes it seem like she's here and not anywhere at the same time. "Death will be a great adventure," she'd said. I almost expect the photo to wink. I lay the carnation against my cheek, its silky petals reminding me of the bird feathers Grandma and I used to find on our walks and take home to look up.

I grip my bracelet. Finally, tears blur my vision. Out of nowhere, Mom hands me a Kleenex. I think of questions I should have asked Grandma. What do I pack for a weeklong hike? Why do manatees do barrel rolls? How did you know you were in love? I think of all the reasons I need her. To tell me about my mom as a kid. To show me the ocean's secrets. To show me how to make life an adventure. What will I do without her?

The mournful organ music holds my hand and twists my heart. I look down at my brother, who's drawing on a Magna Doodle. I'm glad he's occupied and not crying. He's the only person here who doesn't know she's gone. Or maybe he's the one who has it all figured out. Just stay in your own Tinkertoy world where nothing can hurt you.

Then again, he'll never know Grandma Miller, never paddle her canoe among the manatees. I should be thankful for all the years I had with her, I know; I should be glad I'm luckier than Memito.

But a stone sits on my heart. When I was little, I thought I wanted to grow up; now I wish I could unknow things. I wish

I could slide the Magna Doodle's eraser bar and redraw this whole year.

Mom squeezes my shoulder. "It's time," she says, and we take our carnations to the front. Each person lays a flower in front of Grandma's picture. I place my flower and look into Grandma's eyes. Her gaze radiates wisdom and love and every good thing I can think of. She wants me to be happy, I know. But I'm not sure happiness will ever be the same.

I linger at her picture until Mom leads me away by the hand.

As I walk back to the pew, the sight of Raúl sitting between his parents makes me frown. He looks so comfortable, a knee touching one parent, an elbow touching the other. Anyone can see that he belongs to both of them. The whole family looks like a matched set. Eyes and hair the same color. Spanish on their tongues. Heat behind my eyes turns from tears to anger—not at them, but at us. They should go to Guatemala, not us. My family looks like furniture bought at a thrift store. Dad and me darker, Mom and Memito lighter. Spanish a fabric we ran out of.

Without Grandma Miller, I'll be shoved onto a plane. Yanked out of my country. Dropped into a boiling pot of trilled r's. *Grandma, why did you leave me?*

Aunt Jess hugs me once more before we go. "Quijana, I'm so glad we all have each other. I want you to visit more, okay?"

"That'd be great," I say automatically, not feeling it much, but trying to look appreciative.

"When spring break comes, I'll take you to my favorite places in Fort Worth—Spiral Diner, Sundance Square, the Kimbell Art Museum. We'll have ice cream, okay? I know it won't be the same as Florida. . . ."

"I'd love it, Aunt Jess." This time I mean it. I understand. With a little surge of panic, I hug her again. We have to enjoy each other while we can.

At home, I'm looking forward to being alone. What I'd really like to do is play the guitar or take a long walk with Jayden. Both impossible. "Can I go out and swing?" I ask Mom. I imagine singing to myself out there, letting part of me slip into the sky. But before she can say yes, neighbors arrive, hands full of casseroles and cobblers and pots that plug into the wall. We say "thank you" so many times that I run out of sincerity.

It's not until late that night that I discover I'm hungry. I serve myself some pizza and peach cobbler, and it's good. Good enough. But the torn place inside aches worse than ever.

THIRTY-EIGHT

I WAKE UP IN THE MIDDLE OF THE NIGHT thinking of ways to stay home from Guatemala—tie myself to Aunt Jess's red oak tree, lock my bedroom door and refuse to come out. Dreams take over, and I run up and down aisles of the Latino grocery store, finding no exit. The back wall becomes an ocean where I see Grandma standing on the back of a whale. She gets smaller and smaller as the whale swims out to sea.

When I wake, my heart is pumping fast. *School,* I remind myself. *Just make it through the day.*

Memito is on the dining room floor when I walk in for breakfast. He's turned his Tonka truck upside down again, and is spinning one wheel round and round. "Time to eat, m'ijo," Mom says. He stares at the wheel, giving it a spin every time it slows down. "Toast?" He keeps his eyes on the wheels. "Memito?" Mom brings the plate down to his level. "Aren't you hungry?" Mom moves the plate into his line of vision, and this breaks the spell. He climbs into his booster chair. Relieved, I eat, too.

I never thought I'd be thankful for our bus driver, Ms. Franklin, but her "No drawing on the foggy windows today!" reminds me that I'm still in Bur Oak, Texas, and not just in Grief, and not in Guatemala yet. Still, when the bus pulls up to the school building, I stay slumped against the window till the last student steps off. Ms. Franklin looks at me in her oversized rearview mirror as I trudge to the front. "Glad you're back, Quijana. Were you sick all three days?" I shake my head and step off into the cold.

"You okay, Quijana?" Señora Francés asks. Some of my teachers know about Grandma because Mom called the school.

"Mm-hm."

She says something else, but I'm thinking about last night, the crying I heard through the bedroom door after supper. My mother without her mother. How will she ever fill that hole? How will I? On top of that, Dad still seems distant. He hugged me yesterday, but he's not playful or crazy with me at all—no winks or hair tousles or random songs. When I broke his guitar, I broke something between us, too.

The only thing I'm looking forward to is seeing Jayden and Zuri.

"Quijana," Zuri says, giving me a hug.

"My QuiQui," says Jayden, hugging me, too.

The cafeteria is an ocean of noise. As we sit down at our usual table, I try to tune in to Zuri's voice. "I took pictures of my notes from yesterday's class. I'll send them to you."

"Want some chocolate?" Jayden lifts his lunch sack. "I could share."

Notes and chocolate feel like those umbrellas they put in grown-up cocktails, papery and pretty and useless in a downpour. But I know my friends are trying to help. They don't know what else to say. I don't really either. "Thanks, guys." Everyone eats in silence. The chocolate actually does perk me up.

"So in other news," I say, spinning my apple like a top. "I tore up the bus ticket."

"Oh, no. That was so much money! And the huipil," Zuri says.

"I know. I feel terrible that I, like, wasted it, sold it for nothing. Or sold it at all."

"And it was so beautiful," Zuri says.

"Man." Jayden shakes his head.

"So how will you get out of going to Guatemala?" Zuri leans forward.

"I won't." Saying it out loud makes me feel even worse.

"I know." Jayden brightens. "You can be super rude, a total pain. Talk back to your parents, don't do your chores. Then they'll punish you by making you stay home!"

I smile my first real smile in four days.

"She can't stay alone." Zuri shakes her head.

"Why not?" Jayden says. His voice goes serious. "Quijana, have you ever burned the house down?"

"No, but somehow I don't think I'll get the okay to spend two weeks alone." I laugh bitterly. "I've lost so much sleep over this stupid trip. When I picture stepping off the plane, I want to throw up, but I think I really do have to go."

"You sure?" Jayden says.

"What else can I do? It's not how I ever pictured Christmas, but . . ." I twist my napkin and curl it around my finger. I can't even bring myself to tell them about how Dad's still mad. Then I'd have to explain the whole guitar situation.

Zuri pushes her empty tray to the side. "Hey, the choir concert is Monday, right? At least that's something to look forward to."

"That's right." I look up. "You guys still coming?"

"Of course!" Zuri says.

"Sorry about Monday-night football," I say to Jayden, trying to be a friend.

"We're excited!"

Walking back to class, I feel a twinge of guilt. Grandma's gone, yet here I am making plans and even laughing. Going on without her.

When I walk in from school, the house smells of cinnamon and sugar. Mom has put up our Christmas decorations—all except the tree ornaments. Stockings hang from the mantel, snowmen sit on the end tables, and green garlands swoop around the room.

"Wow, Mom." I don't know whether to be happy or worried about her. This must have taken all day.

"I thought we could trim the tree tonight. Does that sound fun?" Her eyes are hopeful. "I tested the lights. And I baked cranberry cake," she says. That's her specialty! But why today?

She must see surprise on my face because she explains. "I turned in my last research paper today. I graduate on Saturday!"

"Oh, yeah!"

Her smile fades, and I know she's wishing Grandma could have been there. Grandma was always a big fan of Mom's master's degree. Aunt Jess isn't here either; she's gone to Florida to clear out Grandma's house.

"Dad'll be home soon," she says. "How about some Christmas music?"

It's probably good for Mom to start a new season. It's probably good for all of us.

Memito's lining up blocks end to end across the living room floor. Seeing me, he pulls me by the finger to his roads and gives me a car. I don't feel like playing cars, but I sit on the floor and start rolling the car down the block road. I'll give it five minutes, I figure.

Mom finds a playlist, and singers belt out "Jolly Old Saint Nicholas" through the speakers. Just then, Memito stops his car, jumps up, and runs to his room. "Mom? Did you see that?" I call into the kitchen.

"See what, Qui?"

"Memito just ran to his room."

She's wrapping the cranberry cake in foil. "So?"

"I think he ran away from the music."

She sighs. "He used to love music. Your dad plays—used to play—all the time. I'll go get him and see." She wipes her hands on a dish towel and disappears down the hall. The next thing I hear is Memito's yell and a banging on his door.

Mom comes back alone, her hair in disarray. "You're right. He won't come out." She turns the volume down and looks down the hall. Then she clicks it all the way off—and we watch Memito's door crack open. He crawls, for some reason, back down the hall toward us, and starts lining up blocks again like nothing happened. Mom looks at me and shakes her head. "This is so . . . I mean it makes no . . ." She blows air through puffed cheeks.

I don't know which words she needed, but I know what she means. Memito used to be a little city laid out on a grid. I knew all the streets, every intersection. Now I am lost. Nothing's where it used to be.

A memory fades in. We're at the park last summer, and Memito is covering his ears and whimpering as the ice cream truck cranks out its repeating song. I hear one grown-up say to another, "What's wrong with him?"

I try to remember if Memito squirmed at Christmas music last year. Does all music sting his ears, or only singing? Or only certain pitches?

I imagine life without music. Silence deleting every song in the world. My choir music transformed into pages of rests, my music files two gigs of static. I imagine Memito walking into kindergarten with noise-canceling headphones.

Another quirk to add to the list.

But doesn't the list add up to something by now? We still eat dinners with the main light off. There are the words he doesn't know, the bell he couldn't hear at all, and now music he hears too well?

I take out my phone. *You're getting warmer,* says a voice in my head as I Google *child sensitive to noise. Warmer,* it says, when I change my search to "sensory integration," a phrase that's bolded on every page. Finally, a site lays out Memito's issues like a row of matches.

"Mom!" I run up to her as she rinses the mixing bowl. "Read this."

She turns to me and enlarges the text on the screen. She reads, nodding. "You think Memito has autism."

"It fits everything!" I can't believe no one has raised this as a possibility before.

But Mom's too calm. "I see your point. A lot of this fits." She hands back the phone with a grim smile. "His preschool teacher did talk to us about it. Back in September, she even did a screening. But it was decided that he made too much eye contact for this to be autism. That's how we ruled it out." Mom dries the bowl and puts it away. "Quijana, come sit for a minute."

I follow her to the living room, but I stay standing. I'm not convinced. What's one test? The website not only lists symptoms, it talks about why Memito was normal until age three—something called regression. If we can figure out what this is, we can treat it, maybe cure it. We could get him back.

"I know you're worried about Memito, but you've got to let us handle it." She rubs her eyes and sighs. "We've been to the doctor, and pre-K did their screening. To tell you the truth, I just don't think they know what to call it. His symptoms are all over the place."

This jars my brain. How can they not know? Grown-ups are supposed to know the important stuff, like why my brother is slipping, curling into himself more every day. "Can't they do anything?"

"They're trying, sweetie—we're trying. You know we are. Speech therapy to get him to talk. Occupational therapy to help his motor skills, and the brushing, well, I don't know if it's working. It's supposed to make him less sensitive."

"But is he getting better?"

Now Mom looks away. "We'll have to wait and see, Qui." She pulls her pitch up at the end, giving the words a determined sunniness.

I'm not willing to wait and see. "He's supposed to know over a hundred words by now." I know she knows, but language delay is an important clue.

"I know, Quijana."

"So what are we going to do?" I don't care that tears are leaking onto her cheeks. I don't care that I'm hurting her, even when we're all still missing Grandma terribly. "We can't just sit around and *wait*!"

"There's not much more we can do." She reaches out to touch my shoulder, but I pull away.

"We have to do something," I say, my voice rising.

Her tone sharpens. "Quijana, we are."

"It's not enough! Memito was fine, perfectly fine until something changed. We have to figure out what happened to him!"

Now my mother stands up. She's not taller than I am anymore, but I find myself stepping back. "No one knows, Quijana. Do you think I haven't been to all those websites? Do you think I haven't lain awake every night, worried sick just thinking about it? You're not the only one who worries, Quijana. You're not the only one who loves him!"

She's crying for real now, and I am, too. Memito is oblivious.

For some reason, this makes me feel better. Not better about Memito, but better. We're walking into the flames together. Maybe she's been there, burning with me, all along.

Mom is blurry through my tears. I step toward her. She takes me into her arms and strokes my hair. My heart wrenches, and I lean into her body. I wish she could solve things like she used to.

"Can't I do *something*?" I ask. "Please?"

She doesn't answer right away. One second flips by, then another, and I realize that her silence is the answer. We haven't fixed anything, but the feeling that I'm a lone firefighter has faded. She squeezes me harder, keeps petting my hair. "Even if he never talks," she says at last, "he's still our Memito."

THIRTY-NINE

I WRESTLE INTO A DRESS for the second time this month, feeling not at all pretty and not excited either. Mom gets her master's degree in English this morning, but all I can think of is having to sit with Dad and Memito for over an hour in the audience. Dad and I still have a force field between us. Grandma would probably tell me there's a door there somewhere, but I'm still not ready to find it.

I peek out of my bedroom and check the hall. No Dad. I cross over to the big bedroom, where Mom brushes on blush and checks her teeth in the mirror. "What if I had oatmeal in my graduation pictures? Yikes!" I watch her pull on a blue graduation gown and pin her mortarboard cap in place. "Hey, you could wear the huipil today. It would match my blue gown."

I'm pretty sure my breath stops. *A lie always surfaces, as oil floats on water,* warns an inner voice I recognize as Don Quixote's.

"It would make your dad happy," Mom adds. Huge gulp. "But that dress looks nice, too." *Whew.*

Our eyes meet in the mirror.

"He loves you, you know," she says.

"I know."

"He's not so much angry as hurt." She turns to face me. "You need to talk to him soon, Qui. I'm trusting you to be mature and handle this thing with Dad on your own, but it won't go away by itself. You have to actually do something about it."

I guess she's right. And hurt? I hadn't thought of him as hurt. I thought he was sulking, but if Mom's right, he's waiting.

She slides tinted Chapstick across her lips and presses them together.

As I watch Mom, I realize I haven't really looked at her in a while. Her eyes are shining, and her hair is glossy. "Mom, you look beautiful!" I pick up her phone. "Can we take a picture?"

"Thanks, sweetie." She looks genuinely happy on the screen as we take our selfie. "Mother and daughter. And when you graduate," she winks at me, "we'll do another one just like it." If I *make* it to graduation. I can hardly imagine getting through Guatemala.

"Are you nervous?" I ask, posting the photo with a caption: *Love this grad! English is her superpower!*

"Oh gosh, no," she laughs. "The hard part is done. This is a celebration."

"But so many people will be watching you."

"Well, but only you guys will be looking at *me*." She smiles at me in the mirror. "And you're my fan club, right?"

"Right." Dad and I may not be fans of each other, but we're both fans of Mom.

Though the auditorium is crowded, Dad, Memito, and I find good seats toward the middle. I make sure Memito sits between me and Dad. The graduates all look alike in their caps and gowns; I can't tell which one is Mom. But when Dad points her out to Memito, I see her bright face and feel a surge of pride.

A woman in a floppy hat takes the podium. Her white hair and frank style remind me of Grandma Miller. "I can't tell you that your field will be easy," she says. "But I can tell you that you are prepared. This class has strength of mind and strength of spirit. That strength is what we honor today." She seems like a fellow ocean lover.

Mom crosses the stage, tall and sure, looking like a woman who can make the world better. Dad and I shout and clap. Like swimmers in parallel lanes, we're doing the same thing, even if it's not exactly together. Memito catches the spirit of the moment and yells, "Yay!" Mom waves to the audience, and joy rises through my body.

At home, Dad has made a special lunch of black beans, buttery rice, and a tomato-y Guatemalan dish called pepián. Mom's invited one of her classmates, Julie, to join us, so we're all on our best behavior. Julie sees Dad at his warmest, Mom at her friendliest, me at my sweetest, and Memito, well, being cute Memito. I think we're all relieved to have someone easy around, someone from outside our world, and the happy chatter lifts us all.

I watch Dad all through lunch. He's acting so well that even I am convinced he's not mad at me. When he tells his favorite story about me—the time I helped a boy learn multiplication by using piles of acorns—he performs the tale all theatrically, just like old Dad. "Quijana. We're so proud of her." He gestures with both hands as if he's presenting me onstage.

But when he meets my eyes, his smile fades. And when Julie leaves, all the color in the house seems to go with her. I wish I could say it was Grandma's death making Dad subdued.

But I know it's still me.

FORTY

MONDAY NIGHT FALLS CRISP AND STARRY–perfect weather for my choir concert. I only wish the weather in our house were perfect.

Once the babysitter arrives, we drive to school. It's my turn to be onstage, but I'm way more nervous than Mom was. I know all the music well—Mr. Green made sure of that—but I still have a scurrying feeling in my stomach. Tonight's my first time to sing in front of real people in a real auditorium. We practiced on this stage last week, but it was echoey then. Now the audience murmurs, charging the air. I realize that I'm actually excited to begin. I straighten my dress and lift my hair behind my shoulders.

Now the whole choir is lining up in the wings, arranging ourselves in the right order. The guys look spiffy in their black suits, and our matching dresses make all of us girls look pretty. The prettiness feels spread around, instead of concentrated in just a few. I try to focus on the fact that not just popular people or even the best voices matter tonight. All that matters is the music.

When Mr. Green walks out, applause pours down. It's louder than I expected. As he delivers the welcome, I peek around the kids in front of me. In the auditorium, faces are staggered like rows of letters on a keyboard. I wonder where Jayden and Zuri are sitting. Then the lights go down, and the audience is a rumbling, black sea. The sea hushes when we walk, row by row, onto risers onstage.

Mr. Green smiles at us and bends his knees. This is a signal to bend ours, too, so we won't pass out. He takes a deep breath and exhales; we do the same. This pushes some of the nervousness out. My heart surges, then settles. Mr. Green raises his baton, bringing the whole choir to a hushed focus.

Then the air turns magical. My skin tingles as every person in the room shares the same held breath. I feel the moment itself—the what's-next—connecting us. We're all— each singer, each listener, even the dust motes in the air— held in the same single spell. The tingle moves to the top of my head, and I know we're about to do something amazing.

Mr. Green cues the accompanist. And then it's happening.

As I sing the first note, the audience disappears, and I give myself to the song. I climb each phrase and ride it down. We bounce each note in the fast sections and crescendo into strong tones for the big ending. My favorite piece starts, and soon tinkling highs give way to warm lows.

Oh, Shenandoah,
I long to see you.
Way hey, you rolling river.
Oh, Shenandoah,

I long to see you.

Away, I'm bound away,

'Cross the wide Missouri.

The last note ends and echoes. Mr. Green lowers his hands, and applause erupts. The stage lights shine like sunlight on my face.

In that warmth, my heart opens wide. I'm in tune with all the universe. But then a thought pinches my heart. Two of those clapping hands are my father's. It's been almost three weeks since I broke the guitar, and he's never shouted, never threatened. Mom's right. He's not mad; he's sad. He could have stayed home tonight, but he came. My stomach drops. I have to apologize.

The next song springs me into a fast phrase. I hop from note to note, and alongside the tune runs the idea of talking to Dad. As I sing out stronger and stronger the rest of the night, I'm more and more sure I can do it.

We get to the last song all too fast. I wish I could stay in it forever. And then we curve into the next phrase and fly to the final line. The last note pops, and the audience sits stunned. Then they roar with applause, whoops, and whistles.

Backstage, Zuri's the first to find me. "You made me cry! That last one was beautiful." She gives me a long hug. "Oh my gosh, I hope they recorded it. I want a copy, okay?"

I'm glowing, pleased with the performance and happy at all the joy in the room—a hundred people smiling and gushing.

"Me too!" shouts Jayden, swooping in for a squeeze. "My favorite was the a cappella piece." Jayden's fingertips meet his thumbs and he jiggles his hands in the air like a chef describing a precise taste. "Tight harmonies and no piano. Just pure voices. Very nice!" Seth, of course, is behind him.

"Thanks, you guys. I was so glad you all were out there." I realize that I even mean it about Seth.

"It really was great, Quijana," Jayden says.

"Yeah, that was better than football," Seth adds. I think he might be exaggerating about that, but still, my vision of our threesome is stretching to add a fourth.

"Thanks, y'all," I say. "Hey, come see my parents."

We grab our coats and jostle through the crowd. "Isn't that your dad?" Zuri says.

It sure is. Dad's wearing a native Guatemalan shirt, and it's the most colorful thing in the room. "That's him all right."

"Sweetheart, you were wonderful!" Mom says, squeezing my shoulders.

"Beautiful, m'ija," Dad says.

"You both know Zuri," I say, "and these are our favorite actors, Jayden and Seth."

"Good to see you again, Mr. Carrillo. Great shirt," Jayden says, shaking hands.

"No kidding!" Seth says.

"¡Gracias, chicos!" Dad's natural friendliness can't hide.

"Nice to finally meet you, Jayden. I've heard so much about you." Mom takes his hand in both of hers. "I saw you in the play, and Seth, you too. Amazing job. Zuri, how are you?"

"Yes, Zuri, where have you been hiding? It's so long since we've seen you! Come over any time. Don't be strangers," Dad says. "Our door is always open." Dad's warmth feels just the right temperature this time.

"Thanks, Mr. Carrillo," Zuri says. "Don't you think it was, I don't know, like being lifted out of your seat? I just closed my eyes and let the music . . . carry me."

"Me too," I say, touched by practical Zuri's emotion. I know what she means, too. Onstage, every problem fell away. Music took me where it wanted to go. "It was like riding the wind."

"Okay, crazy wind-riders," Jayden says. "We're going back to Seth's to catch the end of the game. Be sure to get me a copy of the concert, QuiQui."

"I will," I say, waving.

"I better go, too," Zuri says. "Dad's probably waiting out front."

We hug, and I'm luckier tonight than I have been for weeks.

Mom keeps her hand on Dad's shoulder on the way home. He tilts his cheek and rubs her hand. They love each other. I think they even love me.

When we turn onto Central Avenue, lined with street-lights, I can't decide if we drive from shadow to shadow or from one shower of light to the next. I still sense sadness in the front seat. I can't figure out what to say about the guitar. But I know one thing: I'm not angry anymore.

At home, I'm floating through bedtime prep—brushing my teeth and washing my face—when I hear my phone's magic-wand sound. It's Jayden.

You still up?

Yes.

Seth's going to come over during break.

Sounds fun. Why is he telling me this?

No. Call me?

I call him.

He picks up right away. "So after your concert, he said, 'Let's get together over the break,' and I was like, 'You should come over after Christmas.' He said, 'Cool.' But then I'm driving home with my parents, and I need to tell them, you know, but I can't. I just sit there. And then we're home."

"Where are you now?"

"In my room. Like a coward."

"Your parents don't like Seth?"

"I mean, they met him at the play. I'm sure they think he's fine."

"They know you guys hang out, right?"

"Sure, but . . ."

Now it hits me. I try to step around the wrong words. "They don't know that . . . you like him."

"Right. Qui, I've never told anyone. I knew I . . . *was,* you know, but I never planned or said, like . . ."

"It's okay. I know."

"I know you know."

"Well, duh. You totally like Seth, not any girls. Not even Zuri."

"You mean, not even you."

I can't come up with a response to that. I can't deny that my heart is still a little bruised.

"But I do like you, Qui. You're my best friend. Zuri's like my sister, but you're the one I call, you know, like now."

This moment tastes like a cough drop, half medicine-y, half sweet. "You're my best friend, too." It sounds better than I thought. In fact, it sounds good. I remember hearing that love is built on friendship. Maybe friendship is built on love.

"So, what should I do?"

"Can't you say Seth is a friend?"

"But he's not." Jayden sighs. "I should tell them, right? I should come out to them." His voice sounds pinched, like his throat is tightening. "They probably know anyway." He doesn't sound sure at all. He sounds scared.

"But Jay, you *don't* have to do this now. I mean, Seth should come visit, but there's no rush about your parents."

"But don't you think . . ."

"Look. There's no, like, requirement, to tell them now. If they know already, then they know. If not, that's fine too. The right time will come along. If it's freaking you out, forget it and just tell them when you're ready. That doesn't make you a coward."

Jayden's quiet. Silence soaks second after second.

"You okay?" I listen for his breathing.

"No, you're right. It doesn't have to be tonight. It doesn't have to be this year." I hear him let out a long sigh. "Right."

"It doesn't have to be *next* year!"

"Yeah." He almost laughs. "When I'm ready." I can tell he says the words through a smile. I'm glad I could be there for him, and I'm even gladder that he's relieved.

We hang up, I plug my phone in, make my last lunch of the fall semester, and load my backpack. It's strange how I'm rooting for Seth now. I want Jayden to smile.

On my way to bed, I check my phone one more time. There's a text from Jayden.

Thanks, bestie!

I send back a thumbs-up.

In bed, I lie awake savoring memories of the concert. Mr. Green's first downbeat, our round vowels making each tone ring, hitting the highest note, and the delicious applause. I also remember Dad's voice: "Beautiful, m'ija." From a wise part of myself that feels newly awakened, I hear, *He set aside his sadness for you tonight.* I promise myself that before tomorrow ends, I will apologize.

FORTY-ONE

WHILE I GET DRESSED FOR SCHOOL, I'm trying to think of ways to apologize to Dad tonight. The guitar can be repaired, but this distance between us—I want to repair that, too. I'll have to get him alone, and then . . . what words should I start with? Then I realize there's something else I can do. Something I have to do.

I arrive at the bus stop early. It would be easier if the Latino boys arrived before everyone else, but they don't. Everyone takes their usual places on the sidewalk. The boy who said "Mexicans!" three months ago saunters to the middle. I've learned his name is Garrett. Everyone is looking at their phones. Except me.

The Latino boys walk up, stopping a little ways off, like normal. Are they even Mexican? They could be from lots of countries. El Salvador, Honduras, Bolivia. Even Guatemala. They could be my cousins.

I step closer to them and smile. "Mucho gusto," I say to them, which is what you're supposed to say when meeting someone.

"Encantado," says one. "Emilio." He gives a little head bow.

"Felipe," says the other.

The other kids look up.

"Which way do you live?" I ask.

Emilio points down the street and curves his hand to the right. "Linda Lane."

"I'm up there." I gesture up the street with my thumb. "Did you just move here this year?"

"It's LIN-da," Garrett breaks in.

The three of us turn our heads, questioning.

"Not LEEN-da."

"Chill, Garrett," I say. "'Linda' is Spanish for 'pretty,' anyway. The English name comes from the Spanish in the first place."

"Okay, Tijuana," Garrett sneers. A few kids giggle.

I narrow my eyes at him and don't answer.

"Her name's Quijana," says Emma, the girl who stepped on her own shoe back in September.

Several kids have put down their phones. Emilio and Felipe step up on either side of me, forming a line.

Garrett looks at us, then turns, dismissing us with a wave and sucking air between the roof of his mouth and his tongue. He walks off by himself.

The other kids have rearranged themselves into a rough circle. We're one big group—except Garrett, who's back on his phone, or pretending to be. He probably wants to look busy and important, like he has a billion urgent messages to read. We know he doesn't.

The bus doors open, and I climb on feeling good. I've made up for what I didn't say and didn't do. With Dad, I'll need to make up for what I *did* say and *did* do. Talking to the boys was good practice, but it'll be harder with Dad. I can only hope that'll work out as well as this did.

The day passes in a blur. The best part is going to choir, where Mr. Green passes around little bags of M&Ms in a huge bowl and we watch a video of the concert. It's weird to see myself on-screen, an earnest face in the second row. We sound even better than I remember.

All day, my thoughts keep circling back to Dad and what I'll say after school.

I try out phrases in my head as I walk home from the bus, hoping that the right words will come.

At home, I find Mom in high gear. She's installed a dimmer switch on the dining room light for Memito, is baking a lentil and sweet potato casserole, and has Memito wiping the table. She's been full of energy and smiles since graduation.

"Mom." I take a deep breath. "I'm ready to talk to Dad." I push extra determination into my voice, even though I'm nervous, too.

"Oh, Qui, I'm super glad. You'll both feel better, I know it."

I decide to tackle the apology after supper. Everything smells too good to wait, so we eat as soon as Dad walks in. After washing dishes, I'm anxious to get this over with, but then he gets on the phone. And then he gives Memito a bath. It's nearly bedtime when I steel my nerves and knock on my parents' bedroom door.

"Come in."

I push, and the door swings open. They're both reading on their little couch, Mom sitting cross-legged, Dad stretching his legs out in front of him, ankles crossed. He lays his book in his lap.

I clear my throat. "Dad, can I talk to you?"

"Certainly." He closes his book, marking his place with his finger.

The words dry up in my throat. I open my mouth, but the room feels suddenly hot.

Mom looks back and forth between us. "Should I leave you two alone?"

Somehow that would be worse. I'm sliding under a wave. "Can we take a walk or something?" I remember our late-evening walk with Memito a month ago. Everything felt easier then. "We can take flashlights again."

Dad's eyes start to smile. "How about the backyard?"

We put on our coats, step out the back door, and look up at the stars, standing side by side in the cold air. I see his breath. He must know what I want to say, but he doesn't speak. I look at his profile and, in the moonlight, notice gray hairs near his temples. I've been thinking he wanted some other kind of daughter—a girl more Latina. Maybe I wanted some other kind of dad—more American. Neither of us can trade.

"Dad." I close my eyes and say it slowly. "I'm sorry I broke the guitar." I open my eyes to see his head is down. "I was angry. I don't have an excuse. Before I could think or stop myself, I had done it." He waits. "I'm ashamed that I hurt the guitar you brought from Guatemala—well, destroyed it. And I never should have yelled at you either. Or said all those things. And now I miss singing. Your singing. And you and mom singing." It's true. Life hasn't felt lively since it happened. "I don't know why I felt so angry about playing for Abuela. I could have at least tried. It seems silly now."

He's quiet for a long time. Then he says, "You're such a good sister." He's looking at the sky, but all I can look at is his face. "Such a wonderful daughter." Surprise lifts me, almost pulling me out of my shoes. I thought he would yell, or scold me at least. When I think of the splintered guitar, I feel like he should.

"Hijita. You don't have to sing in Guatemala. You don't ever have to play guitar. It's just . . ." His voice wavers. "I wanted to give you something to make your life sweeter."

I blink. I wonder if I'm hearing correctly.

"Here in the States, it is not so easy to keep the customs, to even pass down memories of places far away. We cannot visit Guatemala often. Is it any wonder that it is as foreign to you as, what is it, Timbuktu? I blame myself about the Spanish. I missed the chance to give you that. Now we are left with songs. And the guitar." He looks down at his hands. "When I saw you holding it, I admit I was hopeful. I hoped to still give you something of your heritage. Something of me."

I meet his eyes. He blinks tears away, and my own eyes moisten. "Dad," I say.

He opens his arms, and I step into them. I squeeze him hard. He hugs me and kisses the top of my head.

In his embrace, I feel all the strain and worry fall away. "I love you."

"I know, m'ija. I love you, too."

I pull back. "I've only earned twelve dollars."

"I'm not worried about that," he says. "It might be time for a new guitar. I know a store, remember?"

Before we go in, I look up at the stars hanging low and glittery. Tonight, each one seems reachable.

Back inside, we can tell that neither of us wants to go to bed quite yet, even though tomorrow is a school day. "I'm going to have some hot chocolate," Dad says. "You want some?"

"Sure."

"You know, your grandma's the one who taught me to use a microwave. And how to wash dishes, too. At home, my sisters did that, but your grandma—she set me straight, said men in America help in the kitchen." He laughs. "She never let me forget that!"

In three minutes, the microwave dings and we each take a mug. "It's hot," he warns. We sip our cocoa at the table. The warmth in my belly spreads to my whole body. Dad usually comes up with a quote to end nights like this. Just as I'm thinking that, he speaks up. "As Cervantes says, 'You are a king by your own fireside, as much as any monarch on his throne.'"

Right now I wouldn't trade places with any king.

FORTY-TWO

ON THE LAST WEEKEND before our trip to Guatemala, Mom and Dad and I spend all morning cleaning house for a party. We're celebrating two events at once: Mom's graduation and Christmas, with no presents.

I fold paper napkins into fans on the table, then check on Memito. He's whirling on his Sit 'n Spin in the living room. I'm hoping he'll enjoy the day and not get overwhelmed when Tía Lencha's crew and Aunt Jess descend on our house for the buffet-style supper.

My cousins circle the dining table, which is crowded with homemade tamales, tomato rice balls, handmade tortillas, and fresh guacamole, plus a treat that I helped make—strawberries dipped in white chocolate tinted green to make them Christmas-y.

Mirabel grabs my arm right away and starts giving me the scoop on her new boyfriend. She was right. Brian likes her. "He gave me a snow globe on the last day of school." She says it quietly, but her eyes sparkle. He sounds so sweet. It's the perfect Christmas gift.

"And it plays music!" Crista says.

"I'm surprised you didn't bring it along," Raúl says with an eye twinkle.

"*Tss*." Mirabel switches back to sister mode long enough to roll her eyes at him. "What about your guy, Quijana? Did you find out if he likes you?"

I take a deep breath. "I found out."

"Well?"

"We're . . . just friends."

"That's too bad," says Mirabel.

"No, it's not," snarks Raúl. "A friend will last longer than Brian."

"But love is better than friendship," Crista says wispy-like, as if she's just stepped out of a theater after a romantic movie.

"You sure about that?" Raúl shrugs. "I got no one to tie me down. That's the way to be."

"You don't know anything." Mirabel waves him away, but I think he may have a point. I don't see him worrying about how to dress, how to walk, how to be liked. I don't worry about that with Jayden either. And most friendships do last longer. I hope I'm friends with Jayden all my life.

"I don't know, I might be on Raúl's side," I say, and Raúl nods at me. I get the sense that I've finally said something he doesn't think is totally lame. "Want to see my room?"

All three follow me down the hall. "Nice idea," Raúl says, pointing to the manatee poster on the ceiling. "I'm going to do that." He plops on the floor.

Crista squeals at the sight of my stuffed manatee, then runs over and hugs it.

Mirabel perches demurely in a chair by the window. "So, you're obviously into manatees."

"Yeah, I've actually seen them in the wild. In Florida." It sounds dorky, but I can't help getting excited.

"Did you swim with them?" Raúl sits up straighter and looks at me.

"Yeah, I snorkeled. And kayaked. You can't take power boats near the manatees."

"So you actually swam next to them and breathed through that tube thing?" Raúl seems genuinely impressed.

"Grandma Miller took me." I nod toward the picture. It's weird to think they know her only from the memorial service.

Mirabel gives me a sad smile. "I bet you miss her."

I nod.

"Um, can someone tell me what to expect in Guatemala?" I ask. "Besides the constant Spanish."

"The food!" cries Raúl.

They all shout out favorite foods. "¡Elotes! ¡Plátanos fritos! ¡Chiles rellenos!" That's roasted corn on the cob, fried plantains, stuffed chiles. "And homemade tortillas! ¡Mangos!"

I laugh. "Okay, sounds like I won't starve."

"Hunger is the best sauce in the world," says Raúl.

I recognize the phrase. "Where'd you hear that?" I ask.

"Oh, my dad says it. I think it's from a book."

Now I remember. It's from *Don Quixote*. "My dad says it, too." Raúl and I lock eyes and nod. "Hey, does everyone wear those, um, huipils? Abuela sent me one."

"Oh, no, don't worry about what to wear," he says. "Those are mostly for native folks in villages. In the city, everybody dresses the same as here."

Whew. Maybe no one will ever know I sold mine.

"You're so lucky you get to meet Abuela for the first time," says Mirabel. "She's so sweet! She'll spoil you with cafecitos and limonada con soda. Little coffees with milk and lemonade with fizz."

"Yeah, I'm excited." I'm scared. Is that the same thing?

"Papi gets embarrassed because she always tells stories that make him look cheesy. Like how he and your dad used to help each other serenade girlfriends. They'd take their guitars and sing in harmony outside the girls' windows. For real."

"Wow," I say, a trickle of guilt sliding down my spine. Was that the same guitar I stepped on? Was Tío Pancho harmonizing with Dad when he first sang to my mom?

"Kids! ¡Comida!" our mothers call.

"I'm glad you guys moved here," I murmur. I don't think anyone hears me, but I don't mind. It's still true.

We all eat dinner perched around the living room, then Crista and I sit on the floor at the coffee table to mess with a jigsaw puzzle.

On the couch, Aunt Jess, who isn't married, argues with Tía Lencha, who is. "The wife," says Aunt Jess. "It's the leading role every girl auditions for, but I don't want the part." Aunt Jess talks with flair, maybe from teaching sociology classes at the community college.

"What about children?" Tía says, gesturing with her arms, leaning her whole body into the word. They turn to face each other.

"My life is perfectly happy without children of my own," Aunt Jess says. "Besides, I have a niece and nephew."

Lencha's shaking her head. "You don't know what you are missing."

"Ah, but do you know what *you're* missing?"

The aunts think Crista and I aren't listening, but I catch Crista's eye and wink. She understands. We know they'll say more if they don't know we're paying attention.

"Who will take care of you when you are old?" Tía asks.

"I'll call on you!" Aunt Jess says triumphantly.

It's an old argument. They have it every time they see each other. Maybe Tía Lencha feels sorry for Aunt Jess, but I like Aunt Jess as she is. She takes me to the art festival every year. She lets me order what I want at the food trucks, and we dance at the music pavilion.

I imagine her life in more detail: Aunt Jess coming home from classes to read books and talk with friends. Aunt Jess writing her blog. Aunt Jess taking out-of-state trips with no car seat and no diaper bag.

My mother breaks in. "The point is we have a choice."

"And what about . . ." Tía Lencha drops her voice. "A little heat? In the bedroom?"

"Lencha, las niñas," Mom whispers and looks over at me and Crista. We keep our eyes on the puzzle.

"Just asking." Tía Lencha's playing innocent.

"Not every married person has what you have," Aunt Jess says. "But don't worry about me. I'm too busy for all that."

"Winter nights can get cold," Tía singsongs the last word.

"So can relationships," Aunt Jess says, mimicking Tía's tune.

"Enough," says my mother. "It's time to talk New Year's bash. We'll be in Guatemala until the second of January. Who wants to host something after that?"

I tune out. This puzzle is almost done. It shows a young couple carrying presents out of a wood-fronted store, musicians on a street corner, and children peeking out of a sleigh. It's a happy scene, but I don't see anyone who reminds me of Jayden, or an Aunt Jess type. I'm not sure who I am in this picture either.

Okay, what would the puzzle of my life be? I'll have Zuri and her mom window-shopping; Jayden and Seth driving a sleigh; Aunt Jess hauling a Christmas tree on a sled. Tía Lencha, Tío Pancho, and the cousins can be carolers. My parents will hold hands on a bench; Memito can make a snowman. And me?

It comes to me immediately. I'll be singing and playing a song in the town gazebo. Maybe I'll give myself a friend or a helper. Or a husband. Maybe not. But in every version of the puzzle, I can imagine myself singing. Singing and smiling.

"What about a song?" Tía asks Dad. "Una canción para la graduada." *A song for the graduate.*

"Hey, where's the guitar?" Raúl says.

My father opens his mouth, then closes it. I wish for a snowman to materialize in the living room to make everyone forget the question. As Dad's face turns red, I stand up. All eyes are ping-ponging between me and my father.

"I broke it."

Dad's head nods, but everyone else's turns to me. "My goodness!" says Aunt Jess. "How did that happen?" Other voices pile on. My mother stays quiet.

"I, um, stepped on the neck." The words come out thick from my throat.

"You *stepped* on it?" Raúl squints, as if sure he hasn't heard right.

I try to think what else to say. A wordless ocean surges in my ears. I can't explain what happened. What would I say? *I was really mad?*

"An accident," my father tells them, swallowing.

An accident? Not even close. I guess it'll stay our secret.

"And that means—" He fastens his eyes on Mom's and says, "I owe you a song, Kim. A graduation song."

This is all my fault. I'm melting in shame. Neither of my parents looks at me. They only look at each other.

"*For she's a jolly good fellow!*" starts Aunt Jess. "*For she's a jolly good fellow!*"

The whole room joins in, and I'm glad Memito is in his room.

I sit back down to the puzzle, but I'm not really looking at it. I find I've been staring at a pine tree that's completely finished except for one piece. I hope we do get another guitar. Soon.

FORTY-THREE

AFTER SCHOOL, I DROP MY BACKPACK and open the fridge. Mom's at the wall calendar, writing something.

"Is your last week of school going well?" Mom asks, turning around. "I started packing. Four days! I can't believe it's so close. You're going to love Lake Atitlán!"

I still wince when I think about Guatemala, but Mom's obviously excited.

"Hey, and guess what?"

"What?"

"We made an appointment for Memito with the Child Study Center. They're going to do a full evaluation—I told them all his symptoms and everything. I don't want to get your hopes up about any miracles, but they may be able to tell us something new."

"That's great, Mom!"

"Play with him for a while, will you? While I start on his suitcase?"

Zipping Memito into his coat, I let myself hope that we'll learn more about how to help him.

We head into the garage for sidewalk chalk. It's cold enough for gloves, but I hate getting chalk dust on my mittens. In the frosty air, my bare hands soon turn red.

At first we scratch lines and arcs on rough concrete. I can't draw anything fancy, just hopscotch squares. Memito likes them, though. He hops through the boxes, which gives me an idea.

I make a straight line, thick like a balance beam, and he walks it, putting one shoe ahead of the next. Then I place circles like stepping stones down the sidewalk, and he jumps inside each one. I add train tracks, zigzag trails, curves. Soon we have an obstacle course of chalk shapes. I'm an artist-engineer, a playground designer. The perfect ending pops into my head. A spiral.

Memito knows just what to do. He winds into the middle and looks at me.

"Puh," he says, meaning up.

"All done!" I say. "Now go back." I walk over and show him how to turn around, thinking he'll retrace his steps, but he stands still. He's arrived at the end. Spiraled to the center. The only way out is teleporting "up" with his big sister's help.

It's funny to see his mind stalled like this. He's stuck, and a sneaky thought makes me think of leaving him there.

"Puh," he says again and holds up his arms. His bottom lip pushes out, and I lift him up. His arms wrap around my neck, and I press him close. He smells like baby shampoo. With his soft cheek against mine, I don't care how many words he's supposed to know. I don't care if he goes to a special class or learns to read when he's eight or never. All the have-tos he's supposed to follow puff away like breath in cold air.

And just as I'm thinking this, Memito wriggles, hugs my neck, and says clear as a bike bell, "Quijana."

It's the longest word he's ever said. I feel crowned. Maybe he will talk someday. But I'm starting to see what Mom means, too, about doing what we can and still loving him as he is.

In a big-sister glow, I watch him jump from chalk square to chalk square. He does it in his own quirky way, sometimes with two feet, sometimes with one, sometimes tromping on the lines.

For some reason, the colored lines and circles of my chalk course make me think of my Jayden song. I sing it all the way through under my breath. It's still a good song, even if I'll never sing it to him. I guess I could start a new one. I walk wide circles in the driveway, humming, looking into the bare treetops, trying out lyrics. *We pedaled up the sunny hill / one hot October day.*

Memito pulls down my old jump rope and runs it back and forth on the sidewalk like a streamer. I'm tempted to show him the right way to use it, but I don't. He has his own ideas.

The lake shone bright with ~~tinsel streaks~~ *floating* ~~stars suns~~ *sparks / We . . .* hay, ray, stay, ballet?

When my song snags on a rhyme I can't find, I decide to leave it for later. Like Memito, like me, the song's future is still forming. Right now, we're all unfinished. And unfinished is fine.

When we go in, my cold hands hurt with warming up.

"Hey, sweetums," Mom calls from the dining table. "Aunt Jess is back from Florida. She brought this over for you," she says, handing me a padded envelope. "It's from Grandma Miller."

Confused, I squint at it.

"There's a postcard inside, written to you, and a necklace of some kind. Aunt Jess was cleaning out Grandma's desk and came across it." Mom smiles.

I'm distracted for a second because it's just occurred to me that my Unaccompanied Minor letter would still have been delivered to Grandma's. "Um, did Aunt Jess mention any other mail at Grandma's?"

"No. You mean mail Grandma meant to send? Or mail she received?"

"Uh. Either, I guess. Never mind."

Before Mom thinks of another question to ask, I take the envelope and walk to the table.

It's so light it feels empty. I freeze for a second, wondering how to feel. Happy and sad pile on top of each other as I open the flap. I pull out a postcard of a mermaid statue and a thumb-sized mermaid on a necklace, her tail sparkling teal and blue, flowers wreathing her shoulders. The statue on the postcard perches on a rock and looks out to sea. On the back it says *Den lille havfrue*, which must be Danish for The Little Mermaid, since it says Copenhagen, Denmark, at the bottom. And there's Grandma's handwriting, bold strokes in dark ink.

My dear Quijana,

I look away for a second, not wanting to reach the end of her message. Not wanting to say goodbye again. Not wanting to cry. But I'm already crying.

My friend brought this to me from Copenhagen, but I want you to have it. Remember how we laughed to learn that manatees inspired mermaid legends? Well, this one is lovely. Like you, she is special and beautiful. See how she longs for the ocean, her true home? That's where I am going, isn't it? Even if the surgery goes well, I'll be leaving you soon. But I'm happy to see what's ahead. Remember, I will stay close to you, Quijana. Think of me in quiet moments, and you will feel my love flowing over you. Keep swimming, dear one. Do everything for joy. I love you, G'ma Miller

I can hear her saying each word, and I run them through my head over and over. I look up at Mom. She's carefully not looking at me, letting me have my moment.

"Thanks, Mom." I hold the card to my chest as I walk to my room. Inside, leaning against the closed door, I reread her words. *Think of me in quiet moments.* I sit on my bed and look at her wise eyes in her picture.

Dad taught me to meditate when I was little. He grew up praying only in church, but now he "pulls up a chair with God," as he says, whenever he feels like it.

Now I remember what he taught me. I try to relax my feet, my stomach, my shoulders. I watch my breath. *Inhale joy, exhale worry. Inhale thank you, exhale goodbye. Inhale yes, exhale yes,* until breath is a stilled lake I float on.

Soon I feel my heart lighten and my head go airy. I think of Grandma Miller, and love warms me. She doesn't seem far away, but very close. I'm almost tempted to believe what she said about staying close to me. Instead of missing her and feeling sad, I'm happy in this wide-open moment, my mind a place I can trust.

The postcard flashes into my mind, with the little mermaid looking toward the ocean. And though I'm sitting on my bed, in my house, in my town, I'm also a ray of sunlight spreading across Denmark's North Sea.

I open my eyes and put on the mermaid necklace. Her open arms remind me of something else Grandma said: *Embrace the adventure!*

I walk out to the living room and find Memito pulling his suitcase in circles, Dad washing up for supper, and Mom rummaging in the fridge.

"That is such a beautiful necklace," Dad says.

"It's from Grandma."

"I heard." He winks.

Mom's phone rings, and she hands the Romaine lettuce to Dad. "Why do people always call at suppertime?" Dad says, frowning.

"Hey, Jess," Mom says. "Yup, started packing today. I have a list of my lists!" Her voice drops in volume for a few seconds. Then it's loud. "Unaccompanied Minor form? What are you talking about?"

Oh boy.

My parents stalk toward me as I slink into a chair at the dining table. Embrace the adventure, all right.

"How did a form granting you permission to ride a BUS to FLORIDA get into Grandma's mailbox?" Mom's as much bewildered as angry. She keeps shaking her head and throwing her hands in the air, like she can't imagine such a thing.

Memito senses tension and runs to his room. Great. Without him, the spotlight will shine entirely on me.

"I don't understand," says Dad. "What is going on, Qui?"

"I'll explain," I say, sighing.

And so I give up. I tell them everything.

"Sold it. As in, *sold* it?" Mom's still in shock. "And Ms. Thomas knew?" Again, her hands go up. "How could you?"

"On eArtisans."

"No. I mean, How. Could. You."

"Quijana," Dad says, "your abuela paid good money for that. She paid with love, too. She went to the market and picked it out especially." His forehead creases, and I worry that he's about to cry. I feel worse than when I broke the guitar. We're back to his being hurt and me being the cause.

"I know, Dad. I'm sorry." I press my lips together, then continue. I tell them how I biked to the bus station and bought the ticket. "And then they needed a form and a signature," I explain.

"Good thing!" Mom says.

"And I didn't want to forge your names or anything."

"Dear God." Mom presses her eyes with her fingers.

"Quijana," Dad asks, sincerely puzzled. "You wanted to avoid Guatemala that much?"

I wince. The truth is that I still don't want to go.

"And they let you buy the ticket?" Mom says.

"Well, I had to show my ID, but yeah. If you're over twelve."

"Well, *that* makes it okay." Mom's sarcasm is clear. "I know we've ridden the bus together," she says, "but how could you possibly think that . . . You know I'd have had the police stop that bus immediately. A twenty-eight-hour ride?" Mom's voice squeaks as her pitch goes higher.

"But I was going to leave a note. And Jayden was going to walk me to the bus station. I figured you wouldn't worry." It's kind of too bad that I never got to try my plan. "Plus, I was going to call at eight-thirty a.m. from Pensacola." They don't see the beauty of it, obviously, although it's actually sounding crazier to me, too, as I see their faces. "I was going to bring snacks," I say, tentatively.

"Unbelievable." Mom puts her palm to her forehead.

Dad blinks and shakes his head. He's frowning, but then his expression changes to one I don't totally recognize. He's tilting his head and looking at me closely. A smile tugs at one side of his mouth.

"Snacks," he says. He starts chuckling. "Snacks!" He throws his head back with a full laugh.

Mom stares at Dad. "Nothing about this is funny."

"I'm sorry. But such an elaborate plan," Dad says through laughter. "The garage sale, the website, the ticket, the letter." He's lost it, cracking up. "She could be la presidente!"

Mom, chin juts out, but then she smiles.

"Snacks!" says Dad again. I can't tell if he thinks snacks are smart or silly.

And now Mom is laughing, too. Shaking her head at first, then full-out laughter. They're laughing—both at me and with me.

I look from one to the other, confused.

"She thought of everything, Kim," Dad says. "But you left one thing out, m'ija. We would never have left without you. Never. And if we had, we couldn't have enjoyed the trip. Not with you somewhere else."

I think I'm still in trouble, but I smile anyway.

Dad puts his arm around Mom. "We raised a resourceful girl. Determined."

Mom isn't over it yet, but she doesn't disagree with Dad. "We'll talk about this more later," she says, and then Dad says, "Come," and pulls me close with his free arm.

It's the first time in a long time that I've trusted their love for me. They love me for who I am, crazy as I am. They love the Quijana they have.

FORTY-FOUR

THE SCHOOL BUILDING IS BUZZING TODAY. It's the last day of regular class before finals. Jayden walks backward as we go to lunch, telling some complicated story involving water balloons. He's already almost run into three people, partly because of his wild hand gestures, partly because of the backward walking. I laugh, but Zuri is subdued.

"So what's everyone doing over the break?" Jayden asks, taking his usual stool at our table. "I'm staying home. No trips. Bo-ring."

I elbow him. "Not boring the whole time."

"Yeah." He's shining even thinking about Seth.

But Zuri just sighs. Jayden and I look at her.

"My sister's coming home from college for Christmas."

"What, is she an ogre or something?" Jayden asks.

Zuri rolls her eyes. "*No,* she's bringing a boyfriend."

"Mr. and Mrs. Ogre?" I ask.

Zuri sits up straight. "Oh my god, don't even joke about that! She better not! She's way too young. She has her whole life to get married. It doesn't have to be now."

"So . . ." Jayden makes sly eyes at Zuri. "I take it you're not a fan?"

"He's going to ruin Christmas." Zuri slouches. "He'll eat all the pork—my mom's special recipe from the island. I just know it."

"And that's what you're worried about?" I ask.

"No. It's just, I want to see my sister, you know? Not him."

I try to think of something helpful. "Can you do something with just her? Like go to the mall or ride bikes or something?"

"Or could you send him on a long errand with bad directions?" Jayden says, smirking.

Zuri lets herself smile. "I mean, she was my sister before she was his anything."

"Now that's what I'm talking about!" Jayden says.

"I'll switch with you," I say, finishing the last bite of my sandwich. "We fly to Guatemala *tomorrow*." My stomach still curdles when I think of it.

"How long is that flight?" Zuri's eyebrows pull together like she's trying to see Guatemala on a map in her head.

"Four hours."

"How's your Spanish?" Jayden asks. "Is Señora Francés going to be proud of you or disappointed?"

I shake my head. "I'll sound like a two-year-old."

"You'll be okay," Zuri says. "We've been back to Barbados twice. Of course, everyone speaks English there. The hardest part for me was saying goodbye again."

"I think you'll have fun," Jayden says. "At least Guatemala's something different."

"That it is," I say.

"If nothing else, just take a billion pictures and send them to me so I can live vicariously."

Maybe Jayden's got a point. I still feel dizzy thinking of all the Spanish I won't understand for two weeks, but part of me will be glad to be a different me in a different place, starting a new year. I somehow forgot that eventually, in just two weeks, the Guatemala trip will be done, and we'll be back to school. "When we get back, it'll be a new year."

"Everything keeps changing," Zuri says, frowning. "Nothing stays the same."

I try to think of something that does. "Your own courage," I blurt out, remembering a Cervantes quote.

"What?" Zuri says.

"The guy who wrote *Don Quixote*." I can't recall the exact words, so I paraphrase. "He says you haven't lost everything if you keep your own courage."

"Mmm," she says, unconvinced. I'm not convinced myself. Courage—that I could use. And how can I keep it if I don't have it in the first place?

The bell rings to send us back to class, but we can't leave like this, feeling anything but courageous, on our last lunch together before break.

Jayden rummages in his backpack. "Hey, look." He holds up three Popsicle sticks.

"Popsicle sticks?" I ask.

"Extras from a project." He pauses. "Or . . . they appear to be." He says this in a magician's voice.

Zuri gives him a what-the-heck-are-you-talking-about look.

"They might look like ordinary Popsicle sticks," Jayden says. "But these—these are courage sticks."

I raise my eyebrows.

"Hold on." He brings out a red marker. In all caps, he writes COURAGE on each stick. "This is for courage while sitting next to little brothers on airplanes, trying to speak Spanish in a foreign country, and eating food you've never seen before," he says, handing me the first stick. "This is for the courage to handle boyfriends from hell, dwindling supplies of pork, and big sisters who forget, *if only momentarily,* how important little sisters are." He places the second stick in Zuri's hand. "And this one's for hanging out with the Sethster, missing my friends, and facing the lineup of unplayed games I may have to try, now that there's no homework."

Zuri and I look at each other with raised eyebrows. This is so cheesy, so silly, so Jayden. She breaks into a smile as she shakes her head. "You are such a goofball, Jayday."

"Tell me you don't feel better already," he says.

"I do." She nods.

I hold up my stick. "This goes in my carry-on bag."

"Mine goes here," Jayden says, putting it in his coat pocket.

"How about this?" Zuri tucks it into her bun.

"Perfect," Jayden says. "Now we're ready for anything."

FORTY-FIVE

THE NEXT MORNING, we board the plane. I scoot to the window seat and look out over the wing. I watch suitcases ride a conveyor belt into the cargo hold. My roller-bag is down there somewhere, but my courage stick is tucked in my back-pack under the seat in front of me, and I'm wearing both my mermaid necklace and my sea turtle bracelet.

Mom and Dad talk in Spanish across their armrests, each in an aisle seat. Memito sits next to me, and the window seat I begged for feels farther than I want it to from my parents.

"Don't be nervous," I say to Memito, but really to myself. He's wearing a weighted vest to quiet his nerves and doesn't look at me, but just flips through a book Mom gave him. Why should he be nervous? He doesn't know where we're going; he's never talked to Abuela on the phone and wondered what she's like in person; he doesn't know that two whole weeks will pass before we're home.

Home. For Dad, Guatemala *is* home. I hope some-one hands him a guitar while we're there. He hasn't played for almost a month now, and I know he misses it. He tries to serenade Mom over morning coffee and sing Christmas songs, but it's not the same. More than once I've looked at the empty guitar hook and wished it could be filled again.

And it will be. I'll pay for it. Thinking of pet-sitting and raking leaves, I touch my mermaid necklace, my determination glittering.

I think of Grandma Miller and one time when we were walking along the shore after dark. The waves, instead of black, glowed fluorescent blue as they crested and fell. "Is that real?" I asked.

She laughed. "Magical, isn't it?"

The sand looked strewn with blue Christmas lights as the tide washed in and out. Wading in, our feet stirred the water's surface and twinkles surrounded our ankles.

"That's bioluminescent algae," she said.

They looked like underwater fireflies. I didn't know something real could be so fairylike.

I fasten my seat belt. A tide of excitement rises through me as the plane pushes away from the gate. An announcement says to turn off our phones, and I see that Zuri's sent a selfie with her sister in front of a Christmas tree. **Quality sis time!** I send her back a thumbs-up, **You two look great!,** and a Santa hat. **Bon voyage,** says Jayden. I power down my phone as Mom and Memito watch a safety video on tiny screens on the seat backs.

But Dad leans forward and winks at me, and a glimmer passes between us. Sometimes I feel more like Dad than anyone else in our family.

We roll down the runway and pick up speed. Memito grabs Mom's hand. My mermaid necklace presses against my throat, and acceleration presses me against the seat. The plane's engines roar. The nose tilts up, and we swim up streams of sunlight into the sky. No one can see it, but I'm sparkling.

FORTY-SIX

ALL MY LIFE the word "Guatemala" was an empty room. Now it begins to fill.

Purple volcanoes. Pink flowers tumbling over walls. A blue bus chugging by, so overcrowded that men hang out the open door. A shoeshine boy, his brown box of supplies at his feet. The colors turn my eyes into kaleidoscopes. It's like Grandma said: *You'll see amazing things.*

We park at an archway that leads to my aunt's front patio, and I bite my bottom lip. I hear a yell: "¡Están aquí!"

Sun warms the top of my head as I step out of the taxi. Then my ears fill with musical voices as people run toward us and start a merry-go-round of hugs. I say, "¡Hola!" over and over. It's practically the only greeting I know, but somehow, it's all I need. Name after name rolls into the air until a streamer of names seems to drape from one end of the patio to the other. Each person speaks to me in double-speed Spanish and gestures. Raised hands, clasped hands, one hand stirring the air. I smile in reply until my cheeks ache from smiling.

"¡Pasen!" someone shouts. Inside, we stow our luggage as one tío carries away the coffee table; another shoves the couch against the wall. Within minutes, a CD spins and marimba music bounces into the air. Uh-oh—Memito. But he's just clutching Mom, and he doesn't cry. Fingers snap, shoulders shift, hips swing. Spanish words fall like confetti around me. I realize I don't need to know what they all mean. When the song ends, everyone's talking and laughing. My body feels light, buoyed by the room's high spirits.

Platters of papaya and mango float toward the dining table over a sea of heads, and one of my tías and a cousin emerge from the crowd to set the platters down between a stack of napkins and a pile of forks.

I bite into a mango and wipe the juice from my chin. Mangoes don't taste like this in Texas! Then I look around the table at cousins of varying ages. Maybe I can give them something, I think. I pick up a napkin and start folding. I make a bow tie for each of them, and their eyes shine. A boy of about ten keeps meeting my eyes, then looking away. Finally he says, "May the Force be weeth you."

English! I guess the whole world knows *Star Wars*. I flash him a smile. I try: "Obi-Wan."

He cups his hands over his mouth and breathes loudly.

"Darth Vader!" Several voices join mine, and I'm ready to go through the whole character list when Tío Marcos claps and hands a guitar to Dad. Dad grasps the narrow neck, sets the instrument on his knee, and strums with a flourish. His smile reaches his eyes.

Tío Marcos has his own guitar, too, and the men sit facing one another, adjusting the tuning pegs. When all the strings sound like one guitar, a melody flies up from Dad's fingers. Four weeks, and his fingers haven't forgotten a thing. Tío plays chords and a baseline. I've never heard a guitar duet before, and it leaves me breathless. The harmonies intertwine and cast a spell over the room. The littlest cousins sit still and listen. Even Memito is rapt. Dad and his brother look at each other and not their guitars; they must have played this song many times. As I watch them, rhythms perfectly in sync, each anticipating the other's strum, something heals inside me. This, *this* is what my father was trying to give me the day he brought his guitar to my room.

I can finally picture him here. Mom's always talked about how he and Tío Marcos started a band. I've heard how Dad shined shoes, played street soccer, and knocked on the door of a famous newspaper columnist just to meet a living writer. Now it all becomes real.

A familiar-looking woman with a long, gray braid steps through the open doorway, and the music stops abruptly. Dad sets his guitar down and crosses the room in two steps. He takes her in his arms. "¡Mamá!"

They share a hug forever, her eyes gleaming brightly. Is she crying? I can't imagine not seeing Mom for years and years in a row. I'd be crying, too.

People make way for Abuela and offer their seats. She chooses the middle of the couch, and little cousins scramble up to kiss her cheek. I hang back, not knowing if I should approach her.

Mom brings Memito and sits beside her. Abuela's careful not to startle him. She speaks to him in upswinging phrases. At first, he burrows into Mom's shirt, but soon he turns his head to watch Abuela. Finally, he reaches out to touch her braid. She hands its end to him and says something that makes everyone chuckle. Then her eyes search the room and find me.

"Abuela," I say, hoping my one word is enough.

"Ven acá." She stands and spreads her arms wide. After a strong hug, she takes both my hands in hers. "Quijana," she says. "Mi Quijanita." I breathe in her rosewater scent as she studies my face. "Como la mía," she says, which immediately translates in my head: *Like mine.* And it's true—her nose is the shape of mine, her face the same oval. She sits on the couch, pats a tiny space next to her. I thought I would be nervous when this moment came, but all my jitters melt in her warmth.

Putting her arm around me, she gives a little squeeze, then notices my necklace. She holds it in her palm and tilts her hand to make the colors shimmer. "Qué bonita." *How pretty.*

What is "mermaid" in Spanish, I wonder. She answers my unspoken question.

"Sirena." She nods toward the mermaid and meets my eyes.

"Sirena," I repeat. "Mermaid." I pronounce the word slowly.

"Merr-med," she says back. "De tu Abuela Miller." *From your Grandmother Miller.*

A mist springs to my eyes. She must have heard the story from Dad. I nod, not trusting my voice.

"Muy especial." *Very special.* Her eyes pour love into mine. I'm relieved that I've been able to understand her so far, but I can see that words don't matter as much as I thought. I feel like I've known her always.

In Mom's arms, Memito's eyes keep closing. Dad comes to stroke his hair. "Mientras estoy dormido, yo nunca tengo miedo."

I recognize the quote from Don Quixote: "While I'm asleep, I'm never afraid." His words bring back Grandma Miller's message, *Don't let fear narrow your life.* That's what she said when I complained about coming here. I remember thinking I would hate Guatemala. I look around at the friendly faces— como la mía—and feel Abuela's warm hand on my shoulder. I don't hate it. It feels like a place where I could belong.

Mom and Dad start down the hall to put Memito to bed. The guitar lies against the arm of the couch. An idea flashes. "Dad, wait."

Everybody looks at me. I try to stay confident.

"Um, quiero cantar para usted," I say, looking at Abuela. *I want to sing for you.* I pull the guitar onto my knee and try out the strings. They're metal, which means they're stiff and hard to press, but I try my three chords. They come out clear. The

316

room hushes. I take a deep breath and start. I know my song is a little cheesy, but the words take on new meaning, saying them to Abuela:

The more I know you, the more I want to know you more.

And when you fix your eyes on me,

I feel my heart expand, fly free.

Without your love, I'm incomplete.

Togetherness makes life more sweet.

Your life inspires; I want to bloom.

A better me lights up this room.

The more I know you, the more I want to know you more.

"¡Me encanta!" Abuela clasps her hands in front of her heart.

Dad's eyes dance.

"Me gusta mucho tu cancion," Abuela says. Her smile lights up the last dark place inside me. I want to be nowhere in the world but here.

A late supper brings savory scents from the kitchen. In the kitchen doorway, two older cousins, a boy and a girl, stand patting tortillas and flipping them from one hand to the other.

"¿Puedes hacer tortillas, Quijana?" He's asking if I can make tortillas. I think back to Tía Lencha's, and Mirabel teaching me how to use enough water to shape the harina.

"Sí," I say, standing up. I can.

GRANDMA MILLER'S WISE WORDS

QUOTES FROM *DON QUIXOTE*
BY MIGUEL DE CERVANTES

QUIJANA'S POEM, "APPLE-JUICE POPSICLES,"
based on Ms. May's assignment to write a poem inspired by
"Blackberry Eating" by Galway Kinnell

> I love to go to the freezer in late July
> and paw among the ice-cube trays and bags of
>   broccoli
> to find the upside-down, tapered sweetness of
>   apple-juice Popsicles,
> the handles standing at attention, their sugared
>   plastic spines
> holding crystalled ice. As I yank one Popsicle and
>   lift it to my tongue,
> drips of juice trickle, the slushy tip gives way
>   between my teeth,
> and a syrupy cold melts in my mouth, leaving it
>   stunned
> like tunes sometimes do, certain sappy songs that
>   sashay and slide,
> which I hum, sing, and slather on the air in the
>   juicy, sweet silences
> after Popsicle-eating in late July.

POEMS QUIJANA HEARS

Supplies:

- Play-Doh (homemade is fine)
- photos
- timer (phone or hourglass)
- sense of humor

1. Divide players into teams of two, three, or four.
2. Lay out (or display on-screen) a grid of photos that feature the players. Use an odd number of photos for an even number of teams, and an even number of photos for an odd number of teams. Use more photos for a longer game. Nine or ten makes a good starting number.
3. Decide who goes first through a coin toss.
4. On their turn, a team designates the sculptor for the round. The sculptor chooses a photo to recreate, without revealing their choice, then turns their back to the photos. The sculptor has three minutes to make forms, figures, or shapes that prompt guesses from the team. No number or letter formation is allowed. A point is awarded if the team guesses correctly before the time is up.
5. Play moves to the next team.
6. The job of the sculptor should rotate between team members.

Tip: Make your own house rules!

Bald eagles: Our national bird, many bald eagles really do live in Florida and start nesting in September, always near water. They usually choose a high pine tree and sometimes make a second nest in their territory just for variety, like a vacation home. Quijana noticed the bald eagle on her passport, but she likes watching real ones through binoculars from the car—a great place to observe from, since you don't disturb the nest. She can also watch the webcam footage of one pair named Romeo and Juliet at: https://www.nefleaglecam.org.

Bioluminescent algae: This magic is real. I took a kayak tour of Merritt Island to see these dinoflagellates—single-celled organisms that flash every time the paddle moves the water. I've also walked along the Mosquito Lagoon shore in summer with Quijana and watched the glowing tide sweep in and out. Her eyes sparkled as much as the water!

Crocodile: These shy reptiles only splash around if frightened, and they sit with their mouths open to regulate their body temperature, not to scare people. Their message to humans: "Please leave us alone." Since crocodiles gulp their food, they can't eat manatees. Quijana is happy about this, and she finds it funny that a manatee can just nudge a croc out of its way if they meet in a swamp.

Gopher tortoise: These large land tortoises share their burrows, which are big and comfy enough to attract other species. So many animals live with them that they are called a keystone species. Like Quijana, they attract friends by doing their own thing. They actually need occasional brush fires to clear out high vegetation around their homes. Then they can eat the low plants and not have to steer around trees. Folks who live in Florida can report any injured gopher tortoises they see to the Florida Fish and Wildlife Conservation Commission at: http://myfwc.com.

Manatee: These gentle, vegetarian "sea cows" usually weigh more than one thousand pounds. They sometimes play in the water, doing barrel rolls and swimming upside-down, but spend most of their time resting and eating. The manatee is Quijana's favorite animal.

Sea turtle: Quijana's bracelet shows a loggerhead sea turtle, but three types (leatherback, loggerhead, and green sea turtles) nest on Florida beaches. It's important to keep lights off during hatching season so that baby turtles paddle to the sea instead of toward electric lights. Sea turtles can live up to eighty years, and they migrate hundreds, or even thousands, of miles to lay their eggs on the beach where they were born.

Spider orchid: These perennial, knee-high plants create a long bristle on the end, filled with little flowers. Each one has long, slender petals that extend from an oval with two dots. No wonder Quijana thinks they look like fairies wearing hoods!

Woodpecker: The United States hosts many varieties of woodpecker, and while they like insects and seeds, most of them love my suet feeders. I buy suet cakes (mainly animal fat) at the store, and Quijana puts them in the wire cage feeders. We hang them from a branch and watch the woodpeckers enjoy themselves!

ACKNOWLEDGEMENTS

GUITAR STRUMS, UNENDING APPLAUSE, AND THANKS TO:

Agent Katie Grimm, for seeing a book that didn't exist yet in the early manuscripts, for faith in Quijana's voice, and for frankness at the right moments.

Editor extraordinaire Taylor Norman, whose first thirteen single-spaced pages of analysis made me see where else Quijana could go.

The whole Chronicle team, especially Ariela Rudy Zaltzman, Claire Fletcher, and Jamie Real, for fine-tuning that made all the difference. Nadia Hernández, whose artistry and attention turned this book into a beautiful reality.

Erin Watley, Ph.D., of McDaniel College, for her thoughtful, sensitive read of Quijana's story.

The Roots Coffeehouse group, for reading, rereading, and critiquing with tough love. Algirdas, Lynette, Melanie, and Suzanne, I couldn't have done it without you.

Urania Fung's NE Arlington Writers' Critique Group, whose comments and catches helped me fix the false notes and make the book sing.

Charlotte, whose encouragement helped me persevere and also fine-tune the sensitive moments Quijana faces.

Trich, who helped me break the guitar!

Sharon Morrow, best seventh-grade English teacher ever, who read an early version, showed twelve-year-old me how grammatical music is made, and inspired Port 3.

My sons, who ate cereal for supper when deadlines loomed, and who always remind me what really matters.

Mom and Dad, whose bicultural home let me live this story and whose love gave me the confidence to write it.

THE OTHER HALF OF HAPPY

DISCUSSION GUIDE
BY CINDY L. RODRIGUEZ

1. What is the meaning behind the title *The Other Half of Happy*? What is the other half of happy, and how does it relate to the characters in the novel?

2. The Carrillo family's concerns about Memito's changing behavior grow throughout the novel. By the end, the family is still investigating what's going on with him. The author does not "solve" this problem by giving us a definite diagnosis. How do you feel about that, as a reader? Is it okay to leave this issue unresolved? Why or why not?

3. When her father asks for an "esprinkler" at Home Depot, Quijana says, "Sometimes I wish Dad didn't have an accent" (11). Later, when a student makes fun of Zuri's British accent, Quijana says, "But who makes fun of people's accents? That kid has no class" (136). Why does Quijana feel differently about her father's accent than she does about Zuri's? Is this type of dual thinking common? Do we act a certain way with our family and a different way with our friends?

4. Throughout the novel, Quijana often wonders why her family can't be "normal" or "regular." From her perspective, what would her family look like or act like if they were "normal" or "regular"? Is there such a thing as a "normal" or "regular" family? Why or why not? Why is this kind of thinking problematic?

5. Quijana is named after the fictional character Don Quixote, whom Quijana describes as a failure. Her parents argue that he makes an effort, and that is what matters. Do you agree with her parents? What is the outcome when Quijana tries something new or finally tries something she has been avoiding? Do you think her name is an appropriate match for her personality? Why or why not?

6. How are Quijana's friendships with Jayden and Zuri important to the story? In what ways are they good friends to one another? By supporting her plan to run away, are they being good friends or not?

7. Mr. Carrillo faces particular struggles as a Guatemalan-born man living in the United States, and Quijana faces certain struggles as a U.S.-born girl of Guatemalan descent. How are their struggles similar? How are they different?

8. What are some of the ups and downs Quijana experiences with her father? How is their relationship different after the incident with the guitar? How do you anticipate their trip to Guatemala will change their relationship?

9. Early in the story, Quijana says, "Grandma Miller says to never apologize for who you are, but who even am I?" (55). Does Quijana have a better sense of who she is by the end of the story? How has she grown and changed? Later, she says, "Right now, we're all unfinished. And unfinished is fine" (298). What does she mean by this?

10. How is Quijana's relationship with Grandma Miller similar to her relationship with her abuela in Guatemala? How are the relationships different? What kind of impact do you think Grandma Miller will have on Quijana? How does Quijana's relationship with her abuela change during the story?

11. What role does music play in Quijana's life? Are there things you turn to in the way Quijana turns to music? Why, and when?

12. What do you think about how Quijana handles the situation with Jayden once she realizes that he can't like her as more than a friend? Have you had a friend go through a similar struggle with their identity? What did you tell them? Is there something that you wish you had done differently?

13. When Quijana receives the huipil from her abuela, she says, "It's totally beautiful. And totally out of the question" (7). Why is it out of the question? How does starting junior high school impact her decision to wear the huipil?

14. Quijana experiences criticism from other members of the Latinx community. She is called a "coconut" and a "pocha" by other Latinx students, and her cousin questions why she calls her father "Dad" instead of "Papi." As a result, Quijana feels like she's not a "real Latina." Why does the author include these examples of intra-community criticism?

15. Quijana witnesses a white student making racist remarks to other Latinx students at the bus stop. At first, Quijana does not say or do anything. By the end of the novel, however, she approaches the Latino boys and stands up for them. Use the bus stop scenes to discuss what it means to be a perpetrator, a bystander, and an upstander. What role or roles have you played in similar situations in your life?

SNEAK PEEK

SHINE ON, LUZ VÉLIZ!

BY REBECCA BALCÁRCEL

CHAPTER 1

SO THERE'S BEFORE it happened. Before I learned to use crutches. Before I needed physical therapy. Before, before, before.

Welcome to After.

I grab a trash bag that's almost as tall as I am. LAWN AND LEAF, the bag says. Perfect for raking out the whole soccer section of my closet. Perfect for clearing out Before.

Soccer shoes? Into the bag. Shin guards? Into the bag. White-and-blue uniforms? The bag. Three trophies, one for being the top scorer in the whole Tri-Cities Junior League? Bag. I can't look at this stuff anymore.

Then there's the ball. Am I keeping it? No way.

Well?

No.

Okay, fine. I can't let go of my soccer ball yet.

I'm not supposed to dribble it in the house, but I pop it into the air with the toe of my shoe and bounce it on my good knee. The knee that bends easy as a Slinky. Clean joint, perfect tendons. I'm thankful for one healthy knee. Really, I am. But I'm sad, too. I used to have two of them.

I shove the ball to the very back of my closet, behind a wall of cardboard bricks I used to make forts with.

Now for the posters of my soccer heroes.

I yank out each pushpin. Down falls Abby Wambach, top scorer of the U.S. Women's Team. Down goes the World Cup team photo, every neck with a gold medal, and captain Megan Rapinoe raising the trophy high. I crumple the posters into big wads and stuff them into the trash bag.

Mom says to stop looking back, so here I am trying, but it's hard to forget. Sometimes I flash into the past. A memory will photobomb my brain. Like that run. That last-day-on-the-soccer-field run.

It plays over and over in my head, a YouTube video on continuous autoplay. Legs pumping, feet churning up the grass, my body a missile speeding toward the goal. . . .

I know the accident happened. Obviously. But at the same time, it's like I'm still running. The goal getting closer, and Mom cheering in the stands. Dad shouting, "Pour it on!" which makes me run even faster.

Some "me" kept on running, but I couldn't go with her. It's like she went on without me, to where I was supposed to go. Now we'll never find each other.

Instead of scoring, I felt a leg sweep under me, my body spinning backward, the blur of another jersey, and pain spiraling out from my knee and ankle. Doctors would later tell me my anterior cruciate ligament tore, my shin broke, and my patella fractured. All I knew then was a dark tunnel, my vision gone, and the screaming pain growing louder.

So maybe I am almost used to it now. The leg, I mean. The pain meds and the therapy and the discussions about whether to do surgery. At least I can walk. No more crutches or canes. I'm left with a "wobbly" knee, they say.

Which means I can't play soccer this spring—or maybe ever. I lost the thing I was best at. The thing that filled three evenings a week and Saturday mornings and gave me automatic friends, at the local league and at school. The thing that made me special.

Now I'm plain Luz. Vanilla girl instead of raspberry swirl.

And now Mom and Dad freak out if I race someone to the bus or charge up stairs two at a time or even walk fast, if you can believe it. They say my knee could "give."

But the knee's no biggie. The thing that bothers me is Dad. He hardly talks to me anymore. It's like he can't get over it. I guess I'm not surprised. He coached me my whole life. I held a soccer ball before I held a spoon, they tell me. Eleven years is a long time, even to a grown-up.

I haul my trash bag of soccer stuff to the living room, where Dad's up a ladder, putting a new light fixture on the ceiling fan. Does he see me at all?

"Can I help?" I ask. "Maybe hand you some tools?" I'm kind of good at mechanical things. I installed my own kitty-cat light-switch plate, and I can build anything from LEGO bricks, with or without the directions.

"All I need is this screwdriver," he says.

"Can I just watch?" I say, remembering how he used to let me "help" replace a door handle or change a light bulb.

"If you really want to, Lucita."

Which is my nickname. He doesn't say it with a smile, though, and my heart wilts a little. He doesn't notice the trash bag in my hands, though it's right in front of me and big as a Texas sage bush.

Before, before, before, he was the head coach of Tri-Cities Youth Soccer. After, after, after, he's just Dad the landscaper. He quit coaching the day I got hurt; another parent took over. He works his landscaping business, called Véliz Verde, even on Saturdays now.

So fine. I didn't want to help with some old ceiling fan anyway.

I pull on my red jacket and head outside with the trash bag. My plan? Put my soccer life on the curb, let the garbage truck haul it away, and dump the past into the past.

"Luz!" Mom shouts. "Be careful on the driveway."

Be careful, be careful, be careful. *I know.*

CHAPTER 2

I FACE SIDEWAYS and take our super-steep driveway slowly, good leg first. I hoist the trash bag with both hands. It lands with a satisfying thump.

A voice carries from across the street. "A little early for trash day." It's Mr. Mac, pulling winter covers off his bushes. He points to his wristwatch as he says "a little early," but his eyes smile.

"Yup," I say.

"Never known you to be early. Must be important. Or smelly!"

That's what I like about Mr. Mac. He figures you know what you're doing. He figures you've got your reasons.

Mr. Mac isn't his full name. It's Mr. MacLellan, but we're buddies, so I get to say Mr. Mac. He was the first neighbor we met when we moved in, and guess what he brought as a welcome gift? Not cookies, not tuna casserole, not some boring welcome card. He brought a lamp that turns on when you clap. It also works when I snap. Practically magic!

Mom calls him Gadget Santa because he's always giving us gadgets, like a motion detector that chimes when Zigzag goes out her cat door. Plus Mr. Mac knows stuff. When I graduated from crutches, he showed me *his* banged-up knee and how to use a cane.

Turning my back on the trash bag, I call over, "It *is* important. It's my old soccer stuff."

He nods his hatted head, and the sun glints off his round glasses. He's quiet for a second. "That's a prickly one to swallow, all right."

It sure is. It won't be easy looking at my bare bedroom, but it's better than looking at a room that makes me sad. "That's a fact," I say.

"Do you remember Stephen Hawking, Luz?"

"The physics guy who talked through a computer?"

"That's him. He said something about intelligence. And he was a smart guy. Test scores, or even high grades—that's not what intelligence is. According to Hawking, it's being able to adapt to change."

I let that sink in. "You mean my leg?" I glance at my trash bag. "So is this me, um, 'adapting to change'?"

"As best you can, right? And life *is* change, I've found." He resets his hat, which has a solar-powered fan built into the top. "Not that it's easy, of course."

I think about the soccer ball still in my closet, and I know that I'm not all the way "adapted." Of course, I might play around with the ball again, just for fun. But what if being a star was what made it fun? And Before Dad showing me his soccer secrets, which After Dad doesn't do. I'm not sure soccer can ever be fun now.

Mr. Mac points to his open garage. "Look what I found," he calls.

He picks up a large remote, extends the antenna, and a red toy car zips out. I love that little thing. Little Red, we call it. He lets me drive it sometimes. Now it crosses the street, zooms right to my feet. Welded to the roof is a shallow box, kind of a tray. Mr. Mac made that part himself. Inside the box tray is a black electronic device—maybe an old, old phone?

I turn it over in my hands. Rectangular buttons line one edge, four black and one red.

"Explore it. See what you can make of it," Mr. Mac says, zooming Little Red and its empty tray back across the street.

"Will do!" I give him a wave and climb back up the driveway, turning the mystery object over in my hand.

Mom meets me at the door. "What do you have there?"

"I don't know." I push one of the buttons and a whole side of the device springs open.

"I haven't seen one of those in a long time," she says.

"Mr. Mac said to explore it."

"Mr. MacLellan's always got something interesting for you, doesn't he?" Mom says, pointing at my bare head. She always wants me to wear a hat if it's the least bit cold.

I ignore her gesture and hang my jacket on its hook.

"So, come here a minute. We need to talk."

"What about?" I say, pressing another button on the black thingamajig.

She disappears into the house, her words fading as she goes. "We'll talk about it as a family."

As a family? There's only three of us. Mom, Dad, and me. What's the big deal? This is not what I want to do with my Sunday afternoon.

From the black gadget, I pull out a plastic rectangle—sort of a cartridge. It has two holes in it, with tiny teeth, like gears. "Can this talk-meeting-thing wait?" I call as I head toward my bedroom.

"No, Luz," Mom says from the kitchen. "Dad's already in the dining room."

I set the black device on my bedside table and turn back. Then I stop. I stand at my bedroom doorway. I let a second go by. Then two.

Dad's been so quiet lately. So gone all the time. So busy, busy, busy. Part of me wants to stand here and make him wait. Make him think about me. Make him wonder where I am and if I'm okay. But of course he knows I'm in my room. He knows I'm basically okay.

Except I'm not.